Taf

Taf

ANNIE CALLAN

Cricket Books

A Marcato Book

Chicago

Text copyright © 2001 by Annie Callan
All rights reserved
Printed in the United States of America
Designed by Anthony Jacobson
First edition, 2001

Library of Congress Cataloging-in-Publication Data

Callan, Annie.
    Taf / Annie Callan.
        p.   cm.
    "A Marcato book."
    Summary: Thinking she has killed her half brother, twelve-year-old
Taf flees her abusive home and sets out to find her long-missing father,
and on her way from Idaho to Pendleton, Oregon, she discovers not only
adventure and sorrow, but also a number of people who love her.
    ISBN 0-8126-4933-8 (cloth)
    [1. Runaways—Fiction. 2. Coming of age—Fiction.]   I. Title.
PZ7.C12977 Taf 2001
[Fic]—dc21
                                                                2001042079

For Hallie, Emma, Laura, Lily, and Claire,
and for all questing spirits out there.

Taf

Part 1

The Great Silkie of Shule Skerrie

In Oroway there sits a maid
and to her baby she sings,
Little know I my child's father,
far less land or sea he's living in.

Then in steps he to her bed fit
and a grumbly guest, I'm sure it was he,
saying, "Here am I, thy child's father
although I am not family.

"I am a man upon the land.
I am a silkie on the sea.
And when I am in my own country,
I dwell it is in Shule Skerrie."

It was not weel, sang the maiden fair,
it was not weel indeed, quoth she
that the great silkie from Shule Skerrie
should have come and aught a bairn to me.

Then he has taken a purse of gold,
he has put it upon her knee,
saying, "Give to me my little wee son
and take thee off thy nurse's feet.

And it shall come to pass
on a summer's day
when the sun shines bright on every stone,
I'll come and fetch my little young son
and teach him for to swim the foam.

"You will marry a gunner good,
and a proud good gunner, I'm sure he will be
and he'll go out on a May morning
and he'll kill both my wee son and me."

And lo, she did marry a gunner good,
and a proud good gunner, I'm sure it was he,
and the very first shot that ere he did shoot,
he killed the son and the great silkie.

Chapter 1

I loved to see them come. Soon as winter skies began to lift, I'd
stand on our porch, head tilted up to the sky for signs, for that first
arc of black on the horizon, like a squiggly line, the brave one heading
them homeward, as I imagined, and the others in a long dreamy
drizzle behind. Sometimes you'd hear their raucous cheers first and
rush outdoors to watch the chalky line zigging across the horizon,
and you'd wait and wait and wait, knowing that the vision would
expand, each bird growing before your very eyes, until they were full
size, and you'd watch them drift down among the cattails, setting
the whole field aflutter with the beating of their wings. And when
they'd landed, nothing, only a faint rustle in the reeds here and
there. I'd lie on my back in the grass, and thank the skies for bring-
ing spring to us again.

Us was my mother Jean, my stepdad Hank, and the little twins,
Joey and Todd. My real dad had gone west. Ma said maybe he got
bored living by the Idle River. He used to lean over my bed and
croon. I remember the spirals of smoke singing out of his mouth.
Only his songs weren't always about fathers and daughters, but full
of wild horses and cowboys and wide open sky, not a house for miles
and miles. He said, who cares that his blood was old country, with

a name like Will Stetson, sure, what else could he be but a cowboy? I imagined him out there on the prairie, mustache blowing in the fierce wind, and he steely on his horse, his spurs digging into the stirrups. Noble and poised as a statue.

All that was left of him was a scrap of blanket and a falling-apart book of fairy tales and ballads from Scotland. Ma said the blanket was made from the skin of two otters. "Your father came across it in his navy days," she said one time.

"Probably won it in a bet," Grandma from the old country put in. She was still alive then.

"He did not," Ma came back at her quick. "He brought it back for the girl. Wasn't he always wrapping her in it and having me read her tales of the silkies?"

"For his own benefit, more likely." Grandma said. "That lad's head was stuffed full of fairies and make-believe. What use did it ever do him, tell me that?"

And Ma did what she always did when her mother-in-law annoyed her, tightened her lips like twine round a hay bale and stalked out of the room.

The silkie was everyone's favorite story in my dad's tattered book. He was a seal who lived near an island over in Scotland, and somehow he could slide out of his skin whenever he had a whim to be human. *I am a man upon the land. I am a silkie upon the sea.* That was the chorus, for it could be sung as well as told, but the line that always tugged at my heart was scribbled in pencil just under the title: *It was an empty oyster-and-pearl afternoon.* No one knew who'd written it, but I'd read it over and over, imagining a kind of creamy peach day, hazy clouds carrying secrets of long-gone fathers and fair maids who give birth to seal-children. The poor seal and his son came to a sorry end, and Ma said that was the part my pa took to, 'cos it was the true story of life. Ma seemed to enjoy whatever Pa did.

"Do you believe in silkies, Grandma?" I asked her once.

"I do not!" She said, and set down her knitting. "But sure, they exist all the same."

There weren't actually any fairies in Pa's book. But there were plenty of shapeshifters, folks who could turn into animals any old time. If it felt like a good day to fly, say, they'd sprout wings. I wished sometimes I could be that horse my pa rode off on, so I could hold him the way he'd held me. But what was left of his blanket wouldn't cover a saddle; he'd been gone nearly seven years already.

In 1915, you could count the motorcars you'd see on two hands; mostly the mayor and his cousins drove them. But Hank got his hands on a great big one somehow, and used it to haul eggs and motorcar parts and any old thing from the Idle River all the way up to Monmouth and the towns in between. That was his route, and he'd be gone for long spells, as Ma liked to put it. I loved his car, the vast space of it, almost a house on four wheels. And the view! You could see forever, fields and fields of wheat stretching miles ahead of you. He built a little sleeping bunk, a hard plank up close to the roof, and I'd crawl in there and watch the world speed past, pretending I was a great floating hawk out in the snags, scouting for prey.

I didn't ride often with Hank, 'cos he said the road was no place for a girl, even though I was probably close to thirteen, and he liked to pick up folks needing a ride anyway and hear their stories. He said he knew mine only too well. I thought, you're wrong there, Hank. You've no idea what goes on inside me, all the aching thoughts and dreams, all the far-off places I go to in my head. Taffy Hero, I'd call myself, and slip me into one of those Scottish folk tales, let them take me wherever they were going. If the page of a story was missing, I'd just add my own five cents, and between the two, I'd been halfway round the world.

But there was no use telling him, I knew, for he had me figured as the spit of my own daddy, a useless waster. The only thing that gave him pleasure was to yank on my hair. It was one long braid that swished down past my hips, and he loved to pretend it was a cow's tail he could tug on. "They'd spot you in a lineup, little Miss Taffy," he'd say every time. "Can't miss hair the color of fire." Ma said it was closer to wild strawberries, the shade, just like my dad's.

Hank kept a picture dangling on a chain from his rear mirror, a woman with yellow hair and hardly any clothes, and his eyes could watch her bob about for hours. When he said he knew her well once, I asked, "So, how come you're still interested then? If you know her story, then she's no better to you than me."

"No," Hank growled low in his throat. "No, you haven't a clue, kid. I know you like the back of my hand, I knew her by the front of it." Sometimes Hank was hard to figure out.

When he'd be gone, Ma would get busy cleaning up. She'd have us gathering sheets and towels and underwear in big bundles and heaving them on our shoulders down to the river for washing. Some folk in the town thought it was common to use river water for laundry, but Ma said it was efficient and what's more, cheap. Her own mother, she told me, had lived in a tin shack right on the water itself, and only had to lift the toilet lid to go fishing. Ma was born to love the river, I knew it, just as my pa belonged to the land. The way she got into the scrubbing, whipping away at Hank's shirt collars till her fingers were red raw, you'd have to marvel. "Gets the job done the way you want it," she'd tell anyone who happened past.

Joey and Todd were only toddlers. You could chase around the hut for hours, tickling them when you caught them, and they'd giggle up a storm. That sound, their laughter, it was like bells chiming, so sweet that it lit up the room. Things were easier when Hank was gone. I never said that to Ma, 'cos she would get all tense the moment he walked out the door. She'd start counting the days till he was due back, and her eyes'd be glued to the cracked watch that hung by the door. "Do you think he's all right?" She'd ask, her forehead all fret lines. "He's usually home by this hour."

"Ma," I'd have to tell her, "he said he'd be gone till Thursday, he'd an extra run up to Annesley, remember?"

"Mmm," she'd mutter, still glaring at the watch like it had the answers to all the problems in our life.

I don't remember exactly how it started that terrible day. Hank had been home for a few hours and he and Ma were in their bedroom with the door locked. I was playing with the twins. We'd been out in the fields picking daisies and dandelions until Joey started sneezing and I had to bring them both in. I hated listening to the noises in the bedroom; I could hear the lash of something, maybe a stick, and screams and then crying and Hank yelling in that voice that made the walls shake.

I tried reading the fairy tale of *Mossycoat* to them, but they weren't interested in magic garments just then. Todd grabbed at a page like it was breakfast and it tore right out of the book. "Toddy! That's my papa's only . . ." But the page was a fist now, useless, like half the stories in that book. The spine hardly held what was left in one piece. Soon as I'd snatched the paper back, Joey began sneezing again. Not one or two wheezes, but a chorus of achoos, like a bird stuck in a bush. His eyes looked puffy. I wrapped him in the Navajo shawl Hank'd got in a trade from someone in Arizona and rocked the little squabbler in my arms. But Todd was not happy to be ignored and he started bawling, louder and louder.

"Keep that noise down out there!" Hank bellowed through the rickety door.

"I'm trying." But the more I rocked little Joe, the more upset Todd became. That's the way with twins maybe, they can sense what the other is feeling, like they're connected at the heart.

Anyway, I picked up Todd in my other arm and rocked them both, but they were heavy things for a scrawny twelve-maybe-thirteen-year-old, and my arms couldn't take all that weight for long. I don't know how it happened, but I was in the middle of the silkie song, *and in steps he to her bed fit, and a grumbly guest, I'm sure it was he, saying, Here am I, thy child's father, although I am not family*, when suddenly my left arm slipped, and just like that, Todd was on the stone floor, crack, thud, bounce, and then nothing, nothing.

My heart was crumping inside me as I knelt down, keeping Joey crooked under my other arm. Todd's eyes were open a bit and they just stared, stared like two ghosts from the other world. "Todd, Todd!" I screamed, thinking somehow the louder I yelled, the more chance I'd have of waking him. "Wake up, boy, come on!" But he just lay there, like a broken doll. Then Joey started in on the crying and I couldn't bear it any more.

"Ma! Hank! You have to come."

"Shut up there, girl, for God's sake!" Hank shouted out. I could hear the bed creaking.

"Please Ma, I need you!"

I thought I heard Ma hiss something, and then Hank's voice, "Damn you, woman, and your sillyass daughter. You're going nowhere till we've finished this." And the bed moved again.

I lifted Todd's fingers into my hand, I remember that, and I remember how one of them twittered, just like a baby wren, and his eyelashes beat for a second, two wings, and then stopped. I bounced Joey on my right hip to try to ease his tears; he was all hot and his baby face puckered in a knot of steam, me still clinging to Todd's tiny hand, until I realized, my heart double beating, that it had gone cool. It was a pale weight in my palm.

I could hear movement in the next room, and Hank's cough and I thought I heard my mother sniffle.

"Just you wait, kid," Hank threatening through the door. "I'll kick you up and down Foley's Alley, see if that'll keep your gob shut for a while . . ."

I'd had his beatings before, mostly when he'd had a few rums, and I dreaded to think how much harder he'd hit if he was sober. I could hear the lock drawing back, and there and then, I decided. I took Joey out to the porch, set him between the two rickety chairs, he still bawling like a cow in heat, and I legged it across the fields, my bare feet scraping and scuffing off stones. I ran and ran, snagging my dress against cattails and brambles, straight through the pond, my ankles tingling in the chilly water. I could hear the geese scatter and wing up in surprise, aar-aarking in my wake.

I didn't stop till I got to Foley's field and then, from behind the thick elm that separated our land, I looked back, and saw Ma on the porch, a tiny figure like a skeleton peering out, and Hank raising his shotgun. One last dry whinge of Joey's carrying to me on the wind, and then one, two, three shots scouring through the air. I peeked out just once, just in time to see a goose flop to the ground, and a haze of gun-smoke fogging the field where all my dreams till then had begun and ended.

Chapter 2

It took almost three weeks to get out of Marlow County. I hid in hayricks and barns and old toolsheds as I moved from field to field. It was the oddest feeling, drifting like that, stopping at creeks to drink and splash my sweating face, prying sour berries off their canes. The blackberries weren't even close to ripe yet, they looked almost green, but I ate and ate, as much as I could stuff in at a go, for who knew when I'd find another meal. It helped that it was nearly summer, and I could manage without shoes for a while.

I worried that the newspapers in Marlow would be flashing my face on their cover. Murderess, almost thirteen, flees the scene. My hair would be a giveaway, so I ripped the collar off my pinafore and made a scarf of it to cover my head. I knew it'd be certain jail for me if I was caught. No one would listen to a kid over an adult.

Though my head was heavy with a maybe dead baby, the further I walked, the better my legs liked it. It was like a scent luring you toward somewhere else, somewhere better, only to find once you reach it, it has disappeared or moved one step ahead of you, so you just had to keep plodding onward. It was like following a trail already mapped out and yet so desolate you felt you were the first person ever to track it.

I knew I'd crossed into the next county when I saw the high wheat-lands, tall golden stalks glittering in the morning sun. I'd never been this far from home, and the beauty and strangeness of it coaxed a loud whistle out of me. Why hadn't I found this paradise before? To my girl-eyes, the fields seemed to be conjured of endless sunshine. I made a nest in the folds of wheat and lay on my back, sucking on a strand, and watched the veils of clouds zig across the horizon. They looked so delicate there against the blueblue of the sky, as if they could vanish in an eyeblink, and suddenly Todd's sweet face floated out of them, his mouth curved up in a U, only the merry pink in his cheeks was gone. He was the color of Marlow marble and the feel of it, I guessed, though he only stayed a moment. A long fork of sorrow raked through my body, and it went deeper than Hank's bullets ever would have, I knew that. I closed my eyes and let the pain have me, until my face was a stream of tears and my throat loosing sounds I'd never heard in my life.

I must have slept then, maybe for a very long time. It was still bright when I woke, though I'd swear it was a new day entirely. Where the tears had congealed, my skin was rough. And yet I felt refreshed, as if the slumber had loaned me a new kind of hope. As I eased my belly up off the kind earth, something crackled, a sur-prising sound. At first I thought I'd squashed a frog, but no, the *kkkkrrr* was coming from inside my pinafore pocket. And out of its deep reaches, I hauled the page from Pa's folk tales that Todd had grabbed at. Oh, dear Todd. I should have let him keep it. It might have been the last story he'd ever get close to. I uncrinkled the paper, stretched it out flat on the grass, almost good as new, were it not so yellow to start with. And my skin prickled under my scarf when I read the words in narrow black letters on top. It was the first page of *The Dauntless Girl*.

The song, a ballad as they called it in Scotland, was about a girl so full of courage, nothing could stop her. Except the fact that there was no page two or three or four. Ma said she didn't know what happened to them, maybe they got used to start a fire one winter. But I preferred to believe my pa took them with him to remind him of his own girl, who was learning herself not to be troubled by anything, even bullying stepfathers. Maybe I hadn't gotten that far yet, but one day.

Seeing that page there in the field, spread out like dandelion butter in the sun, made my heart ease some. With a made-up melody, I half sang, half whistled those words out on the air, and pretended it was my own pa singing them specially for me. *Go down to the cellar, said the farmer to the girl, and fetch me one more beer. That's my girl, my dauntless girl. Don't trip on the ghost by the stair.*

I pressed the beautiful notion into my pocket along with the paper, a piece of my long-ago father, and pulled myself up to standing. It was warm underfoot already. I blew a kiss to the sky that held Todd and I knew it was a kiss goodbye, as I tripped on through the fields, one after the other, my heart filling with a surprising kind of gladness, until darkness came down once again on the land.

By the time I set foot in Addison, Idaho, I'd made myself into a new person: Taffy Stetson, part orphan, father missing, family shipwrecked on the Idle River long, long ago. I blessed the dad I used to have for his wild songs and stories. I must have looked a sight, even though I'd bathed in the river two days before. My dress was no more than a thin rag hanging over me, and my shoes scrapped together with birch bark, but I was jubilant anyway, as I marched into the feed store, asking after work.

A young boy, maybe my age, not too much more, was weighing flour on a scale and he turned to watch me come in. I could see his eyes widen.

"Hello there!" I said, as gaily as possible, plucking my headscarf off. I knew I had to rely on personality to make up for my dusty looks. "Taf Stetson," and I stretched out my hand to the bewildered boy, "I'm looking for work."

"Mom and Pa gone after furniture in Winchester," he said in this slow voice that came out measured like treacle. "Won't be back till Tuesday."

"Oh," I hung my head, trying to look forlorn. "So you can't help me then?"

"Afraid not," he said, but it sounded like something he'd heard an adult say. I noticed he had put down his flour scoop and was eyeing me carefully, as if I were a rare bird landed in his corner.

"Well," I went on, not waiting for him to speak. "I've been on the road for days, come all the way from you wouldn't believe where, just to visit this town. We heard tell of it since we were young ones. Go to Addison, Idaho, that's what they'd say, that's where the good life is." I put on my most dejected look. "And now my poor feet are blistered and raw and nothing's turning out like I'd figured and . . ." Before I knew it, my eyes were brimming tears. Maybe it was just that exhaustion you feel when you come to the end of the road.

"Now hold on here," the boy looked alarmed. "Sit down, why don't you, miss?"

He pointed to a barrel at the end of the aisle and I gladly obliged, for I realized now my legs were throbbing.

"Let me get you some water."

"Lemonade would be better," I said, dreaming of the sugary tartness of it. Already the day was shaping up to be a hot one.

The boy dashed off, wiping his hands on his smock. I helped myself to some raisins from the bin right beside me. Oh, the sweet joy of real food again, my tongue was delirious with the novelty.

"I've brought you a cookie too; you look like you might enjoy one."

"Bless you, bless you," I cried out before I could stop myself, something I heard the church ladies say on those Sundays when Ma dragged me to service, 'cos she couldn't bear being alone. I couldn't think about that now though, when I had an oatmeal cookie with nuts choked in it and little chocolate pieces. My mouth was moist as an Augusta Sunday. I had to force myself to eat it in small bites. But even then, the boy stared at me with interest.

Lucky for me, the bell over the door rang and my angel went off to help a customer. I knew I should keep part of the cookie for later, just in case, but it tasted so good with that pink lemonade, I thought I was in paradise. If this is where Todd is, he's doing well, I thought to myself, and then forgot everyone else in the whole world except me and the beautiful departure of hunger.

When he came back to me, I was licking my lips and kicking my heels against the barrel. I was full of vitality now, and nerve.

The boy sat down on the barrel next to mine. "Where will you stay?" he asked.

"Oh, I don't know, maybe I'll sleep out tonight, it's warm enough." I was still heady from the meal, gay and buoyant and devil-may-care as I'd ever been.

"You'd sleep out?" The boy looked astonished. "There's snakes round here."

"Don't bother me. I come from a family of snakes!"

And the boy laughed, maybe at my boldness, who knows.

"Have you any better ideas then?"

He looked at me funny, but then his eyes flashed and he nodded, a vigorous thumping up and down of his head, licorice hair limping along to the beat.

"Come back at five o'clock, and I'll close up the store and take you there."

"You would?" I was shocked, after all these weeks scrabbling along by myself, to have someone, anyone, willing to help me. A light rose in my chest, the color of May lilacs, and I leaped off the barrel and flung my arms around the startled boy. What's more, I placed a whopping kiss on his ruddy cheek and said, "Friend!"

I had never wished for a day to go by so fast. I paced up and down the little streets of the town, staring in shop windows, trilling songs to myself, skipping from one foot to the next like a child.

I kept stopping strangers on the street, asking, "Is it five o'clock yet? I have somewhere to go to." And they'd look at me curiously, and pry out their watch chains, straining to read the hour. I felt important, like I had a mission, for the first time maybe ever.

When five o'clock finally rolled round, I was standing outside the feed store, feet tapping in anticipation. I could see the boy inside, sweeping the floor. I was tempted to go in and help him, but the minx in me thought it'd be more fun to leap out from the porch and yell Boo!

But then a tall woman with a sharp face marched up the steps to the store and whisked him out after her. He had a brown sack in his hand, and I wondered if it was meant for me. "Alvin, you'll be having supper with me this evening. Can't have you living on cookies and milk while your parents are away!"

"But Aunt Ella, I have somewhere I have to go," the boy said, staring at me sorrowfully as the woman dragged him by the elbow up the street. She didn't even glance in my direction.

My eyes followed them up till they got to the corner and I wanted to cry or pout or even go after them, but all I could do was spit, big juicy wads of it out onto the sidewalk. Until I was overcome with a huge weariness, the kind that hangs over you like a black shawl and robs all light, all hope from you, and the only thing left to do is slide down onto your back and sleep.

"Wake up! Wake up! We have to go now!" The boy was hunched over me as I came to, and I noticed, for the first time, that his eyes were the color of mink fur, soft brown circles.

The light was bleeding out of the sky as we ran, his hand pulling mine by the wrist, up the hill, round the clock tower, and on out beyond the town. My mouth was dry and my sleepy head trying to catch up with where I was. "Almost there," the boy whispered, as he ran ahead. I was surprised to see such energy in him; he'd seemed a sober, thoughtful type, the kind who would ponder as he strolled. The sight of him dashing along on my behalf pleased me.

"Where?" I asked, between breaths.

"You'll see."

And I did. When we got to a bunch of trees, short, fat ones, the like of which I'd never seen, the boy stopped. "OK," he said, "we have to count," and he ran his fingers along the trunks, one, two, three, four, until we were deep in the forest. "Thirteen! This is it," the boy said, and I looked at the wide tree where his hand was. "Miss Stetson, this is your home." He spoke with great ceremony and then pushed against the wood. My heart skipped a beat when a big fist of it fell away and we were peering straight into the trunk. The boy slipped his arm inside and pulled out a small lantern. And before I could catch my breath again, he was flashing it inside the tree. I could see it was hollowed out, maybe dead. There were odd bits of crockery inside it, half an old mattress, it looked like, and books, stacks of them.

"This is my special hideaway," the boy said, and I could tell he was really proud of it. "It's where I come to read and hear the birds and just plain be alone."

"You don't get lonely?" I asked.

"Sure I do, but more so, when I'm round folks who ignore me."

"Oh," I nodded, thinking this boy really could be a friend. We understood each other, maybe.

He climbed ahead inside and reached for my hand to draw me in. We had to squeeze tight together to even fit. It was all lit up like the inside of a huge pumpkin from the lantern. I'd never been in any-thing like it. "How'd you ever find it?"

"Been coming up here for years, just walking, looking, you know. One day, I tapped against this tree and I knew it was hollow; took me a few weeks to carve out the entryway with my pa's hunting tools."

"And the mattress?"

"Aunt Ell's mother's. They tossed it in the town dump. I dragged it out when everyone was in bed and hauled the thing up here on my back."

"You're pretty darn strong, then?"

"You bet. We learned wrestling in school, when I used to be in school." His voice had a sound of sadness in it.

"Why aren't you going anymore?"

"Store," he said, as if that one word explained the whole mystery of life.

I just nodded, content for now to be sitting on a raggy mattress inside a tree, with a boy who was as alone in this world as I.

I remember how we sat in silence a long, long time and how it didn't feel strange one bit. When I woke in the night, the boy was curled in next to me, on his side, and my arm resting of its own accord on his shoulder. He sure wasn't afraid of snakes right then. The two of us clung together like orphaned birds nesting.

"You stay right here," he said to me, Alvin, that was his name, as he was leaving the next morning. "I have to get the store opened, but I'll be back this evening and bring you some supplies."

I wasn't sure I wanted to hide away in the forest all by myself. I was better at moving through it than sitting in one spot. And yet, the warmth of the night's rest and the kindness of a stranger-friend made me yearn to hold onto it.

"I wish you didn't have to go," I told Alvin, before I could help myself. I felt awkward being so forward, but he nodded as if he knew what I meant.

"I'll not be gone long."

With each passing day, that treehouse felt more lonesome. I took to counting the buttery toadstools that stood like hats waiting for a fairy to try them on. Some mornings, I'd sit by the creek, skimming stones on top of stones, building forts out of sticks and wild moss. Some days, I'd pick wildflowers, yellow and white and purple ones, and stick them in the rusted can I found on the bank. If I got bored at that, I'd toss twigs at the birds, but never close enough to hit them, just to keep them on their toes. Ma said it was bad luck to hurt anyone smaller than yourself. And I had to fight off the notion of Todd and his little, useless hands.

In the evenings, Alvin would appear breathless and rosy-cheeked and his pants sopping from the shortcut he took across the Lewiston River. His pockets would be laden down with goodies, ham, bread, cheese, sometimes a tomato. He'd usually bring a jar of tart cider too, though God knows where he got it. Sometimes I was afraid to ask.

We'd have an evening picnic out on the grass, the wildflowers between us, and we'd chew in silence till the sky charred over black and then we'd play Spot the Star as they came out. Maybe it was a childish thing for almost-grownups to be doing, but there was no one to judge, and anyway, why not? You couldn't just ignore all that silver blazing above you.

One extra-hot day, the air seemed still as stones. Until evening at least, and then the rains pelted down in a fury, and the east wind blew so hard that when Alvin and I sat in our house, looking skyward, we could see the tree tips dance.

Once it quieted, Alvin took my hand between his two flat ones, and told me stories. Mostly they were about his growing up, and how his parents hadn't really expected him and that they still looked on him as a stranger. When I squeezed his fingers at the sad parts, he'd get quiet. He didn't want pity and I understood that.

"Tell me about you," he'd ask, and I'd talk about my dad, and how he left when I was five or six, and how I remembered snatches of his songs, though sometimes I wasn't sure how much of them I'd made up. "He had this gingery mustache that came down like a rainbow over his mouth and it'd tickle when he kissed me." Alvin laughed at that. "And a scar on his neck. Ma always said it was shaped like a question mark and how it fit him perfect!"

"Stetson," he laughed. "Fine name for a cowboy."

"That's exactly what he said!" I looked at Alvin, startled, like he'd broken some secret code.

"D'you ever wonder where he is? I would, if it was my dad."

"On a horse, that's where." I was watching the band of stars gathered above me and I jumped when I saw how they ran together like a question. "He's out west, is all I know."

"The West's a big place," said Alvin. "Been reading about how the cowboys took over the Wallowa Mountains and beyond. Pushed those Nez Perce Indians out of their homes while they were at it."

"Wallowa?"

"Yeah, that's down toward Oregon. Pretty country, lured a load of buckaroos down there, my dad says."

"Wallowa." The word sounded funny on my tongue, round and soft and almost, I don't know, familiar. "Wallowa . . ." Like you could lean back and rest in the ow of it.

When Alvin was gone in the days, I started leafing through his books, not that I was really curious, mind. Just tired of counting mushrooms. Even though I knew all the Scottish stories by heart, I couldn't read grown-up books that well. But I enjoyed the pictures. There were loads of cowboys on horses and soon I was searching for my own dad. As if I'd find him up here in the woods of Idaho, inside the leaves of a book.

None of the lined, tired faces looked like my pa, I was sure. His skin was perfect, clear and bright except for that scar. I knew how my dad would look, I realized. I knew I'd recognize him soon as I set eyes on him. There was a horse, though, that looked just right. The book said he was a sorrel mare, lean and elegant an animal as I'd ever laid eyes on. His coat looked like it had been dipped in a vat of fall leaves, and it shone like washed baby's hair. I could see my dad, or anyone else, falling in love with him. Day after day, I'd pore over the same books, not even going outside to bathe, studying each face for hours, looking for a sign.

One evening, Alvin appeared and found me astride a curving tree trunk, as if it were a leather saddle.

"Do I seem dauntless to you, Alvin, brave, I mean?"

"Well, I don't know many folks who up and leave their home without at least a suitcase and a plan."

That didn't feel like the right answer. If I was going to be truly brave, I'd have to leave the forest. I looked down toward the book in my lap.

"He's not in there, Taf, I promise you. Those books I got from a used store; they're ancient."

"But he might be, he just might. Maybe someone snapped his picture soon as he got to Wallowa."

"So that's what you're thinking now? Your dad's in Wallowa? He could be anywhere."

That made me mad. I could feel the heat rising in my belly. "Don't say that!" I leaned out from my perch and thumped him hard on the arm.

"OK, OK, I'm sorry." Alvin took my blows without moving. It made me wonder, afterward, if he was used to it.

I stood up, straight and serious, and looked hard at the boy. "Well, now I do have a plan," I declared, and then swallowed slow as molasses. "I am going to Wallowa!"

Alvin's eyes widened like they had the first time I met him. "Taffy, it's miles off. It's getting on toward fall, it'll be cold . . ."

"I'm going." And just like that, my mind was made up. "Alvin, will you come with me?"

"I . . . I."

"I'm asking you. Will you accompany me or do I have to go alone?"

"How can I leave, Taf? I have my family and the store and maybe school . . ."

"Dumb store, you know you hate it!" I started gathering up things, though I had nothing to take.

"Taffy, please. Please don't leave." Those words tore at my heart, someone actually wanting me, and telling me so, and not just because I was useful. But the voice calling me onward was louder in my head and I knew if I tried to ignore it, I wouldn't have another day's peace.

"I'll sleep the night, Alvin, and take off before dawn." I felt somehow lighter just saying it.

When I opened my eyes again and stretched to the sounds of the owl next door, Alvin was standing outside, his arms clutching a package. "For the road," he said, leaning into the treehouse and kissing my cheek. I saw damp patches at the corners of his eyes.

"Good luck to you, Taf," he whispered. "I'll miss you. Never met a girl like you before." And as I was heading down the hill, he shouted after me, "Will you write to me?"

"Once I find my dad, I'll bring him here to meet you. We'll see each other again."

But my words rang out hollow as the tree trunks.

Chapter 3

The days were growing shorter and the temperature dropping, little by little. At first, I was warm enough, what with the cheese and ham Alvin had packed for me. Fuel, he called it. But soon enough, I had to put on his father's woolen socks. They needed darning around the toes but the heels and ankles were cozy. I stuffed more leaves into the holes and that helped a bit, though it made an awful racket if I moved at all, like a gang of crows fighting over carrion. Sometimes the noise woke me when I turned in my sleep. Alvin had given me a pair of his own shoes, which were wide and made me trip. Still, it was a small price to pay for the dazzle of the sky overhead, how it stretched out like a hood full of grand promises.

I passed through so many small towns, their names began to blur. I learned quickly how to snatch a loaf of bread off the tray in bakeries. I'd enter with the workers right at dusk as the baker was busy ringing up purchases, slip a loaf under my elbow and out the door. My heart did a little leap each time I edged outside, and then it'd dance with me all the way down the street as I tore off warm yeasty hunks and shoved them into my mouth. Better than any meal in a fancy hotel, I sang to myself as I hurried. If there was any left when I got to a field, I'd have a sit-down, maybe squeeze the juice of a plum, or if I was lucky, a peach, onto the bread, and I'd suck on the concoction like it was melting butter. These are the days, I'd tell myself, just me and the great sky above me.

You never get what you expect, my mother used to say, until you expect what you get. I thought it a peculiar notion but right then I wondered if the accident with Todd had been the only way to get me on the road and bring back my dad to where he truly belonged. I knew Ma missed him even now. It was as if laughter marched right out of our house soon as he did. Something in Ma had shrunk since he'd gone. Maybe that accounted for the way my feet wouldn't sit still. If that was the case, then surely, surely Todd wasn't dead after his fall. One day we would all be a happy family again, put our mistakes and our travels behind us, Ma'd smile wide again and forgive me for running away and, best of all, she'd tell Hank to take off for Monmouth in his automobile and keep driving.

But soon the weather turned so cold that it'd wake me up. In the mornings, I could almost peel frost off my face, and my toes were all tingly. I had to use my hair scarf to blow my nose. "*October died, and December was born.*" That was the first line of *Mossycoat*, and I could have used one just then. The way I remembered the story, this coat was woven of moss and gold thread, and whoever put it on had all their wishes granted. But sadly, this wasn't a fairy tale. It was early winter settling in on a poorly clad runaway girl.

It was closing in on dusk one day when I stumbled over a huge boulder in a field and landed smash in a heap of hard sticks. I pulled myself up, throbbing, but as my eyes adjusted to the leaving light, I found not sticks, but row upon row of animal carcasses. I could have been in a coffin without a lid. My arms shook with weakness, or maybe it was the sound, the crack and snap of leg or neck or hoof no matter how I moved. The beckoning dark made each bone glow into a ghost. I climbed over each one, as steady as my half-frozen feet would let me, terrified I'd collapse into the open grave, and never get up again.

Finally I crossed into another field, and came to a tumble-down building, where a man was relieving himself against a wall. I waited for him to finish and blurted out about the carcasses.

"Dead elk," he said, moving away. "Froze last winter."

There was a truck of some sort sitting there—it looked like the kind Farmer Dan back along the Idle had—and the man climbed in behind the steering wheel. I could hear squawking chickens in the back, and I lifted up the latch at the rear and clambered in beside them, a flurry of feathers and scrambling in the process. Soon as the hullabaloo settled a bit, I found an empty corner and lay myself down like a worn-out dog, and let sleep carry away all ugliness, for it was too heavy for my heart to carry.

The truck was rumbling loud along the road when I came to again, and a man's croaky voice was singing up front, *Give me one good woman and I'll give you a dollar bill* . . .

Wherever he was going with his chickens, I let him take me there too. We must've gone a long way, for it went dark then light before the truck slowed down. I lifted the hatch in the back and jumped out, tumbling along in the dust. Look at me now, Dad, I wanted to shout, see how I'm doing. Soon as your dauntless girl finds you, we can trade our adventures.

But even though the sun was out, I was shivering inside, and I hoped this winter would be kinder than last one was to those elk. I walked and walked till my feet warmed up at least, though they were raw, and one big toe kept bleeding.

I passed a few towns on my travels, but I hardly ever stayed long. One day, I came across a huge sign on a little store, J. Begley & Sons, Slaughterers in Spokane, Washington, since 1910, it said. I don't know if I was more surprised by the business or the place.

I'd only ever heard tell of the state of Washington in geography class back in school. It had seemed lifetimes away to me then, and here I was strolling through it as if I belonged.

Somehow I managed to keep moving toward the Oregon border. I'd follow the smell of farmyards, for they usually had a barn or a stable where I could borrow some hay to rest my busy legs in. Those months blurred into one long day of cold and cloud and little more than the edge of hunger luring me on.

By the time I got to a particular town beyond Three Creek, I was shaky with weariness. Out on the ledge of a house sat a jug of fresh milk. I could see the steam rising off it. And it cried out to me, in that same insistent voice that kept me moving, moving. It was more pushy even than Miss Mantz, who had once tried to squeeze elocution down my child-throat. And I was upon the jug in seconds. Hardly had I lifted it than a round woman with a rolling pin came charging out the door of the house. "What the—!" she shouted at me and I turned, jumping back a bit, and dropped the jug smack on the concrete. Milk ran in warm rivers round our feet.

"You bold girl!" the woman shouted, the bun of her black hair bobbing madly about on her head. "You've ruined my china service."

I just stood there, my heart clinking around inside me. Todd was hovering over me again.

"I'll make you pay for this." And the woman swung her pin at me, brushing my arm. I almost wanted her to hurt me, to beat me into a pulp, like Hank used to. I wanted to be freed of this cold heaviness that was bearing down on me. Hit me, please go ahead and hit me, I wanted to tell this woman with the knotted face and wild hair, punch away everything till I'm stripped bare. But nothing would come out of my mouth.

I was still standing there when a man appeared at the doorway. His eyebrows jumped up into his forehead when he took in the scene. "What's going on out here?"

The woman pointed to the sill as if that explained everything. And maybe it did, for the man limped over to me and took hold of my shoulder. "You'll pick up every scrap of china off the ground, you hear? Every last scrap."

I nodded, and tried to bend down toward the shattered pieces. He held onto the hem of my dress so I couldn't get away. Not that I intended to this time. I wanted to pay off my debt, in some strange way. The woman by then had brought out a tin bucket and I carefully set the broken jug in that. As I got the last of it, the man called out Minnie! and a sleek cat came sauntering out, blinking in the harsh sunlight, and busied her tongue in the pool of milk. The man nodded and shuffled off toward the barn.

"What were you up to at all?" The woman's voice was scolding now, but softer.

"I, I was thirsty," I muttered, swiping at my mouth, wondering if there was dirt on it from the damp ground where I'd slept last night. I could see her taking me in, her eyes moving in quick lines up and down my body. "Hmmm," she seemed to say. "Come inside, and let's get you a proper drink. I had that milk set out there to cool. You'd have scalded yourself had you drank it."

I followed the woman inside, not certain what would await me in there. But she just went to a huge urn of milk, dipped a saucepan into it and then set the pan on the stove.

"From the looks of you, you could use some grits as well." The woman started buttering slices of bread on the table. A wave of sadness moved through me and I wondered was it shame.

"I'm sorry," I said in a quiet voice. "I'm very, very sorry."

"Hush now, girl," and she slid a plate under my nose. "Sit and eat and we'll forget what happened. That's the beauty of old age, our memories abandon us!"

And she smiled, soft in her eyes; they were as deep brown as chocolate, almost the same shade as her hair. I scraped back a chair and sat down.

"Haven't seen your like round here before."

Nor I hers, when I thought about it. Her skin was sunnier than mine, and the man's face, from my brief look, had a hue of wet tobacco.

"Place near the Idle River's where I grew up."

"Is it now? You're a long way from home. And to where might you be traveling?"

"Wallowa County, Oregon, ma'am. It's where cowboys live."

She smiled at that. "Wallowa, eh? Plenty of cowboys down those parts all right." She watched me eat and even though I knew she had her eye fixed on me, I forked the grits into my mouth in shovelfuls. I hadn't tasted anything this good since I left home. Home, wherever that was.

"Say," the lady said. "There's a mail coach goes to Wallowa every couple months. Fellow with a team of mules and a stagecoach that likely harks back to the Stone Age. Timmy the mailman, he refuses to use modern vehicles, don't ask me why, because it takes him forever. But if you don't mind rocking your way there, you could go with him. His rates are affordable, and you'd make better time than you would with those feet."

And I knew she'd seen the tattered leaves sticking out of my shoes. For the first time since I'd left, I felt embarrassed.

"Maybe," I said. "When?"

"Timmy'd be leaving, what day's today, Thursday? He'll be off Sunday morning after next. Before dawn, I'd wager. You'd find yourself in Wallowa within a week or two."

I sat, staring at her, my plate scraped clean.

"You don't have to say now. Think." Then she paused. "I'm Bessie. You can go out the barn and help my brother with his cows."

I was only too glad to get out of that kitchen where everything seemed to close in on me. It made me feel warm and sleepy, like if I sat there for long, I might never want to leave again.

"Yes, ma'am."

"Not ma'am. Bessie!" she cried after me as I lit out the door and across to the red barn.

"There she is, the milk thief!" the man said when he saw me, but there was humor in his voice. "You hear that, cows? This girl's after your prize jewels."

I could feel my face heat up, but the man didn't look at me, just kept on his stool, hunkered toward a cow, his arms pulling up and down. White liquid plopped into a metal bucket, like watery snow-flakes. "Come down here and I'll show you how it's done," he said to me, and I knelt down on the hay-covered floor and he pressed my hands round the cow's teat, guiding them to draw milk out as if this was the most natural thing in the world for a runaway girl to be doing.

I felt comfy there; the smells of hay and cow dung were those I'd gone to sleep with many nights. It was nice to be part of it. We must have worked through two dozen cows when Bessie appeared at the door. "Supper's set for Ama."

The man got up from his knees, for he had given me the stool, and wiped his hands down his trouser legs. "Right you are, Bess," he said. Then he looked straight at me. "You want to meet our mother?"

I wasn't sure I was ready for another person. Two strangers being kind to me after I robbed them was enough for one day. He could see my hesitation, I knew. "It's OK. She might look strange, but she doesn't bite."

So I found myself strolling down a laneway with a basket of steaming potatoes and gravy in my arms. And the towering man keeping pace, dragging his limp leg along behind him. I wished Alvin could see me now; he'd be surprised. Dear, lonely Alvin. He could have been my brother, the way we both made do with life's strange circumstance. Only Alvin chose to stay close to home, and I didn't. Maybe there's only ever room for one dauntless person in a story, and maybe he was the brave one after all.

The man's mother sat in a chair in the corner of her tiny house. She was herself a tiny figure, like a burnt matchstick. I thought of Todd and Joey and how bad things can happen to folks who are left too long alone.

"Ama, meet—what is your name?" The man turned to me.

"Taffy Stetson, ma'am."

"Well, Taffy here is helping with chores."

"I'm so glad you finally got someone to give you a hand, *seme*."

"Yes," the man smiled. "You have to be open to the windfalls that crash through your door."

"You do, you do," the mother said. "Come over here, *neska*, till I meet you."

I stood before this tiny, frail creature, who used words I'd never heard before, and let her examine me. She leaned close and took my hands in hers. I imagined she would be freezing cold, but a heat like a wood stove ran from hers to my own. She squeezed each finger lightly, nodding. When I finally managed to look her in the face, I saw that her eyes went in two different directions. One toward her nose, the other straight ahead. Neither of them seemed to move.

"Ama doesn't see too well any more," the man explained.

"This is a good girl," the old woman said. "A girl with *azari*, spirit." She sat up straight, still gripping my hands. "You follow your heart, and that's a good thing, but it won't lead where you expect."

My breath started leaping all over the place then.

"Don't burden yourself with Ama's visions. She's always imagining something." The man was setting the food on the table. "It's probably that whiskey she hides down here."

"Stay for supper with me."

I could hardly breathe, the room was so dark and cold. And this woman telling me things I might not understand or even want to hear. But the heat in her hands was warming my insides and I knew, as surely as I knew I must find my father, that now, this evening, I must stay.

"Go on ahead," I told the man.

"Do you want to eat down here, then?"

"Later," was all I could push past the lump in my throat, and I shivered, a long, cold jumping of skin as he left.

"*Neska.*" The woman spoke quietly; her words seemed to come through her nose. "You'll find a glass and a fruit jar in the corner behind the straw bale."

I'd no sooner set them on the table beside her than she pried the lid off the jar, filled the glass, small as a thimble, raised it to her mouth, and swallowed hard. "Aaggh!" She sputtered and then poured a second. "This round's for you. Drink it while you can, it won't last."

I examined the shining liquid, a sunlit sheen to it. It looked like heated-up water, golden, and I was helpless but to follow the old lady's lead. My tongue sizzled so hard I thought it had caught fire, but then, a second later, a glorious warmth dribbled down my throat and into my belly. Stars seemed to shimmer upward on their way through my head to the sky. Was this how Hank felt after his rum? No wonder he'd have to have two or several or sometimes a half dozen. Maybe I was just dreaming, but if so, I was glad of it. Since Todd had crashed out of my arms, I'd had little more than nightmares and was usually glad to wake up.

The woman's voice cut through my mind's wandering. "Pull up a seat beside me, while I eat, and tell me how you got here." She spoke in a way that wasn't prying or even curious.

I sat on a chipped red stool in front of the old woman and watched as she picked potato pieces out of the basket, the floury bits catching on the sides of her mouth. For a while, all I could do was follow the path of her arm up to her lips and back down again. I was half hoping she'd offer me more of the magic drink. The more I looked, the more it seemed there was a sort of glow, like a sunrise coming from behind her. After a while, I couldn't take my eyes off it.

The woman spoke, between bites. "You're a deep one, I can tell that."

I wanted to ask her what she meant, but she set her food aside, took my hands again, and went on, "It's all right. You didn't do a thing wrong."

My forehead was beading up with sweat all of a sudden.

"Wasn't your fault what happened, *neska*. Remember that."

"I—I . . ." No words would come out from me. I was dry as an ironing board, and hot.

"There is someone though, who will have to do you a lot of forgiving." She said it just like that, as if it made perfect sense. Maybe she could tell how nervous I was starting to feel, for she changed direction in an instant.

"You like moving about, don't you?"

I nodded, even though she couldn't see me.

"It's in your blood. Your blood is strong like a river." She got quiet then, her hand going limp. Then she drew in a long, dark breath. When she let it out, I thought I saw fire for a second, just a flash of a flame. I thought I must be going mad.

"The road may not be the best place for you."

"But I'm happy out there and I want to find my daddy!" Out it came, pouring like tears all over the old lady's ears. "Besides, I can't go back now."

She patted my hands gently.

"Left when I was small. I remember tunes he'd sing: *I am a man upon the land.* He called me Twiddler sometimes, Ma said, and then he saddled up his horse one day and rode off somewheres far from us and if I find him, if I can just hug him, then I'll be able to rest, then maybe we can both settle . . ." And I was out of breath, my head lowering down onto the woman's lap, till she could stroke the length of my hair. I lay there, bent over her, and let my eyes close. I couldn't bear to keep them open any longer.

"Settle yourself here a while, *ume*. For it's certain that you'll follow that road set out for you, and that road can only lead to sorrow . . ." I'm sure it's what I heard as I lay there, dozing, but it sounded more like a fairy tale carried on the wind and intended for a person in a picture book, not me, definitely not me.

"Poor child's about wore out," I heard the old lady say, as I opened my eyes and found her son crouched under the doorway, for he was taller than it. "She needs a solid night's sleep."

"I'll take her back up to the farmhouse, Ama." And he lifted me, my aching carcass of bones, up off her lap and into his big arms and hefted me on his unsteady foot all the way back up the alley.

I don't remember anything after that, except a wild dream where I was standing on the range with a giant lasso and I was trying to rein in the horse my father was on, but it got harder and harder each time I threw, and when it finally hooked round the horse's neck, nothing would budge. The man on the horse was not my father; it was a statue after all.

Chapter 4

It must have been the next morning when I came to, the scent of sausages frying downstairs. I couldn't believe the hardness of the bed. Even back on the Idle River, I'd slept mostly on the worn-out armchair, which sank down in the middle. So this was what it felt like. I pulled my body out from under the heavy quilt, my legs wet sponge under me. It was as if something unseen was cuffing me to the ground. I could hear voices drifting up from the kitchen.

"She's a lost soul, that one, I'd say," the man's voice.

"Does she remind you of anyone?" the woman.

The man coughed, and then a loud sputtering. I creaked down the staircase before I could hear any more. When I opened the kitchen door, the woman turned in surprise toward me, and she had water pooling out of her eyes.

"You all right, ma'am?" I didn't know what else to say.

"She's fine," said her brother, and he started piling sausages onto a metal tray. "Sit yourself down till we feed you."

"You know my name, and it ain't Ma'am." The woman dabbed at her eyes with a tea cloth. "And this here's my brother, Jack. So now you know."

I nodded as she set an enamel dish in front of me, and a fork. "Well, I'm Taf Stetson."

Bessie asked, "Like those pretty taffeta party dresses?"

"Don't think so." I'd felt taffeta before. A girl at school had a ballerina doll, who wore a skirt made of it, and it felt stiff and foreign in my hands. "What does *ume* mean?" I asked. "And *neska?*"

Jack kept smiling. "Mother's a stubborn woman, that's certain. She's from the old country . . ."

"Scotland?" I leaped out of my chair. "My dad's from there too!"

"Is he now?" Jack motioned his arm for me to sit again. "Well, in this world, there's as many old countries as there are people to come from them, I reckon. Ama's old country is Spain. She's a Basque."

I'd heard of Spain. But Basque had the ring of something you'd carry Easter eggs in, very carefully.

"Basque's a region in Spain, has its own ways, though," Jack explained. "Lotta sheepherders came out here from there. Ama married one. She likes to keep the old language burning. Those words she uses, they're just words of affection."

"Like honey?" I'd heard church ladies speak like that to their daughters.

"Sure, honey. Just like that."

It was my turn to smile, at Jack's easy humor. But Bessie never spoke, just ate as if her mouth were solid with grief, half chewing, then staring off, her eyes wetting up every so often, the way Ma's would after Pa left.

Jack broke our long silence. "Girl, we reckon you need to rest up a while. You can stay here long as you need, help us out with the farm a little. We'd be glad of . . . of . . . the company."

And that's when Bessie leaped up from the table and ran out of the room.

I looked at Jack.

"Bess!" he shouted after his sister. Everything felt strange this morning, as if in the night someone had switched round the characters in a story for a prank. Secrets and strange languages and tears; this family would have fit right into my dad's folk tales.

"Bess had a girl," said Jack, looking almost through me, "Lourdes, after that place where miracles are said to occur. She was a good child, a serious child. Seven years old and as good a fishergirl as ever you'd find. She'd ring trout out of the Snake, long as your leg, shame all the neighbors, you'd swear the fish just waited to nip on her line. Lourdes fell in one day, who knows how, never found even a hem of her dress. I reckon Bessie been thinking of her every single day."

"Oh, I'm sorry," I said, but what I was feeling was a muddle inside. I started wondering if my ma ever fretted over my disappearance. Even if she felt inclined, Hank'd probably put a stop to it. And that thought made me even sadder, that there was no one in this lonesome world to mourn me.

I felt selfish because I could see how upset Bessie was, but I couldn't help my own feelings. It was like they belonged to someone else, and suddenly they'd been handed over to me. My stomach hurt, trying to wrestle through each of them. No sooner would one feeling hit me than another would jump in. I didn't cry, just sat there at the table in a dither.

All I could do was repeat, "Lourdes."

"It's a long way from here, France, I believe. But people go from round the world to ask for special favors."

"It's a good name for a girl," I said, and meant it. I wondered if maybe I should try to go there myself, and ask for Todd back and for my dad to come home. But right then I felt tired out, and a trip overseas, well, I could be as old as Ama by the time I got there, and by then it'd be too late.

"You want to help me with the cows again today?"

"I think I should find your sister, talk to her." I hadn't known I was even going to say that, but once I did, it seemed right.

"As you please."

And so I crept toward the room where I could hear muffled sobs, knocking lightly on the door. "Bessie, it's me," I whispered.

"Come on in," I thought I heard her say.

She was lying on her side, on a bed, her back to me. She didn't turn around, so I walked across to her and it felt natural to stroke her arm, and smooth her dark hair, and she started crying even more, and I kept on running my hands softly along the folds of her body, a gentle, almost rocking movement. And she kept on crying, as if she had the sorrows of the entire United States inside her. She held onto her belly, not trying to stop the tears, and I kept on rubbing. "Yes," I whispered. "Yes."

And then, she patted the bed in front of her, as if she wanted me to slide in beside her, and so I did. It was like being in a trance as I eased down and slid into the curve of her belly and legs, so that we fit together like slotted spoons. I thought of the story in my dad's book where the girl, after all her sad wanderings, arrives at the happily ever after. And then Bessie put her arm round my tummy and I could feel her breasts like a cushion on my back and we soothed ourselves in the luxurious peace of deep slumber.

It must have been dark when Jack tapped on the door. "Ladies, you all right in there?" He sounded like a child frightened of what he might see through the door.

"Yes, yes, we'll be out in a minute." Bessie rustled the blanket she'd strung over us. "It's time for us to fix his supper, is what," she giggled, and that made me laugh, and then we were rocking like two children in sheer delight at ourselves.

We never spoke of that day again, but I began to feel almost happy on this farm, in Lourdes' old room, as if I had a place here, as if there was a home for even wild misfits like me.

I took to milking a good quarter of the cows for Jack, and I helped him with baling hay in the barn. Bessie taught me to make onion cornbread and serve it with pickles and mustard. We stopped whatever we were doing, all three of us, midafternoon and Jack fixed a pot full of coffee and we'd sit on the bench against the barn wall and chew on our snacks. Sometimes I wished Alvin could have shared it all with us. It was a good life, I knew it. I felt comfier than I might have ever, but it felt odd too, like I was playing at someone else, not me. I told myself it just took getting used to feeling wanted.

I suppose in her way that Ma loved me. She never said as much, but sometimes when I was fixing supper, she'd pat my hair from behind. So light, I'd jump, and grope for the daddy-long-legs I thought had landed on my head. That'd make Ma laugh and move away, and I'd long to have her hand back, to promise her I wouldn't stir an inch if she'd just stroke her fingers down my back again. But I couldn't seem to find the words; they'd catch in a fist under my throat. She wasn't much for cuddling or anything, and I could understand that, most of the time. Those bitter winters, sure, it was all we could do to keep a fire blazing and our feet from frostbite.

Maybe I just imagined how much Ma smiled when Pa used to live with us. The apple blush of her cheeks. She had startling white teeth, I'm sure of that, before they started to break and fall out. And it was she who read the fairy tales from Pa's book; that's how I learned them. I had most of them by heart before I was six. Memory was a strange thing. *It was not well, sang the maiden fair, it was not well indeed, quoth she, that the great silkie from Shule Skerrie should have come and aught a bairn to me.* I hardly understood what the words meant, yet something in Ma's voice made every story an easy story.

Of course, that was before we lost Pa to the cowboys. Something in Ma gave up then; she melted into herself like hot snow. And

Hank pushing his way into our lives, well, she had no strength to declare otherwise. And soon the twins came along—I'll never forget that long winter of her childbearing; I thought she might snap in half—and Hank became a habit she couldn't break. She still loved me, loved us all, I'd wager. But she hadn't the will left to express it.

One day when we finished our chores, Jack took me on a long ramble, out beyond Three Creek. Owyhee, he said the Indians called it. There were slinky tadpoles darting through the water, as if they had a clear plan about their destination. We hunkered in the creek, as they danced around our shins. Jack showed me how to cup my hands so no water leaked through, and to rest them in the water next to a rock, and before we knew it, I had one, two, three shiny tadpoles sliding between my palms. Bubbles of laughter rose up in me as I drew my hands out into the air, and each creature slid through my opening fingers in a gush of spring water back where it belonged.

Jack and I made a game out of it, catching salamanders, too, and newts, and then returning them to the spring and trying to find where they went. They moved fast though, and would trick us. There were so many stones for them to hide under; once, when I turned over a rock, a frog leaped up on the strength of his hind legs and took off.

I loved that game so much, I'd walk the afternoons away, going there and back, my hands slimy with water creatures. Jack didn't come after that one time, for it was a drain on his leg. So I'd whistle sad Scottish tunes as I moved, to myself and the sky, until the sky grew dark with weariness.

But one evening, my neck and shoulders ached so much, I lay awake all night, squirming on my mattress upstairs, the moon lighting up my room. It seemed to be almost crying out to me to come join its mysterious dance out there in the sky. Whenever I'd close my eyes, I'd see that mail coach waltzing along the road and a great big sign that read Welcome to Wallowa.

Next day, all day I was restless as can be, fidgeting at the breakfast table, milking one cow, then getting up and pacing across to the hay barn, then picking apples out of the crate and tossing them into the water barrel. I couldn't sit still. Jack must have noticed, though he said nothing. *I am a man upon the land,* the line from my pa's book sang itself through me, but somehow I didn't think this was what it meant. To be really on the land, surely you had to keep moving through it.

I thought of going down to see Ama, for I hadn't seen much of her, but that was one place my legs wouldn't carry me. Whatever magic was in that flask, I wanted it and yet the thought of it set me shivering.

I went to bed early, feigning a headache, and Bessie brought me warm milk and a peanut cookie and tucked me in. Then she pulled a sheaf of clothes out of the closet and set them on the chair next to me. "It might seem odd to go round wearing trousers, but farming's dirty work, and they'll keep your legs warm." I nodded and took deep breaths and tried to tell myself that I'd be a fool to give this up. Here was a family who made a place for me, a place that Lourdes had vacated, yet how could it feel right when there was still a hole left back on the Idle River, where my pa, me, and Todd ought to be? Surely I should be trying to fill that.

All of the next week, I kept busy, and one day passed into the next. Often, Jack would fill us with terrible jokes, such as, "What works up a steam? Why, Peaches and Cream. My ladies are sweet as Peaches and Cream." And we'd laugh hard, for this was one of Bess's favorite tunes. You'd always catch her singing it when she was peeling potatoes or doing her knitting in the evenings. Jack's sense of fun was a welcome light in that house. But he'd a serious side, too. He'd sit in the window seat after supper with the radio on low and his brows knit together, shaking his head sometimes and muttering about how bad the world was turning, what with men maybe joining the war in Europe soon, and women on the rampage about alcohol. He said one day we wouldn't be allowed a simple beverage at all, maybe not even milk, and then the cows'd stop milking and then surely the whole of America would shrivel up and disappear. If we hadn't all been killed by the enemy first. If we could only decide who the enemy was.

Bessie, for her part, would tell tales of her childhood over the supper table, how she'd fallen and taken a lump out of her knee, and how all the local women had come round with pastries while she lay up in bed, "for they weren't sure would I die. We didn't know as much about infection back then." And they'd given her nickels and dimes, till she had a whole purse full of coins. "I was only six,' she laughed, "and I was rich!"

"Wouldn't happen nowadays," said Jack. "You could be lying dead in the ditch and not a one would be there to help . . ."

A long silence fell over us, and I wondered if maybe something had shifted with their neighbors after Lourdes' accident.

"Who went with Lourdes that last time?" I almost whispered, for it felt rude to break into the quiet.

"Farmer Mulligan took her fishing, regular on Sundays. Said he turned his back on her only a second to dig out fresh tackle and . . ."

"Don't, Jack," and I could see Bessie's cheeks sucking in toward her teeth.

"The girl wants to know, I'll tell her." Jack went on to say that since then, none of the Mulligans had set foot on this land again. "Used be we'd have shindigs every so often, at the turning of the season usually. A fiddle and some whiskey and everyone out dancing on this floor here. Been real quiet these past years."

"But it wasn't your fault what happened."

"In a way it was, child." Bessie sighed down into her cup. "Expecting one miracle too many."

"Well, I think it was mean of Farmer Mulligan to take it out on you," I burst out.

"Bygones," is all Bess said, and started clearing away the dishes.

I couldn't rest that night at all, my mind churning with visions of Lourdes running along the riverbanks, her hair blowing in the breeze, until she found the spot, and then the beautiful glide of a body through air, spinning and tumbling, holding on to nothing, until it got tired and flopped into the river. I could see the seriousness leak out of her face as she took off from the ground and sailed like a bird, like a wild eagle, soar, glide, turn, dip, plunge.

But then my head would wander to the next bit of the story and I'd puzzle over why the Mulligans chose to avoid poor Bessie and Jack on account of something they had no hand in. It got me to thinking about my own family and how Ma and me had never blamed Pa for taking off. We just wished he'd come back, and that started me pondering if maybe Ma could be worrying about what happened to me after all. She wasn't a mean woman, I knew that; she was just scared, and she let Hank bully her and us kids, probably 'cos she didn't want to lose a second man. But surely that wouldn't stop her missing me. And that idea got my head busy with imaginings—Ma crying herself to sleep each night; Ma screeching after me from the porch till her throat hurt; Ma going to the police and asking for their help—but I couldn't see any of them clearly. It was all a muddle of pictures in my mind, and they were faint as fog in winter.

Still, I couldn't help my feet walking toward the dresser drawer and pulling out a sheet of paper from the pile. I took one of Lourdes' colored pencils from the box on the table and sat myself down, took a breath, and started writing this: "Dear Ma, I'm sorry I had to leave so quick. I miss you and hope you are well. I am well and working for a farmer. Please give Joey a hug for me. Love, your daughter."

Then I added "gentle" before "hug," just in case she might think

I wasn't careful around children. And I couldn't help writing, "And a special hug for Todd." If I could just pretend he was alive, then he would be, surely. I tried to cross the words out again but my hand wouldn't let me. Writing it made me feel better, as if by going back to the past and clearing it up a little made the future shinier than before.

Next morning, I was up before anyone and had the milk boiled and set out on the ledge to cool before Bessie even wandered in, her pink dressing gown pulled tight around her.

"Morning!" I said cheerily.

"Well, heaven's sakes, look who's up and running today!"

"Yep! I have a letter I have to mail. Want some coffee, Bess?"

"Sounds good." She sat down at the table, rubbing the last bits of sleep out of her eyes.

"Where'd I find the mailman?" I asked, and I could see Bessie's face wake up in a hurry.

"The mailman? Why, Timmy's down in Milton-Freewater, has a little corner in the grocery store. Let Jack take it down for you."

"Nah—thanks, Bess. This is one I have to mail myself."

Just then, a cry pierced through the air that sent knives darting through my belly. I'd never heard such a scream in all my born days.

"What the—?" Bess was standing up now.

"I'll go see," and out the door I dashed, following the path of the sound. It was getting fainter and fainter as I ran toward the meadow, and then it faded out entirely. I hopped over the red fence and there was Turner our outdoor dog bent over something, his tongue out, dripping all over a mess on the grass. I could hear Turner panting as if he'd just climbed a mountain, and right between his front paws was a field cat, its coat tawny and gleaming in the morning sun, and its innards spilling out in a heap of bile from his belly. I could still see the fear in the cat's stunned eyes. Turner was sniffing and lapping over the mess, looking very pleased with himself.

"You bully, Turner!" I yelled and screamed and pounced on the dog, hitting him with the clubs of my fists until the bewildered animal scampered away. I fell down on the grass beside the dead cat, staring at its beautiful, wasted coat, and my insides erupted all at once till I'd spewed out a mess to match the cat's.

I carried that picture of the torn animal in my head all day. It just wouldn't leave, even though Bess swore it was natural as life itself. Dogs kill cats kill mice. It's the law as God wrote it, she said. Like big countries squash little countries? I asked. Jack had been telling me how the Basques had fought a long, hard time for their home-land in Spain, and many had to leave and come to America, where they were bullied still sometimes. But even as I knew all that, my heart couldn't accept. The poor cat just trying to get along, and it got pounced on. It was as if I could feel the cat's terror myself.

When I went into town that afternoon with my letter, I asked when Timmy the mailman would be back from Wallowa, and when he might be leaving again.

I can't even say I planned to leave; it was as if I just followed the path my feet elected of their own accord. Which is probably why I ended up going down to Ama's house that same evening. Sometimes my body seemed to act without waiting for my mind to catch up.

The old lady sat in the same chair she'd been in when I'd first visited her, as if she'd never once moved. "Come over and take Ama's hands."

Again I felt that warmth spiral through me, like a summer's heat wave, only it made me feel lively, not tired. Maybe it was that magic drink she kept hidden away. I wondered if she'd offer me another taste.

"How are you enjoying the farm?"

"I like it well enough," I said, for, whatever caused it, I couldn't lie to her.

"You like my son's jokes?" And we both smiled at that.

"You like my granddaughter's room?"

That question surprised me. "I guess. I mean, I think of her a lot, but I kinda feel it's my room now."

"It is. If you'll hold on to it."

"In what way?"

"You're thinking of leaving soon; it's in the pulse of your wrist."

"I am?"

"Listen to yourself. You know."

"You're right, Ama." I said, the light dawning slowly. "I feel I can't stay here much longer, but I don't know what to do."

"Pass me that wooden box from the mantel."

When I laid the old box in her lap, she opened it, without even bending her head, and drew something out. "Here," she pressed a large coin into my hands. It was the shade of night sky. "Use this wisely."

My breath was a tight rag in my throat. I could barely choke past it to say thank you. The coin was cold in my palm; there was a hole right in its center, like an iron man had poked his finger through. "Is it from the old country?"

Ama nodded. "Save it for when you need it; it won't disappoint you."

I was relieved to hear that, 'cos the silkie gave a purse of gold to the fair maid when he wanted his son back, and it was a very high price he paid, in the end. I nodded, closing my fingers round the strange weight. However long it took, I'd wait till I was wise enough to do the coin justice.

"Your life could run smoother if you stayed," she said to me. "There is a young man who has a big interest in you." And her head jerked back and I could see that same glow around her shoulders.

"But you will do what you have to do. . . . You have the power of true love in you. Trust it." And she drew her warm arms back into her lap. I felt cold.

I longed to ask her if she saw my daddy anywhere, or if I could bring her the flask again, but the words wouldn't come. So I sat, shaking, and the old woman said nothing more, just the sound of her breathing, in, out, in, out, like Ma's old watch ticking.

Eventually, I slid my chair back and stood up. "Thank you, Ama, for the gift," I said, as I moved toward the door, my tongue dry as sandpaper. "I'll never forget you."

And even though she didn't turn her head, I'm sure I heard her say, "Don't give up, *neska,*" as I walked out into the startling light. Or maybe it was "Good luck."

That night I had a dream that Lourdes was drifting above me. She didn't seem to be held up by anything, but was free-floating, her face white and grim. My hands were sweaty when I woke. I didn't even know what she looked like—there were no pictures around— but I knew it was her.

Even awake, I couldn't get her face out of my mind. One half of it was clouded over in a kind of fog. I got up to go to the bathroom. Keep moving, I told myself, she'll go away. But she didn't, and my legs carried me downstairs and straight into Bessie's room. She was lying there with her eyes wide open, the tiny lamp shining down one side of her.

"Bess," I started.

"It's all right, girl, come on in here beside me." And I huddled, knees to my chest under the blanket. Bess swung her arm around my shoulder, and pulled my head into the crook of her shoulder. I couldn't get comfy, though.

"Settle down, child. It's all right now."

She didn't ask if I'd had a bad dream, just held me, and I often wondered afterward if she knew more about my restlessness than I realized.

"Lourdes came to me," I whispered. "She's still here, hovering."

"Now, child, don't fret. This is her home too."

"But she's dead and half of her's covered in clouds."

"That's as may be, child." But I could feel her arm twitch over me. "Lourdes was a serious child when she was alive. Who knows if death changes anything?"

"They her pants you gave me to wear?"

"Uh-huh."

"Who was her pa?" I asked, in hopes that talking might make her ghost go away.

"Oh child, I was hoping you wouldn't ask me that."

"Well, if you don't want to."

"It's such a winding story." Bessie breathed deep and then went on. "I think about it every single day and by now, there's no beginning nor end to it."

"Were you married once?"

"I was not," she said. "Had thought to be, but it never happened."

"So it must have been a trial, having a girl and no husband? Kinda like my own ma before Hank. I remember how the church ladies'd turn the other way once they saw us."

"True, true." Bess sighed. "The hardest lesson of my life I learned from that: once a stranger, always a stranger."

Though I didn't understand exactly what she meant, I knew enough to see how Bess was not so different from myself, or even Alvin. We were all born on this soil, American as Turner the dog or the field cat, and I said as much. But Bess said that some folks fared better on the islands of this world. Let the river flow on its course, she said, some of us are destined to watch from the shore.

"I had Jack," Bessie went on. "That made all the difference. Lucky he's past the age for Europe."

"You mean the war?" I'd heard angry talk in the town about young men having to go to Germany, and fight for freedom. Who'd want to wield a gun against a stranger when he could be sauntering through fields, like I had, free as air?

She nodded. "Even if he was twenty, he'd not have to go. Had a bad leg since he fell out a half door working on Mulligan's farm. Got gangrene, he did, and had to have part of it gouged."

"Oh," I shivered, Lourdes' face still glaring down at us.

"Thank heaven for his sense of humor; that may be what saved him. Saved us." She hugged me even tighter then. "We had that stupid door nailed shut after that."

"A good thing," I said, though I wasn't sure it was. I wasn't sure of anything. We lay in silence until the first hint of light cracked through the curtains, Lourdes floating above us like a sign, and then my hands were pulling down the covers and I was crawling over Bessie and climbing out of the bed. It was like someone else was doing my walking for me, as I went upstairs and pulled my old shoes and dress out from the closet and put them on, someone else pushing me down the staircase, past Bess's room, past the kitchen, through the pantry, and out the door. I was moving over the cobbles, as if in a trance, out toward the road, and down to where I knew the mail coach would pass. I was moving like a winged creature, my feet not landing anywhere, just floating along, when I heard Bessie calling lightly from the back door. I turned to find her standing tall and stately, and her lips gathering into a word I knew she wanted me to have.

"Mulligan," she sang across the yard to me. "Farmer Mulligan." And as she moved to walk back inside the house, I saw the cloud on Lourdes' face lift briefly, and I sighed and turned back toward the direction I was headed.

Chapter 5

It turned out that northern Oregon was having a bad year weather-wise, that the Blue Mountains were already thick with snow, and we were hardly out of Milton-Freewater when Timmy the mailman screeched the horses to a halt and yelled, "I'm turnin' back, folks. No way we'll end up like John Craig. Let's hit Pendleton first." And he twisted his horses round so they were turned back the way they'd just come.

The snow was coming down heavy against our coach. It was like an old friend: every year the fields back home would whiten like magic, and I used to build cowboy snowmen with long, happy pipes in their mouths. I leaned my head out the side and let the flakes hit me, flick, flick, flick, tingling my skin. But the horses were afraid and kept skidding to one side or the other, and soon I was bouncing around like a balloon, banging up against the other passenger, whose name turned out to be Mr. Dacey.

"Good, good," he nodded at me, gently setting me upright every time I fell toward him. "I'd as soon head back home while we can." It turned out he lived in Pendleton, where he was a sampler for the woolen mills, and he traveled up and down the bordering states in search of the finest wool he could lay his hands on.

"But I need to get to Wallowa."

"Oh, I wouldn't count on that in the near future, dearie," he said, as if it was something I should already be aware of. "These passes are treacherous long before winter. The *Eagle* reported an entire road crew out here had to quit operations. Safety first, as the scouts say." He must have seen me wince for he went on, "Timmy's a good driver, you needn't worry. We aren't going the way of John Craig."

"Who's that?"

"Oh." The man smiled at me. "Saint John. Let Timmy tell you that story. Anyone else would spoil it."

"I never heard of Pendleton." I rolled my lips into a sulk, as they formed around that new word. It tasted heavy and bitter compared with Wallowa.

"Pendleton is famous for its wool," Mr. Dacey'd tell me over and over on that long jaunt in the wrong direction. "And I help it keep its fine reputation." He had a sack laden with different yarns and he kept me busy holding out my two arms so he could strand the different wools around them. I marveled at the colors, rose and ash and a kind of mud brown but softer, and he'd strand several shades together till I had a rainbow gathered in my hands.

"Which do you like best, young lady?" Mr. D, as I thought to call him, would ask every few hours and I'd pull out a different ball each time, just to distract me.

"It's good taste you have, all right," he'd smile across at me. "What you have round your arms is called WhisperWool. It takes two whole miles of that yarn to make one shirt."

Mr. D snipped off a length of wool from the tail of each ball, and I asked if I could have one. He laughed, and said to help myself. And as we rumbled along, I pried Ama's grand coin from my pocket and strung it on three strands of yarn, and Mr. D obligingly knotted the necklace secure at the nape of my neck.

When the wind and snow eased up a bit, Timmy the driver let me sit out front with him and once he even let me hold the reins of his mules. "Pull right!" he'd shout as we started drifting off to the left. "Now pull left!" And the veins in his neck would get red and bulge, so I let him take hold of the harness again. "Look back at your tracks, child!" Mr. D shouted from inside the carriage and I turned to find a long woven S curving along the trail in our wake. "You need a little practice, I'd wager."

"Know why I take this old coach rather than one 'em fancy motorcars?"

I shook my head, wishing my pa had stayed longed enough to teach me how to ride horses.

Timmy took in a deep breath, solemn, the way you would before an important ceremony at church. "They offered me an automobile once, you know, but I said heck with that. No thank you very much, I'm gonna respect John Craig, and deliver mail the honorable way." He paused to spit a wad of tobacco out on the air. "Bet you don't even know who John Craig is, young girl, do you?"

"Uh-uh."

And Mr. Dacey sighed from inside and muttered something like "Here we go."

"Mr. John Craig," Timmy went on, "was America's finest mailman. He walked over mountains in the thick of winter, just him and his dog and his sack on his back, to make sure people got their letters and parcels. This was long before driving was heard of."

I kept nodding, and ducked my head, for the rain was beating down hard now. Timmy didn't seem to notice. "Now, this one terrible winter, worst they had in years, John Craig heard tell of someone who really needed a parcel delivered. It was a christening gown for the new minister's baby. But there was a wild storm brewing and he could've just stayed put at home, his legs up on a stool, reading by the fire with his dog." Timmy paused here, deep breath, and I felt like I was reading a book with an exciting ending.

"Well, our John Craig never shrank from a bit of snow nor wind, and he pulled his boots on, stuck a cap on his head, and off he went up over the icy mountains. Now the storm picked up, worst they had in years, they say, and our good John stopped for shelter in an old shack he knew to be abandoned."

"Good idea," I said, but Timmy wasn't listening; he was staring straight ahead, as if the story was written out for him on the roadway.

"Well, it must've gotten mighty darn cold," he went on, then took a long, deep breath, "for five days later, they found poor John Craig kneeling down in the ashes of the fireplace, the silk baby's gown wrapped round his dog's neck, poor suckers both frozen straight to death."

"No!" I shouted before I could help myself. And I could see Timmy was enjoying that.

"Yes! Yes!" He nodded. "That's exactly what happened. And it wasn't too far from yer Wallowa either. Gotta be real careful out that way in winter. Crew over in John Day trying to build a clear road to Portland, every last one of 'em downed with the influenza."

"Oh." I was beginning to feel the Wallowas were a lot to reckon with. I could see my own dad frozen solid on his steed, like an ice king, snow falling all around him and not a sound in the air.

"John Craig is Timmy's hero, if you can't tell," Mr. Dacey shouted from inside the carriage.

Timmy nodded, "Yup, I honor him every way I know how. And I ain't the only one. Why, the Oregon Rural Letter Carriers Association . . ."

"Of which he is a member," Mr. D shouted.

"Of which I'm a member, put up a plaque to carry the name of John Craig forever. You get closer to the Wallowas, you ask anyone to direct you there. A fine brass plaque."

"Our friend Tim has stars in his eyes about mail delivery. You'll never see him catching onto modern ways." Mr. D smiled at me as I clambered back into the carriage, for the rain had turned hard and white all of a sudden and I was shivering. "All the better for us, though, eh? We get to travel in style."

I laid the wool in layers on my lap, to warm me.

Timmy stayed out there, huddled over his reins, driving straight into the blizzard, his hat swaying from side to side on his head. Mr. D would hand him out a flask of whiskey every so often, which seemed to pep him up. It had the same hue as the old lady's back in Idaho and I wished he'd offer me some. I sat propped up on a stack of letters, which made a great cushion and gave me a better view of the land as we moved through it. Even through the sleet and hail, I had to gape at the high cliffs and the deep green to whiteness of everything.

"Fir," said Mr. Dacey, watching my eyes dart from one thing to the next. "Oregon is full of fir."

"So long as it's not afraid all the time," I said, thinking how Jack would enjoy that pun and missing him sorely, especially when Mr. D looked at me blankly.

"Well, I'm not from here myself," he said. "Come from Wales, in fact, family of sheepshearers we were. But not enough sheep to keep six young lads employed. So out I came to Pendleton."

I swilled the word "Wales" round in my head. It sounded like a sad place, a place of ghosts maybe.

When Mr. D pointed out that Wales was the left arm of England and that Scotland was its head, I nearly fell off my perch. Before I knew it, I'd told him where my father came from, and about his book of folk tales.

"The only one I'm familiar with, and I'm almost sure it's Scottish," Mr. Dacey said, "is *The Girl and the Dead Man*. Do you know that one?"

My skin got all prickly, as I shook my head; it didn't sound like a happy story. Mr. Dacey said it concerned three sisters who were each asked to watch over a dead man. The first two sisters fell asleep and died because they forgot what they were supposed to be doing.

Only the third, the youngest sister, managed to stay awake. And for that, the dead man sat up and rewarded her with a bottle of cordial.

"And she used it, as I recall, to wipe the mouths of her sisters and bring them back to life, though I think she had to kill the dead man first. It's been a long time."

This girl sounded more dauntless than the dauntless girl in my pa's song. I wasn't sure I liked this story. "What's cordial?" I was thinking of Ama's special potion, and shivered even more when Mr. D said it was a magic drink, probably the whiskey of life people lived and died from over in Scotland. I had a picture of my pa drinking cordial from his flask, and before I could stop it, another picture of him falling off his sorrel mare. I squeezed my eyes until it dissolved.

"So, you like Oregon, do you?" I asked, hoping we could nudge conversation toward more cheerful things.

"S'all right, so it is. I get to travel, don't I."

"And you get paid, too. If I got money for traveling the land, I'd never stop. Or, even if I didn't." I was surprised to hear myself say so, but it felt true. The land was like a big, open lap that held you without complaint; no matter what else let you down, it remained, steady, calm.

"And where are you off to now in your summery dress? Have you relatives in eastern Oregon?"

"Yes, I surely do," I replied, quick as a whistle. I'd left Lourdes' trousers sitting on the chair in her room when they could have been warming my legs. I hoped Bessie wouldn't be offended. "My father lives out here now . . . somewheres."

"Somewhere? You don't know where he is?"

"Not yet," I said to the balding man. "Not yet. But I will."

"Hmmm, can't imagine any daughter of mine gadding about looking for me . . . ."

"I'm sure she would, sir, if you disappeared."

"Perhaps . . . if in fact I actually had a daughter." And he took a deep swig out of his flask.

"Can I have a taste?"

Mr. Dacey looked as if a buffalo had assaulted him. "I should think not . . ."

"My stepdad let me mix his rum for him!" That part was true enough, but I wasn't supposed to drink it. But now something gold and tingly sounded just right. My whole body longed for the deep heat that fruit jar in Idaho gave me.

It was getting dark that first day and I was cold and weary too, so I rested my chin on my chest and soon I was dreaming of a trail of wool, miles and miles of red wool, like a spool of blood seeping from the Idle River to the Oregon trees, and then it stopped, and I couldn't for the life of me figure out where it went after that.

Chapter 6

The sun was high in the sky when I came to the next day, spread out like a map across the mail bags. Even with Mr. Dacey's coat a toasty blanket wrapped round me, my sides hurt—some of those parcels had sharp edges. Mr. D was eating an orange and the tang of it made me thirsty again. I remembered the berries of summer and their sweet juices and how long, long ago that all seemed now.

I pushed out of the carriage and onto the seat beside Timmy. He was chewing on a wad of tobacco, and every so often, he'd work his mouth into a clench and out would come a wad of brown chew spitting through the hole of his missing teeth.

"That's how the Indians'd fire their arrows. Pheet!" he drew a sharp line through the air. "Just like that. Best not be caught unawares." And I wondered if he meant his own tobacco, for I could imagine it'd be a shock to a young girl, say, chancing past, a wet mush slapping into her eye.

Then I caught a glimmer of the whiskey flask lid sticking out of Timmy's pocket. Before he could stop me, I'd slid it out, uncorked it and swallowed a hearty mouthful.

"What the—!"

The fire in my throat seemed to burn in a straight shot all the way to my stomach. Even my head felt like it was soaring in flames. It was different from the way I remembered, but maybe that's how life unfolds; nothing is ever as sweet as the first time. A rattling cough rose up from my chest, and all of a sudden, of their own accord, the corners of my lips moved themselves up into a tight kind of smile. Maybe this was Oregon cordial.

Timmy had snatched the flask back and was gulping at it himself. Then he broke into a noisy laugh. "Spitfire, that's you!" he said. "Don't you know this is precious cargo? You want more, young lady, you pay for it, I don't care how old you are."

"I don't care either," I said, defiant, and suddenly my age or where I was going didn't seem anywhere near as important as the heat burrowing through my veins. "I just don't care!"

Every so often, I'd catch Timmy staring at my neck. I wondered if I still had mud stuck to it. But then he asked what was that strange medallion I had on. I told him all about Ama back in Idaho.

"We'll have to be taking ourselves a potty break here soon. And let them poor mules rest," he said. "They been working hard this whole storm."

And when we pulled over, he leaned toward me and yanked at Ama's coin till it was close to his eyes. "Just what I figured," he said. "I'll be damned."

"What?" I tried to pull my neck back to where it usually sat, over my shoulders and not craned forward like a goose.

"You tellin' me an old blind dame gave you this?"

"You know I did. What's so strange about it?" Though I knew it was a coin you wouldn't come across every day of the week.

"That there," Timmy pudged his fingernail into the hole in the middle. "That there's a bullet hole, whistled clean through it, bull's-eye."

An army of imaginary ants crawled up my arms when Timmy said that. Ama probably had wild stories to tell, and I wished I'd taken time to ask her.

"I'll give you as much whiskey as you want, for it."

Use it wisely, Ama had said of her coin. It must be worth lots, and I doubted she intended me to spend it on drink.

"Never," I said, though the word blurred and doubled on my tongue.

By the time Mr. Dacey came to and leaned out the carriage window, my head was starting to hurt. "Have you no better dress than the one on you? It won't get you far in Pendleton."

"I don't, but maybe I'll just stitch some fabric together when we get wherever it is we're going." The heat swilling round in me made anything seem possible.

"With what, for heaven's sake? Where's your sewing machine? No, you come down to the mills with me and let's see what we can find for you there."

"A woolen shirt, you mean?" I asked, the excitement leaping out of my voice even as I tried to stop it.

"We shall see what they have in surplus."

I watched the sky go dark and light and dark again. Whole days and nights we seemed to travel like phantoms through the icy white air. My fingertips had gone pale at the very first snowfall and they felt like thick lumps of clay after a while, so I had trouble holding anything in my hands for long. Mr. Dacey fed me gumdrops and carrots and slabs of white bread along the way. I wondered how well I'd have survived that long, bitter journey without him. And for a while, I thought Alvin was right to stay put in Idaho, where it was warm, and he could sup on juice and cookies any old time.

It was getting toward dusk when we rode into the little town of Pendleton, orange street lamps like soft gems on a necklace. There weren't many people about on the main street as Timmy shooed the mules toward the water trough. A tavern stood right there, Grave's Trading Store and Inn, and music burst out of it. A mangy-looking dog sat outside, tied to the railing. He looked like he was shaking, poor thing.

"Well, here we are, ladies and gents. Pendleton, Oregon. We're at the end of the line!" Timmy stood up and scratched his behind.

"The end? What about Wallowa?"

"Sweetheart, I'm gonna have me a large jug of ale, unload my mail sacks and find me a warm woman for the evening. While I still can. Way this country's goin', that may not be long."

"But tomorrow, tomorrow you'll go to Wallowa?"

"We'll have to see. It'll cost you your pretty necklace to get me braving those passes in this weather." He jumped down to settle his skittery horses. I was beginning to feel like them, all uncertain and funny.

"If John Craig could do it, why can't you?" I shouted, but Timmy only laughed.

"Young lady, let us adjourn here and take a stroll down to the mills, get you some warmer clothes," Mr. D announced.

For want of a better idea, I nodded, feeling dismal, and jumped off the seat, making the scrawny dog dance up and down, an unholy bark screeching out of him.

"Gently, gently," said Timmy. "Or you'll have every gangster in town out after you with their gun."

"Thank you, Tim, for the ride," Mr. Dacey slipped a few coins into the driver's hand and then gently nudged me down the street, with his arm. We walked through the town, all shut up for the night, only a man with a bottle lounging on a doorstep. The quietness made me shudder. It was OK out in the fields, you could trust the sound of nothing, but a town should be buzzing, shouldn't it, people dashing round with packages and watch chains like in Addison, Idaho.

We had to cross through several back alleys, and once a cat jumped out on us and set my heart thumping. I wasn't feeling too welcome in this strange place; I hoped all of Oregon wasn't like here.

"Almost there," said Mr. Dacey, finally, breaking into the steam of my thoughts. "See those lights down the hill? That's our mill."

"Mm," I muttered. It looked unreal, this bright daze of white light in the middle of the darkness. It could have been a great big ghost, the kind in fairy stories where one thing turned into another if you looked at it long enough.

"There'll be few people there now, only the overtime lot and a couple of lads doing shift, but they'll let us in, lass, and we'll see what we can find for you."

He pushed through the black iron gate and up a pathway to two big doors. "Here we are," he said, as if he'd led me to the queen's chamber, and he hammered on the brass knocker. Out came a boy in a white apron and he took one look at Mr. Dacey and nodded like a water dipper on the loose. "Come in, come in, sir," he said, holding the door wide for us. "I was just finishing up." In the light of the hallway, I could see the boy's skin had a soft yellowish tinge to it and his hair was black as wet soil and tied in a tail down his back, just like mine. I'd never seen anyone like him. When Mr. Dacey introduced us, the boy smiled at me, and his eyes gleamed like two lemon drops, and an arrow darted straight out of my chest and landed on his.

"PickingBones," I said, repeating his name in wonder, but I was too dumbstruck to ask about such a strange appellation.

The boy must have been about sixteen or so, though he was no taller than me. He held himself upright as a church, and it lent him a stateliness you wouldn't expect in a youth. It wasn't till he came close that I saw the silver ring stranded through his nostril. When it caught the lamp glow, my eyelids flickered from the dazzle. The strange boy held out his left hand, for his right was full of little red balls, and instead of shaking mine, he pressed his hand onto my arm and squeezed, and bolts of light shot up my back. "Pleased to meet you."

He bowed like you would at a princess, and I suddenly felt grown up. I felt like a lady, and that tomboy life of mine an act trailing out in ribbons behind me. I felt ashamed of my tattered green dress and my shoes, but the boy didn't seem to even notice them. It was my face he was studying.

I thought the balls in his hand were candy at first, but when he led us through a doorway into a tiny room, more like a closet, he pointed to the table and said, "These are my beads." There was an assortment of brightly colored beads, all sizes and shapes, and they sat in neat little cigar boxes. "I have just finished this shirt for Mr. Hadley," PickingBones said.

"PickingBones is our master beader, lass," explained Mr. Dacey. "He's an expert." The checkered shirt was a dazzle of glittering beads.

"That's for a man?" I asked, surprised.

"Oh, yes, these cowboys like their finery just as much as women. They're lucky to have PickingBones to assist them in their vanities."

"No, I am lucky," said the boy. "My mother taught me when I was a boy, and now I get paid for it."

"Not half of what you're worth," said Mr. Dacey, and I could sense some strain in his voice, like he was holding back from getting angry.

"Well, let me take you out to where the white people work." And then it dawned on me: PickingBones was not white, he was Indian, of course. I had heard about them some in school but I thought they all wore feathers and big headbands and carried bows, not little red beads. Did they all have gleaming lemon-drop eyes, I wondered?

We were standing in a huge room, full of metal machines and bolts of cloth and baskets of wool lined up along the wall. There was one man running what looked like a sewing machine at the far end, and you could hear the whzzzzz, but other than that, it was quiet. When I spoke, the words seemed to echo off the ceiling.

"Where's your spot, Mr. D?"

"I don't really have one, as I'm on the road a lot, but when I need space, it's in the offices up that way," and he pointed to a set of windows up along the ridge of the wall. It looked a knight's tower up there, dark and eerie.

Then Mr. Dacey led me through to another room again and there were tables full of scrap fabric and assorted pieces of equipment. "This is our remainders room. All of the work that can't be sold ends up here and we're free to help ourselves. Have a look, lass, through this pile. See what might work for you."

I moved through a heap of shirts, heavy, thick woolen shirts with big wooden buttons, some of them. They seemed huge, like they were meant for three men, not a scrap of a girl.

"Keep going, there's bound to be one close to your size. We have a regular assortment here."

Finally, I came upon a bright, flowy thing, with yellow and green squares. It was like a tablecloth, only much, much heavier. I slipped it on over my dress, but there were no sleeves.

"That's a cape. How do you like it?"

I felt lost inside it, and maybe that was obvious, for Mr. Dacey handed me a bright red shirt. "Try this one, then."

And though the sleeves were a bit wide and long, it was the best fit of the lot. "Wind up the sleeves, that's what a lot of people do."

"There!" said Mr. Dacey, standing back and smiling, "You look like a real western cowgirl."

"I do?" I was half excited, half terrified, but I thought he was probably only teasing me. I'd a lot to learn about cowboys and other things, I could tell.

"That should keep you warm," Mr. Dacey said. "Wool is stronger than any other fabric. Keeps the heat in, even when it's wet."

"But what's wrong with it? Why is it in here?"

"The front isn't lined the whole way, is it? They must have run out of satin. Most people don't like to feel the wool on their skin; makes them itch."

"Well, with my dress on under, it's fine." I'd never worn a stitch of wool in my life.

"What's that dress made of? Cotton? Did you know that you can bend a wool fiber back on itself 20,000 times before it breaks?" Mr. Dacey said proudly. "Now, cotton," and he took a wad of my dress in his hand, "Cotton breaks after only 3,000 bendings. And don't even ask about silk or rayon."

"Seventy-five each, Mr. Dacey," snapped PickingBones, who appeared in the doorway as if by magic.

"Yes, that sounds right. Are you done for the evening then?" he asked the Indian.

"Done. Let us walk back into town with you."

"Fine, I think we're fixed here."

I was surprised how my heart lurched when the boy said "us." But when we went outside, a dog stood on the top step, his head tilted up toward PickingBone's, tongue hanging out, and his tail spinning as if he'd just been given a bone the size of Oregon. His white fur pressed close to his skin in little curls.

"Ah, Clem," PickingBones tugged at the dog's ear. "Just in time, I see."

Mr. D explained how PickingBone's dog was a cow dog, a heeler who usually kept cattle in line. But he was loyal as they come, and walked with his master to and from work. He'd sit by his side all day long, Mr. D said, only the authorities at the mills wouldn't allow animals beyond the front door.

And so I found myself clad in a new woolen shirt, strolling down a street in the darkness of a town I hadn't known existed until the day before. It made me feel giddy inside, even though I had no idea where I'd sleep that night. I didn't fancy the doorways of this town; too many strange characters hanging around.

"Can I buy you two supper?" Mr. Dacey asked, and I lit up.

PickingBones looked uncertain. "Where?" he asked.

"I was thinking the Rainbow Grill. It's the only place open now. We could get ourselves a good slab of meat, I'd say."

Clem led the way down the hill, leaping and running after sticks his master tossed him. When we came to Main Street, he barked and then sat on the sidewalk as if he knew when to wait and when to move. It was a skill I wished I had learned; it seemed more impulse than sense drove me onward.

PickingBones hung behind me when we walked into the bright cafe. It smelled of smoke and frying, and you could hear loud music coming from the bar next door. But it was warm as summer in there. I blew into the tips of my fingers, then stuffed them inside the sleeves of my shirt. PickingBones kept close to my rear as we stood at the counter, waiting for a table; he was like a walking shadow.

A round woman in a dirty apron came up to us. "All the tables're full. Use the counter."

I looked around in surprise. There was only one man sipping soup beside the window. The place was deserted.

"But . . ." Mr. Dacey tried.

"The counter," said the woman and turned on her heels. "Or nothing."

"Why?" At first, I wondered if she had vision problems, like how Ama's eyes saw things that weren't actually there.

"Because of me," sighed PickingBones. "I'm not white enough."

"That's ridiculous," stormed Mr. Dacey. The color rose in blooms beneath his eyes.

PickingBones moved quietly toward the door.

"We have to eat."

"I'll wait outside with Clem."

"For heaven's sake!" Mr. Dacey was like a kettle steaming by now, but he followed PickingBones, and I in their trail.

The gladness I'd been feeling was leaking out of me. I took PickingBones's arm in mine and said, "I don't care what color you are, you're my friend. Your dog, too."

And he smiled a grin wide as the River Idle and his face sparkled like stars. "I'm really no color," he said. "Chinese-Indian is a made-up breed."

Before I could ask what he meant, Mr. D ordered us to wait right there. "I'll get us some sandwiches from the saloon." And we stood on the sidewalk, shivering together, two misfits, while our champion marched off to save us.

My new pal told me his mother was Indian all right, came out from Idaho when she was a girl, but his father was a fence builder from China. He spoke of a people who came from far, far away, to make a better life for themselves.

"Like me," I said.

"Like you, like me," he said. "Only they came from overseas." These Chinese were short, he said, and had eyes the shape of almonds and skin like summer wheat. He could have been describing himself. Maybe I was just tired, but I had an urge to lean into that wheat and rest for a long time. But he was telling me how folks from China spoke in a tongue no one could understand. "Sounds like birds chirping all at once, when they get talking."

His father could make anything out of bamboo and willow, but people in this country mostly wanted plank fences to keep cattle and sheep apart, so that's what he did.

I wanted to ask why I'd never met a Chinese before him, but he wanted to know where I came from, and where I was going.

"Me? Not sure yet. I just got here." I squirmed on the step.

"I have a cabin up in the hills behind the factory. One day, I'll own a big house, though, with a picket fence and curtains and three bedrooms. And Clem will have his own kennel."

I nodded at the boy, his eyes melting into honey, and wondered why he'd want a thing that would always keep him bound to it.

"Looking for work?" he asked.

"Nah, I'm heading out to the Wallowas soon as the weather turns. I've someone to visit out there."

I could feel the boy's shoulders tighten. "Wallowa? I'd never go there in a million years."

I was startled. No one so far had voiced such a strong opinion against the place that held all my dreams. "What's wrong with it?"

"Plenty," he said. "Pretty place, I hear. Wallowa's where my mom's people came from. Till they were kicked out."

I thought of what had just happened at the Rainbow, and I felt doubly sad. That this beautiful boy already had two places he wasn't welcome, and that one of those places might be where my own pa was right now. I said nothing.

"If you change your mind about work, let me know. There are always odd jobs at the mills, with so many soldiers off fighting. I know how it is to be hungry."

So he had taken in my appearance, this boy who moved with the grace of a bobcat. I'd forgotten for a while how I must look, being too busy taking everyone else in. And I understood for a moment how the world would see me as a dirty, out-of-place girl, not knowing I carried an important mission in my heart. And I considered how much folks could be misunderstood, on account of a certain appearance. Like my new friend. Or my pa. Some people might regard him as a natural-born cowboy with his Stetson and mare, and not know he'd a wife and a daughter who loved him and wanted him home.

"PickingBones . . ." I swilled his name round in my mouth. "It's long. How about PB?"

"So long as you don't mean Pot Belly!" And he nudged me play-fully in the ribs till I was laughing.

Then the door of the saloon swung open and a man in a black jacket came flying out on his back and crashed to the pavement. Clem let out a howl. "Out and stay out!" came a loud voice from inside.

The man lay on the ground, shouting and cursing at the door.

And just as I was about to go see if he was all right, the door opened again and out strolled Timmy the mailman and a sturdy trunk of a woman on his arm. He was leaning in toward her and kissing her neck, his free hand was dancing up and down her dress. I took in a breath.

Before I could figure out how Timmy'd gotten from Grave's Tavern to the Rainbow bar, PickingBones stood up. "Let's sit on the step over there. We don't have to watch this."

I followed him and his dog quietly, my heart heavy now with the sudden weight of the world, things I couldn't even imagine yet fill-ing up and bearing it down. PB laid his vest down on the step to warm our seat. But I could hardly eat the white bread Mr. D brought us, and tossed the crusts to Clem. "I doubt that Timmy'll be heading to Wallowa anytime soon, Missy," he said, and I sat between these two men, feeling lost as I ever had, and pondering what on earth had led me to this strange town.

Mr. D chewed on his bread, looking thoughtful himself. "Cheer up, little one. It's not the end of the world."

"Sure feels like it."

"I know what you mean, like a town you can't ever get out of. Last stop on planet Earth," said PB, but he was smiling. "Maybe the Bitterroots weren't so bad, what d'you say, Clem?"

"Do they have picket fence houses there?" It sounded like an angry place, Bitterroot, no trees and the wind whistling through it. He said it was where his mom came from.

"Not yet," PB shook his head. "Not yet. Plenty of mountains, and not a single fence."

"Well, time's rolling on. I have to get my woolens from the coach and get on home to bed. What're we going to do with you, young lady?"

"I'll be fine," I tried, but I knew my voice betrayed me.

"Well, you could stay in my front room tonight," said Mr. D. "Although not as a long-term arrangement."

"You're very kind, Mr. D, but I don't think so."

"Let her stay in my room. There's a ledge in the kitchen where I can sleep."

"I couldn't possibly . . ."

"Please, Taf, can I call you Taf?"

He could have called me anything, and I'd have been grateful. But the way he spoke my name, it felt like honey pouring out of a jug in sunshine and it melted every cold place inside me. It was the first time in my life that Taf made perfect sense. I nodded.

"My father always said it was an insult to refuse hospitality. Clem could use some decent company for a change, am I right, Clem?" He looked thoughtful then. "Besides, folks will be less apt to gossip, wouldn't you say, Mr. Dacey? They'd not expect any better from a Chinese-Indian who lives in an old cow camp." He didn't sound happy as he said it, a kind of bitter ring to his voice, and Mr. D nodded slowly.

"Afraid he's right, girl. This town is built on gossip. And they'd wonder what a young girl was doing in my house. Maybe you're right, PickingBones. For tonight at least. You look like you'd benefit from a good night's rest. We all would."

He stood up and brushed dog hair from his trousers. And that's how I came to be walking up a dark hill with a Chinese-Indian beader in a strange town that felt like it was hollowed out of ghosts.

Chapter 7

I slept like the dead that night, too tired to argue when PB led me to a mattress on the floor. He'd thrown some colored blankets down on it and said, "Welcome to my home. It's not much, but you'll rest well here. It's quiet." And then he was gone, and when I woke up in the night, briefly, I could hear the light, steady beat of his snores, like bird's cries, coming from the little room next door.

In the morning, PB brought me a tall glass of milk and a red apple. "Breakfast," he said. "I have to get going."

I rubbed my eyes and sat up, hoping that maybe I was dreaming this sorry chapter of my life. PB was on his hunkers beside me. "It will be all right. You'll see."

"Wish I felt so," I said, and had to work at pushing the tears down. I was surprised and mad at myself. Hadn't I been through worse in my days? Why get so sad now? Yet it felt like the world had more problems than I had reckoned on back on the Idle River.

That was the feeling I had when I sat up and took in the bare gray walls, the battered wooden chair, the wilting blue flowers in a wine bottle. The walls seemed to sag outward in places, like an old person's back, and even though there weren't any windows, somehow the chill wind found its way in.

"What'll I do here, PickingBones? I don't know anyone and I've hardly any money and Timmy may never get me to the Wallowas like I figured." I still had Ama's coin, but I had promised to use it wisely, and that meant waiting till I felt wise. Who knew how long that could take?

"Work," PB said, and there was a certainty in his voice that I clung on to, maybe because I was desperate. "Work keeps a person well occupied."

"You sure PB doesn't stand for Pure Bully?" I asked, wanting to make him laugh again, just to see the silver sky streeling out of his mouth.

"Taf-a-Laf, that's you!" he said, and I liked the sound of it, liked it very much.

True to his word, PB found me a job. I was to be employed by Pendleton Woolen Mills, Pendleton, Oregon, as a shirt buttoner. For twenty-five cents an hour, I was to work through a pile of new shirts and make sure each and every button was securely fastened. Easy, I thought, as I signed the white paper in the gleaming office of Mr. Hadley, the boss. I can do that.

And I could. I sat on a wobbly stool at the farthest end of the factory, and pulled shirts out of a cardboard box, hung them up on a hanger and then on a rail above my head. And I started from the bottom, slip one button through the eye, click, slip two, click, slip three, like a song, until I reached all the way up the collar, where I pressed down the lapels and sometimes clicked snaps into place, if need be. It was a slow process and I had plenty of time to think, even as the other machines whirred through my ears. Each shirt that I worked my way up, I thought of my dad and saw his neck rising out of the top, and his head proud and steady as I snapped the final button into place and brushed him down, like a fussy mother.

Mr. Dacey had put in a good recommendation for me with the foreman Hadley before he left on another journey, this time to the city of Portland, he said. I wasn't sure exactly how old I was; Ma always claimed she couldn't remember. "You're either twelve or thirteen," she'd said to me when I last asked, and that was well over a year ago. "Those early years with your father were blurry." Every year I questioned her about it and she'd give me two choices, "You're either six or seven. You're either ten or eleven," till I'd walk away in frustration. She claimed it was the same case with her marriage. Either ten years ago, or eleven. Love must do strange things to a memory, I'd reckoned, and it made me curious how much I really remembered of my dad, and how much I'd conjured out of the air. Anyhow, I'd spend hours in front of the cracked mirror wedge over the sink in the bathroom, counting the lines on my face like I was an old tree, but that made me at least thirty and I knew there was no way I could be that ancient.

Those first weeks in Pendleton, I felt about fifteen, grown up and working, and that's what I told anyone who asked. The labor laws said I could work no more than twelve hours a week, Mr. Hadley pointed out to me at the interview, if you could call it that. He shifted feet like an anxious crow as he talked. And the only question he asked was, "Are you healthy, child? Because if you've any diseases, in mind or body, we don't want you here passing them round." When I nodded in vigorous agreement, he said, "Good," and went on to tell me what I'd have to do to earn my three dollars a week.

I didn't mind the work that much. The time passed like it would any other way, though each day was a day further away from my dad. I had to put him in a drawer deeper down in my heart and just trust that I'd find him when the time was right.

My second morning at the mills, an old lady came round at break and handed me a slice of coffeecake off a tin tray. "Wipe your hands before you eat it," she told me, and kept moving to the next machine. Then I heard someone start up Happy Birthday at the end of the room, and I joined in, though I hadn't an idea whose birthday it was. It made me feel lonesome, remembering the sponge cake Ma bought special for the twins' second birthday. She always remembered theirs. How she cut it into teeny slabs and sank candles into every one of them so we could all feel like it was our special day. "Never know but this could be our last, might as well enjoy it," Ma said, I remember, and her eyes glowy in the flames. "Or, our next-to-last," I'd joke, seeing as she couldn't keep her years straight. The sponge was hard as stones—we got it cut-price 'cos it had gone off—but it was tasty as can be, better even than this one I was chewing on. Who cares about coconut slivers and nuts?

On my way home at lunchtime, I'd stop in to see PB in his special room. He'd always be poring over a shirt, his eyes squinted almost shut and hands moving like a ballet across the fabric. His ponytail would slide down his chest sometimes, a black river. Mine felt like sagebrush compared to his; I took to piling it in a bun behind my ears like I'd seen Bessie do.

If we needed food for supper or any little thing, PB would slip some change into my palm and send me to the store in town. I liked the walk down there; in daylight, it looked like a whole different place. Shopkeepers had their bright awnings out and children dressed in bonnets and frilly dresses would be playing on the side-walk, their mothers chatting away to each other like clucking hens. I'd saunter past, smiling at them, two quarters in my pocket, and my good Pendleton shirt like a uniform that proclaimed to all the world that I was part of this scene.

I got to know Maisie in the grocery store because it was she always rang up my purchases. "My, my, what a girl you are to come all the way from the Idle River." She'd shake her head. "I ain't never been beyond Monument, Oregon, but one day, I'm gonna get me to England. Yessir, that's the land for me."

In the meantime, she had all manner of questions for me about the factory, what kind of work I did, how much I got paid, how I was treated. I gave her a report each time I stopped in. She, for her part, would weigh my butter or sugar or flour a little loose so that I'd get the best bargain. She was round as I was skinny, and you could hardly see her eyes behind the thick glasses, but her mouth was bright and pink like a cherub's and it always curled up at the corners when I walked in. It was her hair, though, that had me smitten, thick waves of it the color of wheat. "Or maize," I said to her. "No wonder that's what they call you." But Maisie shook her head sort of ruefully.

PickingBones was very good about letting me stay with him those first few months. He never complained about having to sleep on a tiny hard ledge next to the door; he seemed so graceful, though, he could perch anywhere. I loved our evening meals together, Clem tucked into PB's lap. I often cooked up a broth of root vegetables like Ma used make, and we'd dunk our bread in deep and swipe the last dredges off our plates with it. On fine days, I'd pick a bunch of the tiny starflowers that sprouted up all over the hill. They were the color of sky, and PB said they were camas, that his mother used the bulb for eating. The tiny blue petals looked tasty too, like you could suck on each strand, but maybe it was just the way PB held them in his sun-skinned hands.

Sometimes he'd tell a story of his family. They were all dead now, he said, except his great-uncle Hay, who was a famous doctor in a town called John Day. "Could cure almost anyone," he said. "Snake bites, fever, you name it. But then my dad got blood poisoning from barbed wire." He rode fifty miles in his friend Wing Wah's wagon, his foot hanging out the side, all swollen, PB said. "Refused help till he got to Doc Hay's and by then it was too late."

I wanted to speak, but no words came out.

"Some say it was a curse, you know, for his marrying an Indian."

"But surely, . . ."

"People have their beliefs—you can't shake them," PB insisted, and anyway, he said, his mother fled back to the reservation in Lewiston, to be with her own people.

I told him he was lucky to have two sets of people to call family, when I wasn't even sure of one. "You didn't go with her?"

PB shook his head. "I wanted to stay, have a good job before we went back, our heads hanging. Mama wouldn't wait. I'd intended to follow her, but she died of a tired heart before I got there." Whenever he spoke of her, he'd get a kind of crack in his voice, and his eyes would grow moist.

I wondered for a flash if my dad was still alive, but why wouldn't he be? Surely not everyone died before their time, or had strange curses on them. I thought of old Ama back in Idaho and her warnings to me, and my skin prickled. It was easier to hear PB's stories and forget my own problems for a while.

"Mama was the wisest person I've ever known." It was she taught him beadmaking the Nez Perce way, for that was his tribe. As a girl, she used to bead all winter, he told me, and then horseback it to Arizona, where she'd trade her wares for leather.

"But isn't Arizona miles and miles away?" I asked him one night, after we'd shared a picnic of crusty bread on his mattress.

"Sure is, but nothing stopped my mama. Owned a .22 rifle and shot beavers for sport. They made good pelts, so she'd have me scrape their hides and take them down to Grave's for trades. Once she snagged an animal, she'd say a quick prayer and walk away."

I'd never thought of a wise person doing those things, but I sat still and let PB explain some more. "It's said she was the best poker player for three whole states. Beat everyone for a year straight. They called her Tulekals Chikchamit."

"What?"

"Woman Placing Money On Cards."

"That makes sense," I said. "Maybe her son should be called Boy Placing Beads on Shirts." I was trying to make him laugh, but PB was serious.

"The one man who beat her, she married."

I pulled my breath in. People sure acted on impulse out west, but then I suppose I wasn't so different. "Did she love him?"

"That's a story for another night."

He looked so sad sitting there cross-legged, this beautiful half-Indian, half-Chinese boy, that I reached over and threw my arms around him in a great big hug. And as the tears fell, I licked each one away, like Clem would, until his face was a flower of kisses. He sat still as a corpse, just letting the tears come to my lips like the first rain of spring.

After he was done weeping, he pulled back gently, picked up our plates and walked to the kitchen. I loved how Clem followed him everywhere, and wished I had a good reason to. I heard him climb up onto his ledge as I lay on the mattress, wondering what wild thoughts he was carrying round in that head.

He and his heeler were gone next morning when I rose, and I was glad in a way. I didn't have to feel shy and awkward round him. At work, all day, as I moved through one shirt after another, I started to see PB's body, not my dad's, inside each one, filling it out, and I'd take extra care with each button, and smoothing out the shoulders. And once, I couldn't help myself, I pressed my cheek into the folds of the fabric and inhaled his smell, must and sage and dampness. And my legs started shivering, for no reason.

I thought about him more and more, and would make excuses to visit him in his room. Once, when I hadn't bothered to pin up my usual bun, he said to me, "Your hair," and brushed his golden hand down the length of it. He told me when Indians died, someone always kept a lock of hair as memory. I walked around for the rest of the afternoon, looking for mirrors to stare at the strands drifting down my front, to find that magical silk he had spun out of them.

That Friday night, after supper, he looked serious at me and said, "Taf."

The softness in that word, smooth like leaves after rain, made my heart tip sideways.

"Mmm?"

"Taf, I don't think it's a good idea for you to stay here any longer."

"Why not?" I'm sure my face looked horror-struck, but I couldn't help it.

"It . . . a girl and a boy, it's not a proper arrangement."

"Am I doing anything wrong? If I am, just tell me, I'll change it. I'm sorry, I . . ." And then it was my turn to cry, only mine were not gentle tears, but big wracking sobs and howls and PB climbed across the mattress and held me in his arms as I shook. "Now, now, it's all right. It's not you. It's me," he said.

I leaned back so I could see his face. It was golden in the candle-light. "How?"

"I . . . you . . . you are very special to me."

He said, after a while, "I'd like to do this . . . and this . . ." And very slowly, very gently, he pressed his lips to mine, and my heart shot up to my throat. I could feel a fire between my legs. And then his hand moved up like a spider that knew its path, toward the swell of my chest and it rested there as if it had come home. I was burning up inside, the heat of his lips like a lit match against mine. It was the feeling of whiskey, when everything feels quivery, only better, much better, than that. We stood stock-still, two statues in flames, until he drew back and said, "I'm sorry. I'm so sorry. I had no right . . ."

"It's OK," I protested. "I like it. Come back."

But he didn't. He grabbed his buckskin vest and walked out the door, and I patted my heart, still warm from where his hand had been, and soothed its wild fluttering.

A kind of hollow opened in my belly then, a dark emptiness. I wished there was wine in that wine bottle instead of a stupid dead flower. I had no idea what to do with my shivering skin, so I crept up to PB's loft, where he lay his sweet head every night. I could pretend he'd be home any minute and would crawl in beside me, and suck on my hair like a summer wheat stalk.

I'd never been up there—it felt like his private place—and was surprised to find a bowl of tangerines right above his pillow. I remembered them from back home. Hank had brought a bunch back after a trip down south, said they were special fruits, and wouldn't let us kids touch them. Even Ma had to behave herself if she wanted to taste the tiny crescent wedges.

And now, here they were looking all comely and crying out, Go ahead, eat me. I longed for something moist on my tongue, and surely they'd be juicy as oranges. What difference would one make, really? If I couldn't have PB, I could have something that had slept right next to him, and in a flash, I'd the skin peeled off and the orange slices stuffed whole into my mouth. The juice dribbled down my chin in a delicious river, but soon as I swallowed, my lips wouldn't be satisfied till they had another one, they were so small, so delicate, and then, a third. And before I knew it, in the flash of an electric bulb, I'd polished off the whole bowlful. And my dress was damp with juice.

I felt sticky and sad and PB's pillow next to my chest was little comfort. Nor were the white hairs I found nesting under it. For a second, I wondered if they belonged to a woman, for they were long and soft to the touch, but that's how I imagined PB's hair to be, if only I could weave my fingers through it. I must have fallen asleep then, only it wasn't like regular sleeping. It felt like I was in the deepest, coolest, most peaceful cave and I'd have stayed there for-ever if a sudden scramble across the floor hadn't hauled me out.

"Clem!" I creaked up to sitting, plopping my legs over the ledge.

I could have been coming back from the dead. Clem's tail was wagging, and I tried to reach his back with my feet, till PB came through the door. His face dropped like a waning moon soon as he saw me; you'd swear he'd seen a ghost.

"Home already . . ."

PB's mouth widened into its own cave then, as he looked up at me. In an instant, he jumped up on the stool and started gathering all the pale hairs that had fallen into my lap. He moved so fast, my breath caught, or maybe it was the dance of his hands between my legs. I was shocked at the heat in them.

He didn't speak or respond at all for a moment. Just clasped the hairs and kissed them like they were his bride, and he dipped the bowl in a pail of water before setting a pear on it and placing it back where it had been. I rattled on about being hungry and that I'd planned to replace the fruit. But he didn't even look at me, only bent down before the ledge in the same way he'd bowed to me when we first met, and muttered some words I couldn't grasp. And then he strode outside and seemed to be drinking of the air as if that would settle things.

I jumped down from my perch and followed him. "I'm sorry, PB. Whatever I did, I'm sorry. I shouldn't have touched your things."

He shook his head, and spoke slow as time. "Not my things."

"I don't understand. Was someone else living here?"

PB sat down cross-legged on the ground, his back straight against the cabin wall. I scooched down facing him, on the other side of Clem. What PB told me made my heart swell up into a cannonball, ready to explode. He said that ledge had been a shrine he'd made to his ancestors, that his father had taught him always to honor your family, living or dead.

"But tangerines?"

"In China," he said, "people make all kinds of offerings. Once you give something, you're not supposed to take it back. It's bad luck."

I felt the tangerines again sliding down my throat, thick and sickening. A shrine must be a very special place. "Back on the Idle River, you see food, you eat it while you can."

He laughed a harsh laugh. "Yes, we're in America now." PB scraped his feet along the ground. "Forget it, just forget it. It's a dumb custom anyway."

I thought of my own family and how we'd never thought to honor anyone, only eat what's in front of you before someone else gets to it. But PB belonged to a world with different rules. I could hardly bring myself to form the words, "And the hairs?"

"What use is a dead person's hair anyway?" PB stood up, as if he couldn't stay still, and walked back inside, Clem and me watching him.

I knew in that instant, I'd have to leave; he wouldn't have it. When would I ever learn the difference between dauntlessness and foolery? I could buy a million more tangerines, but they'd never be the same, and the thirst aching through my body could never be quenched. Like any foolish girl in a fairy story, I'd taken a wrong turn, and I was beginning to understand that once taken, there was no turning back. And some acts, once done, leave you never, ever the same.

Chapter 8

I thought of trying to track Timmy the mailman down, and going to the Wallowas soon as I could manage fare. But something Ma used to say took hold of my head, and refused to budge: Fix what's closest, first. Mostly she meant sewing missing buttons back in the places where it showed. I'd always hated that advice, because it sounded like a church lady lecturing. Yet now the words crowded in my head and I saw suddenly the wisdom in them. If I'd stayed on the Idle River and tried to help young Todd, maybe he'd be fine now. And I wouldn't be feeling like there was no bottom to my belly. Maybe I was afraid of taking to the road again, and finding it didn't offer all the answers I sought. So many people seemed to have journeyed from somewhere else, with high hopes and strong opinions. And they didn't always happen upon what they were after, it seemed to me. Maybe I didn't want to use up my last card.

But the truth had more to do with PB. In the chambers of my heart, he was starting to take up a lot of room, nudging my dad slowly off to the side. Maybe it was because PB was fresh and alive, and close by, and I was starting to like it that way. If I left Pendleton abruptly, PB might disappear forever just like my pa had. What if he changed his mind and wanted me back and I was nowhere to be found? Maybe Ma was right: First things first. Stay close to what you can mend until you mend it. And it pleased me, in a way, to be living by her words.

So I placed my pa in a drawer in that special part of my heart, which I would open again when the time was right, and wandered down to see Maisie. She sat me on a tall stool at the milk bar while she fixed a vanilla sundae that I melted with each plop of my tears.

"You could have a room for a dollar fifty a month at my place." I knew Maisie lived in a rundown boardinghouse near the railway station, though I hadn't seen it. "It wouldn't be much, for that price, but you'd have a safe roof over your pretty head. Plus, we'd be almost neighbors."

That thought cheered me up. I was starting to feel more and more alone in the world. Maybe it was being in a town made me lonely, a town where PB went on about his life without me. Maisie slipped a chocolate drop into my hand and sent me off to investigate her lodgings. When Mrs. Gubbs showed me the single she had available, I could hardly imagine myself there. It stood at the very end of the hallway, almost on top of the railroad track. When a freight train rattled past, the walls shook like leaves in a spring breeze. The room was not much bigger than the coat closet at Bess and Jack's, as I recalled. And it smelled of disinfectant and what was it, rot? It looked as if someone had entertained himself by peeling strips of wood off the floorboards.

Old Ama came floating into my head, out of nowhere, her dark face bent over me, saying, The road is not the best place for you. There's someone who'll have to do you a lot of forgiving. What would PB and his ancestors have to say about that?

I paid Mrs. Gubbs, who didn't live on the premises normally but who happened to be picking up rent checks when I came by. I paid her two dollars, which is about all I had of my first week's wages. She wanted a deposit, "in case you sully the room in any way." At least it would go toward the next week's rent. I'd just have to scrape by on a dollar, but I'd lived on much less, hadn't I? Yet, when I walked out onto the street, and back to tell Maisie the good news, my heart was heavy as mountain rock. Maybe it was the bite in the air after last year's sweet summer, I don't know, but I'd left the warm sun back in Idaho or somewhere, and every step I took in this new life felt chillier.

Maisie was thrilled to have me living downstairs from her. My first evening there, soon as she got home from the store, she brought me a bottle of milk and half a bread loaf and a tin of logan-berry jam. "You'll have to drink tea," she laughed, "now that you're a grown woman with your own place." She showed me how to boil water in a pot on the heating panel. When it made bubbles like the head of the Idle Creek falls, she whisked it off and poured it in one swoop in a tin cup. Then she set a plate of tiny triangle sandwiches before me, and a knife. "Now all we need's some sugar and a spoon of tea leaves and we're all set for an English tea party." She marched upstairs to get them and I sat on the one rickety chair by the pullout sideboard and wrapped my hands round the warm cup. I rested my face over the rising steam, pretending it was PB, my own beautiful PB, swimming up to meet me.

I told Maisie about Alvin and Bessie and Jack and Lourdes. But all she was interested in was old Ama and how she'd said I was moving toward the place of all heartbreak.

"Mercy me!" Maisie leaned toward me, her huge eyes almost bursting through her glasses. "That woman sure was cookin'. Did she mention about your friend in Pendleton who's gonna be famous in England one day?"

Maisie relished the idea of fortunetelling. "You'll get a disease," she'd say, "not bad, but it can only be cured in England and I'll get to go with you as your nursemaid."

I tried to play along. "No, you'll have a bald man fall in love with you and he'll promise to take you to England by ocean tanker, only one condition: you have to marry him and rub hair oil into his scalp every night for the rest of your life!"

"You'll be sorry, little Miss Idle River, you'll be sorry!" Maisie'd tickle me and issue all kinds of dark pronouncements on my future. So many that I began to worry. I mean, what if you said something or thought something so much that it turned out to be true? What if PB was right about those forbidden tangerines? I changed the subject.

She had stories galore about the other residents in our building, I knew, and I begged her to tell some. It got so my head was overflowing with them, and then one day, when I'd had about enough, out of the clear blue sky, Maisie decided to sing. I'd never heard her utter a note before, but this became the shape of our days for weeks afterward: Maisie cushioned on my Murphy bed, me on the wobbly chair, cups of tea wrapped in our fingers, and she spinning out tunes one after the other. She had a voice like water on marble, thin and clear and high. It was the sound fairies might make if they sang. Even if she had a wild folksong going, you'd hear a lullaby dancing under the words, a deep, motherly tone that would smooth out all the kinks of your heart. I could listen to her, eyes closed and dreaming, for hours. And she was only too happy to oblige.

Not all the other tenants appreciated her tunes, but we didn't care. If someone tapped on the ceiling or banged with a saucepan lid on the wall, we'd hit back in the same rhythm, as if we had a musical duet going. No one ever came to the door. Maybe they were afraid of two odd girls who could make so much racket in one tiny room.

It was cold at night, and I'd pull the thin rug from the floor on top of the sheets, and hug my arms round my waist, rocking my sorrowing body to sleep in time with the passing trains outside. Ever since PB had held me like that, my body felt like it was missing something, something it couldn't quite figure out, but the hole was there, waiting, waiting to be filled. And all I could do was rock it.

One night Maisie came downstairs cradling a bag in her hand. "Sshh," she put her finger to her mouth as she shut the door with her behind. "It's time to get you outfitted, girl. You're a young woman now, there's no denying that." And she slid a creamy thing out of her bag and held it up to me.

"What's that?" I asked.

"You'll see. Take off your dress."

"What?"

"Come on, this needs to go on under."

And so I pulled my dress up over my head and Maisie slipped my hands into straps like a horse's stirrup and bunched the fabric tight against my chest. I looked down aghast at the two separate lumps of my breasts sticking out like bullets, while Maisie cinched the thing tight across my back.

"This, sweetheart, is a brassiere, and you'll thank me for it when you're forty, believe me."

"It feels awful," I moaned. "It's like being strangled."

"You'll get used to it. Every self-respecting woman has one, especially the English. Have you ever seen such ladies? Now, there's a people with downhome grace. Besides, if we're going to the tavern, we're gonna have to look decent. Can't be drooping like spent tulips, now can we?"

And she burst into a song about wildflowers trod on, and I moved around the room in wonder. When I put my dress on again, my chest stood out like a soldier's going to war.

"Try sleeping in it for a few nights, dear, break it in. Just like a new pair of shoes."

Which I'd never had. But I said nothing, just plopped down on the bed and deep sighed.

When I went to work the next day, I could feel this man or that's eyes darting down to my chest in one swoop. I tried to keep my arms bunched over my front but I couldn't button shirts that way. My own eyes kept drifting toward the bead room, hoping to catch a glimpse of the honey-faced one who owned my heart, but I saw nothing at all.

I had planned to visit PB that night; I couldn't stand the ache any longer. And maybe it was just as well that Maisie had other plans, I don't know. But she grabbed me, soon as I set the key in the hallway door and her face was bright with lipstick and rouge. "Tonight's the night, pal! You and me're going down to the tavern in search of work."

"We already have jobs," I protested.

"I know, but this is different." And she stood back, her head held high, and announced, "I want to be a singer."

"Oh, sweet Mais, you are a singer. Surely you don't want to sing for folks passed out in their beer?" Inside me, though, a tingle rose at the prospect of the mellow drink that seemed to burn cares clean away.

"I am, and I do," she declared. "I need a larger audience, don't you see, than this dung heap building. They've shut down half the taverns in the state, turned them into milk bars. If that happens here, folks'll want something to replace their drink with, something better. And honey," she swished her head in a rollicking wave, "you better believe that's me! The tavern's just the place. Prelude to the English opera!"

Before I could move another step, she whisked me down the hall to my room, where she proceeded to paint my face in rainbow colors. I felt heavier with each stroke. When she had finished, I was scarlet and beige and bright gold.

"You have your brassiere on? Good. Now, you'll have to wear this dress—it's the only other fancy one I have. Use this sash to gather it in at the waist. I seen Claire LaCherche do that in the moving pictures."

And so I found myself in a gray-green dress three sizes too big for me, a lemon sash bunching it all in like twine round a sack, and my hair caught up in a silver pin at the nape of my neck. When Maisie shoved me in front of the mirror, I stared at the ghost staring out of it.

"How much money do you have?" Maisie asked, pins in her mouth as she fixed and refixed her own hair.

"Half a dollar is all, till payday."

"That'll do. Just so we've enough to buy a drink."

Foolish me, I thought she meant a whiskey or some liquid consolation, but when we pushed our way up to the crowded bar, she yelled, "Two glasses of lemonade, please." And a man without a shred of hair on his head yelled back. "Beerginrum's all we got, gal."

"Oh, I might've known. We'll have us a couple beers, then," she replied quick as a squirrel, and the baby-headed man slid a warm glass to each of us. I looked at the golden liquid a long time; it seemed to be teasing me with its burnt orange brightness. "Disgusting stuff! Don't even taste it," Maisie said, laughing. Her whole body seemed to be dancing, even her eyes behind her glasses. She was coming to life here; I could see it and yet not understand it. There were men in groups playing cards at a table or holding up the wall here and there. I only counted three other women besides us, and they were each of them with a man.

People looked at us kind of curious, but no one spoke. We stood at the bar taking it all in. The beer tasted like a watery brand of that whiskey I'd snatched from Timmy's flask; it didn't warm my insides like I'd expected. Maisie was twisting her head around the room. "Now where's the manager of this dive?"

I threw my head back like I'd seen Hank do and guzzled the glass dry while Maisie marched off toward the stage. There was a big red curtain running across it, like velvet. I sat, disappointed that nice sizzle had deserted me this time. "You wouldn't have Scottish cordial, by chance?" I spoke loudly, but the barman didn't even turn around.

"Hey babe, who let the children in, uh?"

I could feel a thick breath on the back of my neck and turned round. "You a bit young to be hanging out at bars by yourself?" A man in a big cowboy hat was standing so close to me, I could almost have touched his nose with my own.

"I'm not alone," I replied, firmly.

"Got you a special man hiding somewhere, do you?" He started twisting his head around and I could see a long red scar moving up his neck and along his chin. It looked like a horse's brand.

"No," I said, and then, "Yes," pictures of sweet PB rising like wood smoke to my mind. It was a comfort to think of him in this loud, dark place.

"Make up yer mind, child. Yer daddy probably, huh?" And he laughed and his mouth was a big wet cave, only one tooth hanging down, yellow and icicled. I felt sick, and didn't like being reminded of my long-ago father one bit.

I squeezed past him and the other men loafing round and followed the trail I'd seen Maisie take. She was standing at the foot of the stage and, it looked like, arguing with a man in a black suit. "I can sing better than any of your skinnyass women, I promise you that."

"I don't care, lady. We need all the custom we can get, till our young men come home. So we give 'em what they're after." The man was wiping his forehead with a crumpled napkin. "My customers want style, they want oompah, they want something they've never seen before." And he made a gesture like S's moving through air downward.

"Let me try, just once. Give me one chance."

"Not on your life. I'd have to close the place down . . ."

"But you haven't even heard."

"I know what they like and it's not, forgive me, voluptuous ass in glasses."

Before I could stop myself, I had punched him in the stomach. He wasn't going to talk to my friend like that if I could help it. I enjoyed watching him wince and pull his arms over his front.

"Feisty friends you have, I'll grant you that," he said to Maisie, though he was looking at me. "Now if you had a piece of her fire, or even her hair, I might consider giving you a go."

"Damn you, buster," I said, tossing out all those words I'd heard Hank yell at me when I was a child. "Asshole jerk! Pithead!" I could feel the heat and the joy rising in me like smoke. No wonder Hank used them so often. Maybe it was the beer yelling, but it felt good, despite Maisie's surprised look at me.

"Calm down, or we'll get ourselves thrown out."

"That you will," said the man in black, standing back up straight again. "One more word out of either of you, and I'll eject the pair of you off the premises, permanent."

"See, the snake's too spineless to kick us out," I said, as we slouched back to the bar. "Don't pay him any heed, Mais. Far as I'm concerned, you're the best singer this side of the Idle River."

"Hey, thanks pal, but let me defend myself, huh? I'm big enough." Her eyes were misty. "Anyway, I don't believe snakes have spines." Mais's mouth looked like it couldn't decide whether to smile or pout. I was about to give her a hug when she jumped, high in the air, like a spring lamb. "I got it!" she screamed, and everyone turned to look at us. "Why don't we do a duet? That's different."

"Because I can't sing a note, that's why."

"I'll teach you. You often sing the choruses."

"I can't sing, Maisie. Hank used to say my lullabies scared the kids." I loved to sing when I was happy, but it wasn't the kind intended for public display.

"We can work on it." Maisie was busy scheming, fortunately for me. I was busy pushing back the picture of the newborn twins in their cradle and me coughing out a bedtime song when I caught sight of Mr. Dacey coming through the swinging door. Halleluiah, rescue at hand. But when he came over and we sat together, all three of us at a round table, Mr. D listened carefully, shook his head, and then, sipping at his drink thoughtfully, he said, "Why not a trio? I knocked out a good tune back in Cardiff. Ballads and such, mind you, but not a sinner ever told me to shut up."

"Good, good," said Maisie, leaning toward Mr. D, "that's what I like to hear. Didn't I always say, when it comes to style and polish, the British have it every time." Then she narrowed her eyes and hissed real low. "The Three Spines! I predict we shall be the most famous international singing trio from here to Timbucktoodle!"

My heart was thumping hard and steady in my chest. Careful, I wanted to shout, you never know what that crystal ball will do, you don't want to jinx it. I hadn't forgotten Ama's strange glow, nor her heat. What was it she found in that other world only blind people could see into?

"Another round of drinks, ladies?" Mr. D swept his arm toward the counter.

"Sure thing!" I spoke so fast, they both stared at me like two question marks.

"Say, you don't happen to play an instrument too, do you?" Maisie leaned toward Mr. D, and the pair of them laughed and shook on it and it seemed to me then that these two wanted more than just fame; they wanted to balance some score that I was only vaguely aware of.

I had the next day free, and slept through a good chunk of it. Though my head was a wad of steel wool scraped across my brain, I pulled myself out of bed, tossed the stupid bra in the garbage and headed to the factory to pick up my check. It was already closing in on dark and I figured to surprise PB by waiting for him outside his place. Maybe he'd have cooled down; maybe he missed me as much as I longed for him.

I hunkered down on my legs like I was about to pee, right outside his door. To scare away my anxiousness, I launched into some of the tunes I'd heard Maisie lilt, *Come on home, you drunken sailor, come on home, my love, to me, come on home, you lusty tailor, come on home, sweet dove, to me*. I was trying to ignore the off notes or to make up for them with passion, and as I belted out the last verse, making the most of my lungs, a cluster of birds darted out of the bush down the way, like they'd just heard the devil. I was in the middle of a hearty laugh when the door behind me pushed open and I fell back inside PB's kitchen, and straight onto the toes of a woman.

"Eeee," she cried, as I looked at her from below, her arms waving in the air round her head. Her shoes must have been pointed, for my back felt almost dented from my unexpected landing. "Get off me, you dirty thing, get off."

I stood up slowly, taking this stranger in from the ankles up. She had on white socks and a blue dress that bounced out in waves from her waist. It had no sleeves and a narrow V of a neck that tunneled into her breasts. Her face was pink, with surprise or makeup, I couldn't tell. But I knew one thing: she wasn't pleased to see me.

"What are you doing here, child? Scoo, scoo," and she waved the back of her pale hand at me as if she was brushing a dog away. In her other hand, she was carrying a mirror by a long handle.

"I am not a child," I replied, soon as I gathered my senses. "I'm fifteen years old, and I'm waiting for PickingBones."

"Well, well, and what business do you have with my betrothed?"

I didn't understand the word at first, and I thought she meant brother, but my gut told me they couldn't be related. She was as fair as he was dark. She stood there, like a long golden pencil, glaring, and I couldn't bear to ask her what she meant. I couldn't believe how short her skirts were, barely covering her knees.

"PB's my best friend," I said.

"Is he indeed? And I wonder how come he's never mentioned you to me once?"

"Why would he?" I said. "He's got better things to be doing than gossip."

"PB tells me everything." And she looked off toward the sky. "Or at least he will when we're married."

"Married?" My heart was all of a sudden swinging in my chest. I couldn't catch a breath. I felt dizzy.

Part 2

Chapter 9

When I came to, PB was kneeling over me, his lemon eyes staring into mine. His hand gently brushed hair off my sweating forehead. And the sweep of Clem's tongue on my eyelids had me thinking for a moment I had died and this was heaven, PB and his dog and me, all snug in our own little cocoon. I started to smile up at him, but then I caught sight of the skinny girl behind him, and her hand on his back. "Is she all right, dear?"

He didn't push her off, but maybe he was too distracted by me to notice. "You should have said you were coming."

Why did I always seem to do the wrong thing? Did Chinese Indians expect a letter prior to arrival? How much more did I have to learn? I was hoping with all my heart that this was a bad dream, like the last one I'd had in this room. At least those hairs under his pillow weren't hers. Unless she'd gone white-headed with love? That happened in stories sometimes.

"Let her rest a while," she said. "We need to get the fabrics sorted out now. It's not long until the fashion show."

I closed my eyes against her face and saw a horse, riding, riding across fields of clover and mint. I could only hear snatches of conversation. And a lick curled across my forehead and then something warm covered my legs. And everything went black.

"Let's see, which beads would work best on the worsted wool?"

"Do we really have to do this now?"

"Unless you want to do something else," and her voice softer now, almost a growl, "something even more fun . . ."

And a cough from him. "No, show me the swatches, please." And then, much later, "I can't guarantee I'll get all the beading done by Saturday, Miss Hadley."

"I'm Lara, sweetheart, Lara."

"I'll try my best, but sewing on satin is time-consuming."

"You can do it. I want to be the first woman in the United States of America to model one hundred percent iridescent wool. You're going to make me famous!" Her voice sounded like it was blasting through a trumpet. I opened my eyes briefly and she stood there in her slip, a skein of silk over her arm, and she planted a great big kiss on the tips of her fingers and carried it straight to his mouth.

Something dark and burning rose in my belly. It was a thing I'd never felt before, and I scrambled up off the floor, kicking over a cup, and tore out into the night. I could hear PB's voice echoing down the hill after me as I ran. There was a lion inside me and I had to keep running if I was ever to outdistance him. I nearly knocked Timmy the mailman down when I turned onto Main Street.

"Whoa there, girl! What's got you in such a hurry?"

"Can't stop, Timmy!" I hissed, as I legged it past him and down toward the boardinghouse.

"I'll be off to Wallowa any day now . . ." I'm sure that's what he shouted after me, and I could almost hear bells choiring out of my ears, an answer. Maybe that's how life was: if you wished for too much, say your father and your beloved, then maybe you could only have one. Or maybe if you got greedy, you got to have nothing in the end, only your own miserable self and a sack full of tangerine peels.

But still I kept running until I reached my own front door. My throat was dry and thick and I couldn't stop shaking enough to get the key through the keyhole. It must have taken me five minutes to get inside, where I threw my heaving body onto the mattress and punched my fists into it until they grew blisters.

I must have fallen asleep eventually, for I heard a gentle tapping on the wall and thought I was still dreaming. Visions of PB climbing all over that woman were swirling in my head, and I couldn't stop the black spiders chewing away at my insides. I had never felt like this before and thought I might be ill.

In fact I was. I had a high fever by the time Maisie came round, my forehead a puddle of salty water, and she kept wiping it with a damp dishcloth. My breathing was ragged as if there were a crow in my chest pressing down on me. I persuaded Mais to pour me a glass of beer, anything to relieve the weight. For the first time in my life, I wanted to die. I didn't even know what that was, only that it must surely be a better place than here. Me and little Todd, and maybe Lourdes, we could be a team of broken people together.

"What're we gonna do with you, pal?" Maisie smiled down at me. "My bet is you're lovesick. I've seen these symptoms before."

"You have?"

"Sure. They're classic, even the long, pitiful sighs."

"What sighs?"

"Come on! You've been letting out long, deep breaths every two seconds, as if you were carrying the entire weight of Pendleton on your shoulders."

"I am."

"See? You're a classic case. So . . . who is he?"

I didn't know how Maisie detected the source of my sorrow. But I was glad to pour out my troubles, one after the other, to her, except about me stealing the tangerines; I still felt tender about that. She listened, nodding, and then when I got to the part about the woman who looked like a pencil, she shook her head sideways in vigorous swipes as if she was trying to wipe the notion away.

"Oh, oh. You're in love . . ."

"I am not!"

"Sweetheart, believe me, it is love of which you speak. I've seen it at the picture house. Jane Eyre, move over." Maisie shook her head slowly. "But boy, oh boy, do we have trouble on our hands now."

"What d'you mean?" I tried to sit up, but my arms suddenly were matches and couldn't support me.

"First of all, he's Indian. They're not looked on too well round here."

"Chinese Indian, and I don't care."

"I know you don't, but everyone else does. Why d'you think he has his very own room at the mill?"

"He needs it for his beads."

"Wrong, child. They need it—to keep the smell of him away."

"He smells of sweetness and trees and . . ."

"Dearie, whatever he smells like, white folks don't want to know. It might be contagious, and then what'd they do?"

"But that woman, she was white."

"Ah yes, here's where we run into real trouble . . ." Now it was Maisie's turn to sigh. "See, that girl, she must have one major crush on Badger Boy. Like you do . . ."

"I don't!"

"Just like you do. But, and here's the problem, she's Mr. Hadley's daughter."

"The foreman, you mean?"

"The very same. I know 'cos she often comes into the store for nail polish or lipstick. Bright red cherry, she wears, with a big fat liner round her mouth."

"That's it! It nearly dazzled me."

"Well, she fancies herself a model, see. Been trying to get the mills to make women's wear for ages now. Sometimes she sends her dad in to the store to pick up stuff for her. Poor old thing, he looks lost among the makeup jars, but he's like a slave to her. Buys gallons of milk at a go, lords know what for, though I wouldn't be surprised if that hussy bathed herself in milk like Cleopatra."

"I can hardly believe you, Mais. I mean, what'd someone like that be doing with PB?"

"That's my question. You can be sure, though, that her dad knows nothing about it. Forget Germany—there'd be another war right here in Pendleton if he did. He ain't bad looking, I suppose. Seen him come in the old days with pelts for trade, before they hired him on at the mill."

Maybe it was good luck in China to kiss your boss's daughter, or maybe it was bad luck to refuse. I wished this sickness of mine would wipe out my past and PB's past and simply hand over a whole new present. "I'll probably never see him now."

But Mais swept my concerns away with a brush of her hands. She screwed up her eyes real solemn and stared into my eyes. "I predict," she said in a low voice, "I predict that you will see your beloved again and you'll fall crazy in love like bunnies and have a whole army of kids with bouncy tails. And you'll all go bobbing down the hillside frisky as spring. How's that for a glorious future?"

"Oh Maisie, I can't . . ." And whatever it was I meant to say, it got buried amidst the tears scurrying down my chin and onto my dear friend's chest.

"Hush, hush now." And she rocked me till I was empty, dry as antler bone, still.

It was three days before I ventured outside again, and though I was due at the factory, my legs carried me downriver toward the house of warm women I'd heard about. Ho House, was what Mais called it. I knew women received men there, that was all, and I had some inkling that here was where I might find Timmy the mailman.

But when I knocked on the door, an old woman answered it. Her hair was black as coal, a young girl's hair, and yet her face was a tree of lines running every which way. She had on a dress that stuck to her body, so you could see all the lines and bumps of it.

"Well?"

"I was looking for Timmy, ma'am."

"Were you now? Oh, Timmy's a good customer all right. But he ain't here, sorry. Headed back east, last I heard, while the passes were good. Always a man for the urgent, um, delivery."

"What?" My breath was coming at me in bullets, bang, bang, bang. "He's gone? He was supposed to take me to the Wallowas. I've almost enough saved."

"Hon, don't you fret. He'll be back round this way again soon, I'll wager. Likes my girls, he does."

She eyed me closely, like she was reading my soul and I wondered if she could see the shattered ridges of my heart. "You ain't lookin' for work, are you?"

"No ma'am. I'm employed already up at the mill."

"Well, if you ever are, come see Dolores. Ask for Dolores."

I nodded, and backed away down the street. Somehow buttoning shirts had lost its joy. I knew I'd just sit there, picturing a face soft as honey in every one, and the collars would get tears rained on them. I slouched back down Main Street, and suddenly, I was on Court, staring straight into the window of that steamy cafe that Mr. D and him and me had gone into my first night in town. The Rainbow Bar & Grill was a red glow, and I should have kept walking. But there through the glass stood that same mean waitress bending over a man, all smiles and bright eyes. I got struck, by lightning maybe, just like that, and inside I marched, my stomach blazing, went straight for the counter, picked up a white dish and flung it, hard as I could, like a brick against the wall. It cracked into a million pieces, like snow drizzling down to the gray rug. "See what happens when you don't treat things with respect?" I yelled.

The waitress stood there staring for a minute before she marched right over and yelled blue murder, and a hundred other colors. "What d'you think you're doing . . . young hooligan . . . I'll show you respect . . . vandals these days, I ask ya . . ." On and on, I hardly heard, only felt the grip of her thick hand on my wrist and was almost relieved when the policeman came in and marched me away down the street.

Chapter 10

Maisie came to see me in jail. I didn't care, just sat there on a tin stool and listened to the mice running round in the floorboards. When they brought food on a tray, I left it sitting, and they took it away. There was nothing inside me now, nothing, just coldness and dark. What use was it shoveling food in there? Nothing seemed to warm me, not even Maisie's embrace.

I lost my job at the factory, no surprise. Once the rumor got round that I was a convict, no one'd want to look at me sideways. "Where'll you live, girl?" Maisie asked.

"Don't know."

"How much do you have?"

"Don't know."

"What on earth are we going to do with you?"

"Don't know."

Well, in spite of me, two things happened quickly that provided the answers Maisie wanted. I couldn't have cared less if I'd spent the rest of my days behind bars. It wasn't any better in front of them, far as I could see.

The first thing was Mr. Hadley came to visit. I couldn't believe my eyes when I saw him walk through the door of my cell. "I have a proposition for you," he said, and I thought he was going to talk about PB and his daughter, but he looked nervous, not angry, and his left hand was shaking. "There's a job needs doing and you might be just the one for it."

"Well, the other one didn't work out, did it?"

"No, but this might." And he went on to tell me about two little girls who lived with their mother out toward Reith, in a little two-story house. He had a special "connection" was the word he used, with these people. And he wanted the very best for them. Only the woman wasn't too well, see, and she needed to sleep a lot, which left the little girls alone pretty much. And they were growing up with odd ideas about life. And so, he wondered, his lips squeezing like an accordion in and out, so could I possibly look after the children four days a week? He could only get there himself on weekends and maybe one weekday, if he was lucky. I could have a room there and board, and no one would bother me.

After he finished, he took a long breath and leaned forward, staring at me, and I saw something in his eyes, something that said he was begging, not asking.

At that point, he might have been discussing cockroaches for all I was bothered, but Mais kept on at me to take the work when I told her, though she'd never heard of this family. She said then we could still rehearse our music with Mr. D, and maybe even get a gig at the tavern before long. If Maisie got to sing just once, just once, at the tavern, then she'd die happy. It's what she told me over and over. She even sent Mr. D down to work on me. And that was the second thing.

When I first saw the look on his face as he walked into the cell, I felt a faint twist in my gut, like shame. He'd had high hopes for me, I knew, and I'd let him down.

"OK, OK," I said, not able to look him in the eyes. "I'll do it."

"If it were up to me, I'd say no to the whole thing. We can't have a civilized society and go around throwing dishes at people." Mr. D's eyebrows were knit together, I knew it, from the expression in his voice.

"I didn't throw it at her, and you might talk to her about civilized . . ."

"All the same, I'm disappointed in you."

"Well fine, see if I care." But I knew that was just my mouth moving. There was something in me that wanted Mr. D's approval.

"For dear Maisie, who thinks so highly of you, I'm prepared to overlook your past behavior, and to begin our musical rehearsals."

"Noble of you, Mr. D."

"Not noble; it's simple caring for somebody else but yourself."

But it was much more than that, as I found out soon enough.

I was to get out the next day at noon and had intended to head over to investigate the children that needed minding, but Hadley showed up, arms flapping, and said the mother was in a bit of a state, that he'd have to talk to her some more, but that she would, yes, she would settle down again soon. I studied the needles of his eyes, for I felt sure they'd seen PB more recently than I had.

"Hey, Mr. Hadley, you don't have to convince her. I'm not even sure I'm convinced myself."

But he swore up and down that it was the ideal solution and to just give him a little time.

So what now, I was musing as Mais inched her way in the door, just as Hadley slid out, taking off his hat to her, nodding, nodding.

"Thanks, Mr. Hadley, for hiring our girl here. Now, which family is it?"

But he was a black crow, squawking one minute, gone the next.

"There's been a delay," I told Mais, as she sat down on the bed beside me.

"Well, you could probably stay on here. Looks like they've plenty of room."

"Yeah, I might be the only criminal in Pendleton." I was noticing this strange tone drifting into my voice, bitter like a lime, the way Hank my stepdad would talk sometimes. You'd think he meant one thing but then you learned the hard way that he meant the exact opposite of what he said. It was work keeping up with him and I never appreciated it; made me feel I couldn't trust a simple word out of his mouth. I didn't want to end up like that, but I wasn't able to stop my tongue. It was like someone else had gotten hold of it.

"Wouldn't that be a laugh, though? Choosing to stay on in jail after you've served your sentence? We could rehearse in here. I bet the acoustics are pretty good, all these high ceilings."

"You're not serious?"

"I am! I'll go get Donald, I mean Mr. D, to come join us this afternoon and we can have a hoedown right here in your cell." Maisie looked bright and excited and her cheeks reminded me of spring blooms. I noticed her hair was done different, swept up in a big pouffy bun, and just tiny golden curls swirling down round her cheeks. It suited her, but I couldn't even get the words out to tell her.

"I'll be here," I said, turning onto my side and chewing on a straw. "Less they kick me out."

"They won't. I know Sergeant O'Connor, used go out with my mom after Dad divorced her."

"You're joking! You mean you could've got me out earlier and you let me just rot in here?"

"Where would you have gone? Stop worrying, girl. It's all gonna be fine." And she shoved a big bag into my hand. I could smell warm donuts through the paper. "Have a chew on these, and I'll be right back."

And she was out the door, quick as Hadley.

That afternoon, at least I think it was afternoon, gauging by the light through the tiny window up near the ceiling, Maisie and Mr. D rumbled in, pulling a large case on a cart behind them. "Here we are, here we are," Mr. D announced as if it were a circus long awaited. It kind of was, now I think about it, a musical circus, and Maisie was delighted. I had a place to go to, and she had her trio all arranged.

"For you, dear child of the wilds," Mr. D handed me a round disc with little tin colored tassels on it. It shook and filled the air as the tassels rattled against each other. I looked at it in shock, nearly dropping it.

"Haven't you ever seen a tambourine before? Look! Here's how it works." And Mais picked the thing out of my hand and burst into a song, patting her fingers and then the heel of her hand against the edge, and it made a cheerful sound, like children laughing in a summer field, spinning and tossing their hands in the air, and it made me want to jump up and dance. Mr. D must have seen me tapping my foot, because he grinned and said, "Lively, isn't it?"

I nodded, trying to calm my foot down but it wouldn't oblige; the toes were wiggling in spite of me. "You have to promise me one thing, Mais?"

She raised an eyebrow at me.

"You won't call us the Three Spines, OK?"

"Deal!" she laughed. "So that's how you work that one." Maisie handed the tambourine back to me." You just keep up with the beat."

"Easier said. . . . Why don't you play it?"

"I'll be busy singing." She tossed her head like a horse and her mane of curls followed helplessly. "Besides, the tambourine used be a gypsy instrument. Perfect for you."

And as she and Mr. D strung words together, a shadow passed over me, all the people I had known and loved and left. Mom, Todd, Joey, Alvin, Bessie, Jack, Ama, and oh, PickingBones and Clem, the ones I never wanted to leave. Why was it I always ran?

And then I thought of my dad, and the sorrow trailing after him that he knew nothing of, like Hansel's breadcrumbs, only they were hardened pebbles now that could cut your teeth, and going in the wrong direction.

"What should we start with?"

"Dunno," I said.

"I do." Mais of course had her tunes all lined up like crockery on a pine dresser. "See, I've made a list, so that the songs follow in a particular order. Dance tune, slow waltz, tango. . . . We want to get those tavern folks away from their drinks and onto the dance floor."

"Good thinking, love." Mr. D beamed at her as he polished his instrument with a napkin. The way Mais smiled back at him made me nervous. There was something passing between them that I recognized, and yet it spoke of loneliness. And then I realized in a flash, it was me who felt lonely, not them. They were happy, it was obvious. Soon as Mais started into *My Love's Been Done Hurtin'*, Mr. D scraped his bow across his fiddle, even as his chin held it in place, his eyes pushing out of their sockets to get a look at Mais. And she, well, you'd swear there was no one else in the room, nor in the entire world, than that wool salesman from Wales. Two bugs in a rug they were; I could practically see the waves of romance wafting through the air between them. And I felt cold, colder than I'd been in a long while.

"Play, girl, tap that juicy thang!" And Mais was moving now, swaying her round hips slowly as she sang and I bashed against my ridiculous little hand drum, all the misery wadded up inside coursing out through my fingers. *Oh, let that no-good rogue go . . .* Maisie sang. *For I got me a love than ain't gonna hurt no more.* And I struck the tambourine till all of the little discs jumped in and danced off the walls. Mr. D was almost drowned by sound.

"Easy now, easy," Mais paused to speak. "This here's a love tune, gal; let the nice slow sound control the rhythm."

"That's it, that's it!" shouted Mr. D, as I laid off the banging just a little. "Now you have it." And he was as excited as the mares of Missouri in springtime.

The sounds whistled round the room and echoed off the ceiling so loud you'd swear we had a loudspeaker in front of us. And before I knew it, Sergeant O'Connor was at the gate, easing himself in for a listen, a half smile on his miserable lips. And he was nodding his head away, scrunched up against the wall, for there was hardly any room left in the cell. All the available space was being filled up with sound, and then Maisie's voice got real slow and husky, and she moved into another song, this time sad and lonesome, her eyes closed tight and a look of sorrow on her face like I'd never seen, and the room got quiet, only her carrying the heartache of all time on her moist red lips, and everyone in that room in the grip of it.

I set the tambourine down gently and leaned back against the wall, letting my lids droop, trying to find in my own eyes the secrets of grief Maisie sang of, but nothing was there, only blackness and cold. And I sat like that, in a trance almost, while Mais sang her song of despair, and a shining white goose swooped in from nowhere, flap-flapping its wings and rising up through the dark air, light and graceful, and then it was gone and all that remained was a load of tears hurrying down my face. The room had no sound, and when I opened my wet eyes, the first thing I saw was a policeman outside the cell, and he was letting the wall hold him, his arms folded, his legs crossed. He was young for that uniform, maybe seventeen, and broad.

He looked like a forest bear inside his crisp outfit, listening to Maisie's magical voice, but when I opened my eyes, he wasn't looking at Mais, no, he was leaning back against the white wall, a smile on his pink mouth, and he was staring straight at me. My heart did a little jump in surprise. Being watched like that made me uneasy, though his face had a kindness to it, and he had the air of someone easy as the wind. There was something not there in him, something red and angry, that I was used to seeing in folks of the law. No one like that had ever shown up to haul Hank off for a talk. No, there was a mildness to this boy's smile that kindled a warmness in me. And I was so surprised that I started laughing. Lightly at first, then a little louder, and Mais ended her song and she laughed too, and then Mr. D joined in and even the men in uniform, even their mouths were wide open with the laughter. It was as if a magic had entered the room and was circling through all of us and coming out through our throats and our mouths. For the briefest moment, I had a feeling this was where I belonged.

A silence came down on the room then, and we all sat there lost in our thoughts, until the soft-faced boy spoke. "That was beautiful, beautiful. You're a talented bunch." And he was still looking straight at me. I started to shift about on the bed, which set Mr. D bouncing too; it was as if we were drunk on something special.

"Gotta get back to work," the sergeant said, nodding at Maisie. "That's a good sound you guys have. We'll be sure to attend your first show."

"Indeed," said Mr. D. Maisie was all wide smiles and beckoning to the young man to come in. The sergeant had to move out first to make room for him. "Come, officer," Maisie said, in her English voice. "Join the party." And the young man strolled in and came straight toward me, holding out his hand like he was about to meet someone famous.

"I'm very pleased to know you," he smiled at me, a big round gentle smile. "I want to thank you for waking up that Rainbow Bar & Grill for us."

I received his hand and it was warm and full and covered my own entirely. I didn't speak.

"Went by there this morning and who should be sitting in the window sipping at his coffee but Theodore Gull!"

Maisie gasped, then clapped her hands, then smiled. "You don't say?"

"I do! There's a new sign posted on their door now. 'All folks welcome here.' Never thought I'd see the day."

"Well, well," Mr. D shook his head. "You just never know, do you?"

"Gull who?" I sat there, blinking, while this warm stranger cupped my hand between his two big ones and grinned.

"Theo comes from the Deep South. His skin's a tad darker than ours."

"A negro, you mean?"

He laughed heartily, and my hand bobbed up and down with his. "You got it, ma'am. Never been served in there until now."

"Duskier 'n English coal dust." Mais shook her head. "I'll be damned."

"How'd all this happen?" I was starting to enjoy the furnace round my fingers. I didn't want to let it go. It put me in mind of the old woman's heat, only hers was more crackly and sharp.

"Well, let's just say you opened up the matter . . ."

"In a not too diplomatic way," Mr. D put in.

"Still and all, it cannot be denied that our young friend here got the ball rolling."

"And what kept it going?" asked Mais, gathering back her breath.

"A gentle nudge, shall we say, from the law."

"You mean you support what I did, throwing that dish across the room?"

He winced a bit at that and Mr. D said, "Not the act itself, I'm sure. Not the best means to the end, but . . ."

"But it worked!" And the policeman squeezed my hand till it started to throb. "That's the main thing now, folks, isn't it?"

And I knew then I had a pal, in the least likely place of all.

"Officer Robert Dixie at your service, ma'am," he said, and he shook my burning hand firmly. "But please, call me Bob."

I stayed in my cell overnight and feasted on a hearty supper that Bob brought in on a tray. "Only the best of meals for our best inmates." He smiled and set it down on my lap. A giant slab of steak, rings of golden onions, bright green peas. It was the first real meal I'd enjoyed in a while. I could feel my blood starting to move again.

"I could get used to this life," I said, and Bob laughed. He laughed easily, as if all the world were a great big joke to be enjoyed, and it made me lighthearted just to hear him.

Though when I asked if he had a jigger of whiskey to top off the princely meal, his face darkened. "There's better things than jail and hard liquor on the horizon for you, young Taf." I shouldn't have been surprised he knew my name, though I'd been trying to avoid sharing too much of my history. Sometimes it felt like too many complicated stories for even me to recall. "A person with that amount of courage, well, they'll go far. As I believe you will, ma'am." And Officer Bob stepped out of the cell, his white teeth lighting up the wall as he departed.

I wanted to call after him, to tell him it was rage, anger, bitterness drove me to it, not bravery at all, but there was only air around me for ears and so I chewed on my meat in slow, deliberate bites.

Chapter 11

Most mornings I woke up on my own time, no clocks or birds to alert me to the passing hours. But one day I jolted up off my mattress, there was such noise coming from outside. It sounded like a stampede of cows, but it was people, for there were horns tooting and whistles, and songs going. I had to clamp my ears. I wondered if that far-off war had finally arrived in Pendleton. I banged on the bars hard; it annoyed me they were still padlocked, when I was supposed to be free to leave. But no one came. The whole world seemed to be gathered just beyond the station's door, and no matter what I did, I couldn't join them. Hardly more than a body length away, but it might as well have been China.

Eventually I sat back down, my throat sore from hollering, and wondered if the world was about to end, like the Idle River church ladies would sometimes predict. My foot caught the tin mug, and it hit the wall and slid right back to where it started. I longed to be out in the fields again, running, and no walls to collide into. I knew how hamsters must feel, in their tiny cages, racing round on their wheels, trying to escape, until they wore themselves out.

I could hear voices shouting, full of life, and a man's laugh, and then, in a flash, sailing past the tiny window next the ceiling, something red went on its way. I could have sworn it was a balloon. Was this a county party, some revelry I'd not been told of? I was dismayed that Mais or Mr. D or someone hadn't thought it worthwhile to inform me.

I punched my mattress, the walls, shook the railings again, but not even a policeman appeared. What if I committed a crime, and no one to witness it? Though the only damage I could do in here would probably be to myself. It seemed the criminals and everyone else were right outside my door, having a mighty good time, without me.

Sergeant O'Connor finally arrived, a tray of food balancing on one hand. "Sorry I'm so late." His eyes looked twice as big as usual. Before I could open my mouth, he declared, "Today is an historic occasion, Miss Taf. Indeed it is. Today, and I quote, 'President Wilson declared the cessation of all hostilities.' The war to end all wars is behind us. We are a nation at peace once again!" The tray shivered above his hand.

I whistled loud as my lungs would let me. "Wheee-whooo! We're free! We're free!" I hopped around in circles, wherever there was room for my feet to land. And whatever I did right then, I was sure nothing could put out the smile on Sergeant O'Connor's face.

But I sank back against the wall when I realized I may have been the only one in America locked up, when the rest of the world was celebrating freedom. "When can I leave?"

"Now, if you'd like; it was your choice to stay, I believe." But when I ran out into the street, it was quiet. The sidewalk was rainbowed with burst balloons and candy wrappers and long stalks of torn ticker tape, and a man was dragging a crying child home.

The biggest event of the century, and I'd missed it, by about a dozen yards. I slunk back into the jailhouse and flopped back on my bed. I thought of all those soldiers who'd left their homes, and some who wouldn't ever come back, and how fragile a thing peace was, even in my own heart. Sometimes it felt like its own war struggling in there. But tonight I would allow gladness in, like everyone else, for peace was building its nest once again in the world.

Chapter 12

Next morning as soon as the dawn bell buzzed through the block, I hopped off the mattress and banged on the bars. "Time to go!" I yelled until Sergeant O'Connor came marching down the corridor, looking stern. I was disappointed it wasn't Bob. I wouldn't get to say goodbye to him.

"Don't you want breakfast first?"

"No thanks, Sarge," I said lightly. My heart was full of hope this morning and I wanted to make the most of it.

"Well, good luck to you then, girl," he said, directing me toward the huge oak door at the end of the hall. "And behave yourself!"

I walked out into the street, my eyes blinded for a second by the light of the sun. Everything seemed lit up from inside, luminous, and I stood on the steps, my arms stretched to the heavens, and took a long, deep, slow breath in. There was a bite in the air, though, winter already undressing fall.

I traced the route out toward Reith, to the family Mr. Hadley'd told me of. I knew they wouldn't be expecting me just yet, but it seemed best to check on my living quarters early in the day. If it wasn't going to work, better I knew it early and start looking elsewhere for a pillow and bed. Or would it be the fields for me again? And would fields be as inviting now, without PB in them with me?

I let the sun melt the chill inside me as I turned onto the low road leading away from town. I found the house easily; it was the only two-story house on the street. It looked like the curtains were closed, which surprised me, 'cos most folks out this way didn't even have curtains, and besides, it was daylight. But then as I went up the driveway, I could see something else, like paper maybe pasted against the glass. The pathway was rough and uneven, and parts of a broken doll lay strewn across the yard. No one had trimmed the grass lately.

I rang the doorbell and it buzzed so loud and long, I had to pry the bell out of the socket so it'd stop. No one came to the door. I was considering turning around and leaving, not having a good feeling about the whole setup. But then I caught sight of something moving in the window and part of the paper was being clawed away, so that a hole emerged and through it appeared a small eye, fixed firmly on me. It was so low down, close to the ledge, that I guessed it was a child staring out. I went over toward where the eye glared and tried to smile. There was a look in that eye I'd seen before. It was close to terror.

"Hi," I said. "I've come to meet your mother. Can you tell her I'm here?"

There was no response. "Sweetheart," I tried. "Is your mom in?"

The eye disappeared and I got a view of the head and then the eye again and the other eye and the head, all in a quick flash, and it dawned on me that the girl was shaking her head.

"Well, could you come to the door then? I'd sure like to meet you." I spoke as gently as I could, but my stomach was upset and I was chalking up how much I loved Mais to stay on and live in a strange dump like this.

Suddenly, to my left, the door creaked open slowly, and a skinny girl with hair thin as rain leaned out. Her mouth was covered over with what looked like a headscarf. It was smeared with red crayon. I thought I must be dreaming.

"Mommy's asleep," the girl said. Her eyes made beads in her pale face. Her voice sounded like it was coming down a tunnel.

"What . . . How can you talk with that, that thing on your mouth?" I whispered, fire rising up to my throat.

"We got it figured out," and her eyes crinkled as if she was smiling. "After Daddy puts it on so we won't make noise and wake Mom, we just wet it with our tongues, see. Don't taste too good, though."

My throat burned. "Don't you have a sister?"

She pointed inside somewhere and I stuck my head in, fearful of what I might see. A girl, smaller than the one at the door, was standing at the window, still staring out through the hole she had carved. A half dozen crayons lay strewn about her feet, like baby fingers. I stood down from the step and looked from the outside, and there was that dull, frightened eye again peeking through. "Pearl loves to draw. She painted color on my mouth, see?"

"I better not come in." I couldn't think of anything else to say.

"No, we'll be in trouble for tearing at the glass." I didn't know what she meant at first.

"Daddy put it up yesterday. It was hard work, he said, and don't you children touch it."

"Is the window broken?"

"No." The girl shook her head and then started coughing, and the scarf blew in and out of her mouth like a leaf in a March gale. "Mommy ran away yesterday and we kept looking out for her, so Daddy put up the paper. He said, she'll never come home if you children keep on looking."

"Don't touch it, girls," the girl at the window said, as if she was talking to air. There were yellow and red crayon squiggles all over the paper.

"Now look at that hole. You better not say you were here."

"Where's your daddy?"

"Gone. He had to leave after the doctor brung Mommy home. He doesn't live with us."

"Where does he live then?"

"Daddy lives in a henhouse. Daddy lives in a henhouse. Daddy lives in a henhouse." The tiny girl at the window spoke into the paper as if it was her favorite doll. She never moved from her spot at the ledge but kept her eye steady on the dime of light pouring in toward her.

"What's your name?" I asked the girl at the door.

"Pearl One," she whispered, and I could see she was having trouble breathing and speaking. I wanted to rip the stupid scarf off.

"Pearl Two," said the girl at the window, not moving. "Pearl Two, Pearl Two, buckle my shoe. You'll never be done, so my best girl's Pearl One."

In all my travels, I'd never once encountered such a sight. There was a fire inside me and I leaned forward to Pearl One and grabbed the edge of the mud-colored scarf and gently lowered it off her mouth. Underneath was pink and scaly.

The girl's eyes widened in surprise, and her eyes filled with tears. "No, no, no. This is Daddy's game. You can't play." And she raised the scarf up to her lips again, her hands trembling. It hung limply under her nose, and all I could do was throw my arms round her in a hug, and leave.

"You tell your mom Taf Stetson came by. Tell her Mr. Hadley sent me." And I moved my shaking body back down the garden path, and out the gate. Hadley sure had a lot to answer for.

I ran all the way back into town, not even pausing to watch for motorcars or animals. It was as if a lightning bolt lit me from behind. When I got to Main Street, who should be walking out of the drugstore, only PB. For a second, my heart jigged skyward, visions of his hands on me flashing in my head like a cartoon in the Saturday newspaper. But my breath was ragged and tight and no sooner did I recall that soft evening together and the candle lighting us like gods, but then came the scene at the door, two girls with no mouths.

"Hey!" PB turned and saw me approaching, warm steam puffing out on my breath. "Am I glad to see you. I wanted to tell you . . ."

"No time," I said, surprised at myself, but for the first time, it felt like something was more important than PB's love. "There's been a, a tragedy."

"What?" His face, as I passed, had a look of puzzlement. His black brows were purled together over the bridge of his nose.

"Children." My heart ached to burrow deep into his chest but my feet kept on walking, and I turned back to wave him away as I went on down the street, not certain where to go or what in the world to do.

I headed toward the mills, but got only as far as the square of grass they called a park in Pendleton. I had to rest, take it all in. I thought I saw Clem's tail swishing in the distance, but there was no sign of him or PB, and I was half disappointed. Life seemed simpler in jail. I didn't have to worry about my true love colliding into me on the street, and be reminded he loved another. I didn't have to see how some poor folks lived. I could just rot away in my imagination without a care. The world might have declared peace, but war still waged in the small towns of the heart.

The park had a bench, and a little fountain inside a square of bricks. I splashed the water dozens of times on my face, trying maybe to wipe out the memory of those girls' faces. But they remained steadfast and clear, and I knew I would have them with me until I did something to help. I shook my face and held it up to the sky, though there was only a weak sun to dry it.

Hadley was desperate about something, I could tell, but I didn't know what. Part of me wanted to thump him hard with my fists until he said he could make it all better, take those girls out of their dark house and let them talk and laugh and look. But another part of me knew I had to be careful. Last time I gave in to my anger, I landed behind bars. And that was its own kind of trap. I was so lost in thought, I didn't hear PB sneaking up beside me. "Forgive me intruding," he whispered, "but you mentioned children. Is this about Todd or Joey?"

And in a flash, I realized it was. I'd helped ruin two boys' lives, hadn't I? Poor little Todd. I just couldn't let it happen again. PB was wise, just like his mother; he'd know what to do. His eyes glinted gold above me, as I poured out the tale of the strange girls in one long, breathless sentence. PB listened, though I don't know how much he understood, just pressed his arms around me in a warm circle. This time my legs didn't shake. "They're lost, those girls. . . . I know! We could take them to your cow camp." It seemed a perfect answer. "It'd be a tight fit, but there's no cows, and we could . . ."

PB stood back, gripping my shoulders stiffly, like a guard on duty. "We can't just steal children, Taf."

The way he said my name, it came out slow and sticky sweet. I could feel my insides clump together like toffee. "Even if there's no one to steal them from?"

My beloved's eyes narrowed so the light disappeared out of them, and I remembered those tangerines I'd stolen. They had belonged to somebody, not me.

"What else can I do?" I sat back down, away from PB's hands.

"You should see Mr. Hadley, ask him. He will know what to do."

"You won't help?"

"Of course I will, if I can. That house with the picket fence I'm saving for? One day . . ."

One day sounded hopeless to me. One day could be next year, next century. I was tired of waiting for people to act like I expected them to. No one fit into that fairy tale story I dreamed for myself all those years ago back on the Idle River, Taffy Hero and her happily ever afters. It was as if I'd traded one tale for another, darker one, soon as I fled Foley's Alley.

My heart hung low in my body. Clem seemed restless, his pale ears pricked, eager to chase something, a hare maybe, in the bushes. It struck me how his fur was the perfect match to Hadley's daughter's hair. PB stood erect as a lamppost, but it was an awkward pose. "I am sorry about what happened with Lara . . ."

So it was Lara now, no longer Miss Hadley. Oh PB, is everything lost, I longed to ask, but all that came out was, "You're right. The Hadleys have all the answers."

I could feel those lemon-gold eyes on me as I trudged out of the park and on up the hill to the mill. They bore a dark hole in my back.

The sun was starting to move lower in the sky by then. It'd be dark soon. Who would be looking after the girls? Would they go to sleep unfed? What was wrong with the mother that she'd allow them to be bandaged up like that, her own flesh, and go to sleep? What kind of sickness did she have? What had PB been going to say?

My head was sore with questions as I headed up the road toward the mill. That house was a dark fortress, but I couldn't leave those poor mites to shrivel up inside it, alone. Even Todd and Joey had Ma to look out for them. If I don't ask Hadley, I'll never know, I told myself, though I was starting to realize that the answers weren't always the ones I wanted.

When I pushed through the doors into the mill, the foreman was nowhere to be seen. People were winding down for the day, switching off machines, putting fabrics away, tidying up.

Ella, the woman who used to give me cookies, looked over in surprise when she saw me. "Well, well, look what the wind blew in. Good to see you again, girl."

I tried to smile. "Hadley? You seen him lately?"

"Been locked up in the boardroom all day, having their big annual conference. He's got buyers in there from all over."

"How long do you think it'll take, the meeting?"

"Can't say, dear. I'd wager till dark anyway. They usually have a big catered supper 'bout six."

"Thanks," I said, and even though I'd never been in there, I walked slowly, with sureness in my step, toward the boardroom. It had a thick wood door and it was ajar. I could feel the heat of all those bodies oozing out into the hallway and then, horror, Hadley's voice, "So, to conclude, let me summarize the wonderful benefits of wool: Worn next to the body, wool fibers naturally breathe in air and exhale perspiration. The fabric is durable. It's one of few fabrics that naturally warms to icy temperatures."

"Yes, sir," I heard someone say. "But it's not fashionable enough for the city. People want spring in their clothes. With the war behind us, everyone's in a mood to celebrate. They want to be noticed."

"Precisely," came back Hadley, "And that is why we've come up with this. Dear, would you stand, please?"

I peeped my head round the door and followed everyone's eyes toward a woman wearing a vivid green shirt, glittering with beads of all colors—red, blue, silver, gold, white, purple—and they ran in dizzying zigzags all across her front, like a rainbow of rivers in the sunshine. Everyone in the room seemed to gasp, even me, not just at the shirt, and that would have been enough, but the girl too, that pencil-hipped woman I'd last seen blowing kisses at PB.

It was more than I could take, having to face her again, for she seemed the source of all my troubles, and I was about to march in there and scream or curse or spit, but then Hadley said something that made my heart stop.

"This, folks, is the new wave of wool for the, um, fair sex. Our beadmaker, PickingBones, is the premier bead artist in the Northwest. These patterns," and he pointed to the dazzling cornrows of beads across her front, "are his own unique design. He's been working in, ahem, alliance with my daughter, taking her ideas and adapting them to his talents. And see what glorious work is emerging . . ." The daughter beamed and tossed her yellow hair back over her shoulder, like a mane. And I saw how beautiful she was, with her rosebud mouth and flashing lashes, I saw how candlelight would flicker against her hair as it fell on PB's shoulder, and he breathing in her perfume.

I couldn't stop the stupid predictions erupting in my head: the old woman burning my hand with her grip, and telling me PB would love a stupid model and they would run away together and live on berry juice and laughter and I'd be left sorrowing through my old age heartbroken and alone. Or maybe it was the Chinese bad luck finally caught up with me.

I could make out the faint shape of a bird in that outfit, a bird with bead wings flying where I could never touch them. And I suddenly felt stupid, dirty, homeless, mad, a vagabond without a purpose.

Tears dripped onto the sidewalk soon as I stepped back out through the swinging doors. Maybe I did belong in that house of sorrow with those misfit girls, where all the world was kept at bay and nothing, good or bad, could get in. Pretty soon, you'd have to stop caring, wouldn't you? You'd forget there were ever such things as models and beads and stupid, stupid love.

I took the long path back toward that ugly two-story house, and walked the thin wall that ran in a border along one side of it. The backyard was a mess of tall weeds and grass. It looked like no one had been in here for centuries. I sank down among the greenery and it felt good, the softness of the blades against my skin, the brush of them.

It reminded me of the geese and how they always returned to the cattails and wheat back where I used to call home. And I smiled sadly to myself. No wonder I'd been drawn to their constant flight and their landings; I belonged to their tribe, gypsies of the air who made nests of other people's waste. The only trouble was, I didn't have wings and they all had pals to travel with. I was sure feeling sorry for myself, my head dizzy with frustrations, until I finally lay down and slept the sleep of the lost.

Chapter 13

I woke to the sound of screaming. It was a woman's cry, sharp and haunting, like those birds of the night I'd heard about that holler and make a terrible fuss. It sent shivers down my back, but it was cold anyway, the first touches of frost on the ground, shimmering silver in the pale sunlight. I crept up to the back window, but the noise was coming, it seemed, from upstairs. It must be the mother, but who would leave such a woman in charge of two young girls? And my heart somersaulted then with the thought that my own ma had done the same. Gone and left me a moment with two babies and what had I done but hurt or even killed one of them. Poor sweet-eyed Todd. I blew him a big kiss wherever he was, set it sailing on the air like a bubble to find him, before I crouched up against the window ledge.

What I saw through that window snarled those thoughts right out of me: the girls were seated at the kitchen table, spooning what looked like porridge into their mouths from a bowl. Then Hadley appeared on the scene like a ghost, in his gray woolen suit. He looked out of place in that filthy room. But the girls began singing, *Pearl One, and Pearl Two; buckle my shoe*. And the strangest sound came out of Hadley's mouth, it took a moment to figure it was a song. *If you buckle your shoe; my best girl's Pearl Two.* Little Pearl stood up, it was the first time I'd see her move at all. And put on the dress Hadley handed her, reciting the rhyme long after her sister stopped.

"Good! We have someone coming today to meet us. We need to be on our best behavior, girls, our best behavior, don't we now, for Daddy?"

Big Pearl was nodding as he pulled the spoon out of her hand. Pearl Two banged her spoon on the floor. "Best girl for Daddy. Best girl for Daddy."

It all ballooned in my head, the whole scene, Hadley's desperation, his need for someone to take over here, his choosing a petty criminal. This was Hadley's harem, these girls were his, these pitiful girls. And that woman, whoever she was, his girlfriend maybe. And there he paraded around the mill, showing off his pencil daughter when he had two sorry-looking kids hidden away.

I slapped on the window with my fist, and the younger girl dropped her spoon with a clatter on the floor and Hadley jumped a foot, up off his feet and back toward the door. He looked as if death had suddenly leaped out at him, and maybe, in a way, it had. I could see his chest heaving in rapid waves and his face, oh, his face was priceless, eyes like black saucers staring out, like two bad yolks in a gone-off egg.

I banged again, and this time, Hadley put his hands up, right over his head like he was about to be arrested. The girls strained toward the window.

"Who's there?" Hadley said, his eyes closing, as if he could block out whatever evil was chasing him down. "Whoever it is, I'll come out. Just don't touch my girls. If it's liquor you want, I only have sherry."

I felt a desperate urge to laugh, all mixed up with tears, but stuffed it back down my throat. He was a pitiful figure standing there, maybe even more pitiful than me, and that made me want to laugh even harder, the notion that there might be someone in this wild and crazy world who was as foolish and lost as I was. As if sherry was all I wanted, as if a glass of something sharp and hot could make everything better. Then again maybe that was the cure pure and simple.

I heard the window open slowly and there was Hadley, with his long head sticking out. "You!" he said, his face trying to gather back some of its composure. "What on earth are you doing in the backyard?"

"Waiting for you, you old . . . you old," and the laughter collapsed inward, and became a fist churning in my belly. Like how Alvin might have punched when he used to go to school.

"Look, why don't you come inside where it's light, and we can talk?"

When I walked in, Hadley guided me toward a chair in the living room. Even with the light bulb blazing down on us, it felt to me like a dark room. And cold. "Sit, please."

Hadley coughed and took a long breath as I settled myself on the hard chair. The door to the kitchen was closed, and if the girls were still in there, they were quiet. Not a sound stirred in the house, even from upstairs.

"So what's going on here?" I decided to jump right in.

"Just give me a minute," he said. "I'm still recovering from the shock of your sudden appearance." He dabbed his face with a white tissue. "I thought it might have been a mountain lion or someone after a drink, the way it's becoming more scarce lately."

"Spare me, Mr. Hadley, but since when have you been bargaining with animals? But as you mention it, I will have a glass, thank you."

"I was taken by surprise is all I am saying. You can't be too careful round these parts." Mr. Hadley poured a thimbleful of sherry.

"I hope you have more to say than that."

"All right. I asked you here, after all. You just arrived a tad early."

"I believe I arrived exactly on time, Mr. Hadley." I gulped and swallowed, the honey rivering down to my busy stomach. "Now please . . ."

"We have a special situation here. Unusual, so to speak."

"I'll say."

"Please don't interrupt me, or I'll not be able to finish." He was still daubing his temple. "The two girls you saw? They are, ahem, my daughters."

"I figured. They seem to call you Daddy."

"Well yes, the difficulty is, I'm not able to look after them as easily as I might."

I wanted to tell him what I'd seen the day before. But I let him talk, for I wondered how a stranger might feel coming across cold Todd and crying Joey the day I left the Idle River.

"Which is why I hoped you might, you know, help me out?"

"Where's their mom?"

"That, alas, is another problem. Their mother is upstairs, sleeping now. You may have heard her crying earlier this morning?"

I nodded.

"She is, isn't well, as you may have ascertained. She needs to take regular medication, which helps a great deal. But she forgets. More and more, she forgets, and then," he shook his head and looked so tired that I almost wanted to put him to bed, "then hell breaks loose . . ." I could see his bottom lip starting to quiver, like he was about to cry.

"I know you must think terribly of me. You have every right to. But I'm only doing the best I can, what with my career and my other daughter."

"Your career? You mean you weigh up the needs of the family against your job? I may be young, but even I can see that humans are worth a bit more than work is." And then I thought of PB and how much he wanted to earn enough to get that stupid fence around a house.

"Yes, yes, but it is my income that allows me to keep, to support my family, don't you see?"

"So you can keep two families, you mean? Does your girlfriend, if that's who she is, know you have another house in town, and another daughter?" I'd heard about a woman, Mrs. Hill, back near the Idle River who'd kept two families going at once, and she'd have to run back and forth between them. Ma said it was just a vicious rumor made up by bitter men. But I wasn't so sure now. People seemed to do some strange things.

Hadley stood up straight as a rod and stared at me head-on. "Violet, the woman upstairs, she is my wife."

I was starting to feel irritable. No one seemed to be with the people they were intended for. "Then why don't you live here, with your other daughter?" I couldn't bring myself to utter her name.

"You see, we, Violet, my wife and I, had Lara, when we were first married. We were happy then, for a few years. But she is, how can I put it, a delicate woman, and her delicacy made it difficult for her to, ahem, navigate through life. We had to put her in a, a home, if you understand my meaning."

I saw visions of a crusty damp old mental institution; I'd heard my own pa's sister ended up in one back in England. Grandma from the old country said she stopped remembering things, so they had to put her in a place where memory didn't matter. The kind of place where spiders took over the window sills and people talked to themselves for want of an ear.

"But she was so unhappy there, so very unhappy. I couldn't do that to her, keep her locked up and, and . . ." He seemed to choke on his words then. I sat quietly, waiting till he could continue.

"It was an evil place, let me assure you. They did things to her that would ruin an animal. I had to get her out."

"Why didn't you bring her home?" Nothing seemed to add up any more, no matter how much I counted.

"We tried to live all together again. But, but she was with child, with children."

"I don't understand."

"The girls, they are twins. I know, I know, they don't look even close in size. But they are the exact same age. And well, my daughter Lara had problems with three sudden additions to the household. You must understand that it was just Lara and I for many, many years. One develops habits.

"Besides, my wife would have her screaming fits and no one in the house could sleep. No, it was better to give them, my wife and the girls, a place of their own. But I'm run ragged," he was still wiping his forehead, "ragged trying to keep both residences afloat."

He sat there a long time, staring ahead, as if he'd forgotten me, forgotten where we were, forgotten who he was and his hard life. I almost felt sorry for him, the defeat in his eyes.

I didn't move, just watched his face and the shadows falling across it. He could have been a pillar, made of stone, and only the lines on his brow shifting.

Eventually, he spoke. "I cannot do it all any more. It's not fair to the children, to my wife, to Lara. The girls can get rowdy as girls will and their mother needs absolute quiet, absolute, or she'll wake up and scream the house down and then the girls get frightened. No one can help their behavior, but the combination is difficult." And he sighed such a long sigh, it went on for minutes. All the puffed chest of the boardroom was gone. I considered hugging him but sat stiff in my chair. "If the neighbors discover the girls are alone so much, they'll be dragged off to foster homes, I'm afraid. You can understand how my trust in, ahem, institutions, is meager.

"I thought, perhaps, you might be able to play with the girls, help them out some. They have a lonely life tucked away here and some days I only see them briefly."

"Why did you have more children, Mr. Hadley, when one seemed more than enough?"

He looked down at his black polished shoes. "It wasn't my, my choice," he said. "It just happened."

"How come they have the same name? Don't tell me you ran out of ideas."

Hadley took a huge breath in. "My wife . . . Violet . . . my wife doesn't speak much any more, but she was very attached to a particular strand of pearls I bought her for our first anniversary. She, ahem, fingered them a long time after the little ones were born and so I thought, I thought, why not Pearl."

And I thought to myself, as I stood up and went to look for the poor girls, that I'd take greater care in deciding about my own children.

I found them, Pearl One and Two, sitting on the floor in the kitchen, smearing jam in jagged lines between them. The smaller girl had one hand stuffed inside the jam jar and her mouth was a blob of raspberry.

The bigger girl turned to look up at me as I walked in. Her eyes were blue pools.

"OK, now that you're dressed, let's get this mess cleaned up here," I said, trying to sound efficient, as if I knew what I was doing. "I'll help you. Where are the rags?"

The big girl jumped up and ran to the sink, where she pulled out two cloths from a cupboard underneath. "Here! Here!" She sounded excited, as if she'd been waiting all her life for some simple direction that would tell her what to do next.

Little Pearl sat where she was, licking her fingers, some small song running through her lips, her eyes not lighting anywhere. She scared me.

"OK, girls, here's what we'll do. Let's start by making the kitchen sparkling as possible. And if, only IF, we get that done this morning, we can go for a walk. How's that?"

Pearl One jumped up and down, her eyes dancing. "A walk? We get to go outside? A walk? You really mean it?"

"I don't think that's a good . . ." Hadley was standing in the doorway now.

"If you want me to work here, you'll have to let me run the coach my way." And I turned to Pearl by the sink and said, "Yes, I really mean it. Soooo, let's get to work!"

And the three of us gathered up a bucket of lathery water, a mop, some rags and a dustpan, and we whisked through the room, clearing off the dishes, putting away everything in sight. Mr. Hadley stood silently watching us, as we worked our way round the room. And when we got to our last stop, the circle of jam on the floor, he stepped right over the mess, plucked his little dreaming Pearl up in his arms, and carted her out to the living room. "We have to put your shoes on if we're going out." And his voice had a ring to it, a higher pitch, maybe it was happiness, who knows, as he strolled out of the kitchen.

"Fun," said Pearl One to me and I thought how very little fun she must have had in her life to enjoy scraping clean a filthy kitchen. I remembered how Ma used to love cleaning too, and that made me sad and glad all at once.

"Fun," I smiled at her and nodded. "Now go get your coat. We're off for some air."

Suddenly Hadley spoke up. "These girls aren't accustomed to the outdoors."

"Well, if they're with me, they better get used to it. It's where I spend most of my days."

Pearl Two didn't have a coat, or couldn't find it, and she seemed dazed to be even stepping beyond the lintel of her front door. She gripped the bottom of my dress with her fingers. I decided to carry the poor thing, wrapping a blanket over her scrawny legs.

Pearl One skipped about ahead of us, weaving in and out of gardens, zigzagging joyfully down the road. There was a sound tissuing out of her, I couldn't make sense of it, but it burst on the air anyway.

Pearl Two hid under the blanket, her head tucked low, only the crown of corn-hued hair sprouting out the funnel like a carrot top. I hummed a low tune, one of Maisie's, much slower than it was meant to be, but it had a calming sound to it, and I'd a strong feeling we all needed a good soothing at that moment.

As I watched the gleeful stride in Pearl One's walk—pointing at trees and flowers and even weeds—my body grew heavy, this babe in my arms, just like years ago, me and Joey and Todd. And what a hames I made of that. How could I take on two new charges, I asked myself as I wandered down the streets. Yet how could I not? If I didn't, then who on this strange earth would?

Big Pearl would have walked forever, I'm certain, eyeing houses as if they were new toys, but there was a nip to the air, and I was worried about the little one. Do new things slowly, that's what I'd heard. It sounded like good advice to me right then.

When we got back, Hadley was waiting at the door, stepping from one polished shoe to the other. His hands were rubbing against each other like two people at war. "You're back." He leaned forward toward us.

"Of course we are. And better for it too." I set little Pearl down on the fading rug inside the hallway and let her big sister push past us. Up the stairs she ran, "Mommy, Mommy! Guess where we went!"

I could see the color fade from Hadley's face. He turned to go up after his daughter, but I put my hand on his arm. "Can't you let her be?" I said. "We need to talk about this arrangement you have in mind." Still holding his arm, I moved him in toward the living room, where little Pearl had perched by the window ledge, staring. Since when had I gotten so brazen, instructing a man who used to be my boss? But I reasoned that I was only doing what had to be done. Someone needed to take charge round here, and if there were no volunteers, then I'd better step in, hadn't I? I knew what sorrows could come from ignoring the obvious.

"So, I sleep here, feed and look after the girls. What else? Your wife? What about her?"

"She, she's fine, once she has her medication. There are certain medicines she absolutely must take if she is to remain . . . calm. I can write down the dosage and the times for you."

"Doesn't she eat too?"

"Not a lot. She's not fond of food. The doctor said baby's food goes down easiest at this stage."

"Baby's food?"

"I'm afraid so. Her stomach has seized up on her from the lack of sustenance over the years, and she can only manage easily digestible foods. Stewed apples, for instance. Soft cheese is good, when you can get it. And milk, plenty of milk."

Hadley fished in his wallet. "I will pay you for the food and other supplies, on top of your regular salary."

"And how much is that to be?"

"I was thinking . . . two dollars a week, plus room and board?"

I'd earned three, buttoning shirts at the factory. "No," I said firmly, for I knew Hadley needed me and I knew I'd be earning every cent. "Six dollars a week, and I'll do it. Not a penny less."

Hadley took in a long breath and stared at his shoes. I could be out sleeping in fields again tonight, one wrong word from Hadley and I'd be out that door, and good riddance. There was a silence for a brief minute until the sound of Pearl Two shouting upstairs knifed through it.

"All right, yes, all right." Hadley nodded his head vigorously. "You're a saint, truly, to take this on. And I know you'll do an excellent job."

Compared with nobody, anything I did would amount to excellence. Any little gesture to improve these girls' lives would be better than nothing at all. Even I knew that.

"Deal?"

"Deal." And we shook on it. By the time Timmy showed up again, I'd easily have fare saved to get to Wallowa. But somehow the notion didn't thrill me like I'd thought. Something needed mending right here, right now, where I stood.

"I'll move in tonight. But first, I need to do some shopping. Your cupboards are bare as a baby's bottom."

"Ahem, yes, that would be appreciated."

"And one more condition, Mr. Hadley . . ."

"Arthur, please call me Arthur."

"No more kerchiefs, Arthur."

"No, no, of course not." And I could have sworn Todd's round face was out there behind Hadley's, grinning like a Montana cat.

I ventured all the way back to town, five dollars in my fist, with a new sense of purpose. Before, that sense had kept me always moving. I still wanted to find my pa, but for now I had a reason to stay. I couldn't abandon two girls who'd known nothing but abandonment their whole lives. I knew firsthand how it could leave scars inside you even if no one could see them.

Once on Main Street, I broke into a run, wanting to tell Mais my news. Here I was, fifteen maybe sixteen, getting paid for a job I used to do for absolute free. I hadn't been the best of housekeepers, I knew that, and look what I'd done to poor Todd. But maybe, just maybe, this was my chance to make up for my mistakes. I could love these girls like they were my own, and never let them slip out of my fingers the way Todd had. I'd be extra careful and loving and strong. My head was spinning with bright promises as I pushed open the door into the general store.

It wasn't Maisie I found there, though, but the happy policeman. He had a bag of penny candies in his big hand. "Well, hello there!" He beamed at me, sending heat off him like a furnace in winter. "I'm not used to seeing you outside bars."

"Well, you'd better adjust then!" I joked back. "'Cos I'm staying on this side of them, for a while anyway."

"Here, have a licorice." He held the paper bag out toward me. "They're real good."

"Thanks, but no. It's early yet for sweetness." The sherry's tinge lingered on my tongue; I didn't want to lose it. My eyes scanned the store. "Have you seen Maisie at all?"

"Not this morning, no."

"Hmm, that's odd, she usually works today. Hope she's not ill."

I was about to turn round and head down to her room when the policeman touched me gently on my arm.

"Say, while I see you here, I was wondering . . ."

I looked up at his two big dancing blue eyes. "Wondering?"

He shifted on his feet. "Well, the officers of the law have a brass band going—actually, it's very good, you'd be surprised, musicians from all over the state. And well, they're giving a concert this Saturday."

"Where? In my jail cell?"

He laughed, a great big wide laugh that seemed to take in the whole room. "No, it's at the Mason's hall on Court Street. You know, that big gray monstrosity right next to . . ."

"Oh yes, right next to that famous and popular Rainbow Bar & Grill . . ." I was getting into the spirit.

"Might you, would you like to go with me? It'd only be an hour or so and I have two tickets and you might enjoy it, get some ideas for your own musical trio . . ."

He was out of breath by the time he got all that out. I had to smile. This confident, cheerful, huge, candy-eating policeman standing there, nervous and awkward. I found my head nodding, even as PB rose up from the grave of my heart. For a moment, I wished it was him inviting me somewhere, but I remembered how his face had narrowed that day in the park, how he'd said, I'm sorry about Lara. Not even close to how sorry I was. And I found my mouth saying, "Why not?"

"Great!" His voice echoed off the walls of the store; there was so much glee in it, you could almost reach out your hand and catch it. "Can I pick you up?"

"No. No. I'll meet you outside the hall."

And so we agreed to be at the Mason's hall at 7:15 on the following Saturday. I ran the whole way down to Maisie, my heart lightening, for the first time in a long while. I was feeling needed, like there was a place carving itself out for me, not for pity or desperateness, but simply because it wanted to. I could hardly wait to pour out to Mais what happened, and barreled in the door of her lodgings and down the hallway, not even stopping to look at my old room, but straight up the creaky staircase to her place. Her door was open a crack and I pushed it in, singing, *Maisie, Maisie, give me your answer do, I'm half crazy all for the love of . . . Boo!*

But my mock surprise fizzled into the woodwork when I caught sight of Mais in her black slip splayed out on the bed, and Mr. D crouched over her, buck naked and the two of them puce-faced, staring at me with eyes like glazed hams.

"Oh," was all I could say. "Oh."

"Girl, what you doin' here? Why can't you knock?"

"I, I . . ." I eased out the door I had come in, my body all hot and shaky. I kind of knew this is what men and women did together—hadn't I heard Hank and my own mom at it many's a time—but I'd never seen it, nor even imagined Maisie, nor Mr. D, and definitely not together. I leaned up against the wall in the corridor, willing my heart to slow down its thumping, and I could hear shuffling and whispering from the room. I sank down to the floor and breathed deep as I could.

Of course, I thought then, of course, these two were working up to this all month. Swishing through my head, pictures of Mr. D smiling at Maisie in that special way, and she beaming love rays back at him. While I'd been in jail, they'd been getting cozier and cozier. And I felt my stomach heave and then settle and then heave again as I remembered PB's hands dancing on my skin and how good and juicy that felt and I had to sit myself down on the floor in the narrow hallway and swallow down the thumping in my throat.

Mr. D was the first to come out; he had a shirt on and a towel round his waist. His legs were covered in black hairs. "Lassie, I'm very sorry you found us . . ."

"Don't be, Mr. D," I choked out. "I shouldn't've . . ."

"It's all right now. There, there," and he took my hand and hauled me up to standing. Sometimes I still felt like a child.

Maisie came out then, and gave me a great big hug. "It's OK, sweet thing."

"You see," Mr. D had his arm round both of us now. "Maisie and I are in love, lass, and we were just expressing that love when you came along."

"And we love you too, girl, sure we do!" Maisie kissed the top of my head. "Donald's my main man, but you're still the best! Runaway, jailbird, tambourine gypsy: who couldn't love a girl like that?" And I laughed and then she laughed.

"Well, I got a date myself," I announced, and then fell back in surprise that I'd said such a thing. Bob the policeman was only a friend, a companion. It was PB I loved.

"Well, well," Mr. D took me by the arm. "You'll have to come in and tell us all about it."

And the three of us squeezed together on Maisie's bed and I spilled out the entire story of Hadley and his family, of Bob and his candy, of PB's shimmering shirt bouncing up and down on Miss Pencil's bosom. Maisie lapped each detail up.

"I wouldn't worry about her and PB," she said. "She knows she's onto a good thing with PB's designs. She can get some credit for his talent, see?"

"I tend to agree," Mr. D nodded. "But I'm very concerned about the situation with the Hadley children. Sounds frighteningly close to negligence."

"Well, as long as I'm there, I can help make sure the girls are taken care of."

"Well, well, to think I never knew. Hadley's sure a sly one." Maisie laid her warm and hearty hands on mine. "You sure you're up to the task, precious?"

"I'll make sure," I said. "I've some things I want to make up for, or to get right, or something. This can be my test."

"You're an oddball, and that's for sure." And Maisie hugged me again. "Now when're we going to rehearse for our own trio, and you with a young policeman sweet on you?"

"Don't, Mais. You know I'm sweet on someone else."

"Well, fine lot of good that's done you. Enjoy yourself, girl, while you can."

"Yes," Mr. D piped in. "Can you come round Sunday afternoon for a rehearsal?"

I was nodding vigorously when he said, smiling, "But knock first!"

Chapter 14

When I got back to the house, Hadley had gone but the door wasn't locked.

"Girls, girls!" I shouted. "I'm home!" What an odd sensation, to say that. Home was a word that was a mystery to me. A mystery, and a stranger whose face kept changing.

Pearl One came charging down the stairs. "Mommy's resting but she wants to see you. I told her all about you. Except your name. What is it?"

"Taf." But even as I said it, it caught on my tongue. I could still hear PB's mouth making sweet milk of it.

"Laf," said the littler girl, and I had to sit on the staircase for my feet would hardly hold the weight of my heart. Taf-a-Laf, he had said once, Taf-a-Laf.

"I like your names," I tried.

"Me too." Pearl One sat next to me. "I was always Pearl, but little Zoe wanted to be Pearl too, so that's what we called her. 'Pearl too, me, Pearl too,' she used to beg us. You could be Pearl Three!"

She sounded so joyful, I didn't want to disappoint her. "Well, thank you. Why don't we call ourselves Pearl A, B, and C? That has a nice ring to it. Three pearls in a pretty necklace."

"Yes! Yes! Everyone wants to be like me." Big Pearl leaped up and ran to get her sister, who was sitting, legs spread on the rug, staring straight ahead of her. "You're Pearl B, little sis. How about that?"

"Pearl B, Pearl B, that's me, that's me." Little Pearl looked up from her scribbling—she had three crayons going on an edge of a napkin—but her eyes were black and dull.

"It'll be our special secret, OK?"

"'K," Pearl B chimed. And Pearl A added, "So, even though folks call you Taf, your name is really Pearl?"

"That's right. The Pearl Triplets." I smiled at their earnest faces. "Now, first order of business, after I put our food away, is to rip those stupid covers off the windows. Want to help?"

At this, Pearl B stood up and marched on her little feet across to the window and stuck her finger into the tiny circle she'd etched out already and just kept pulling till there was a tear running the whole way down to the ledge. I ran over and helped her yank the rest of it away, and light flooded into the room like a miracle. So much brightness, it hurt my eyes. "Good, good," I said, once we adjusted.

"Mommy might be mad at us," Pearl A said, hunkering down on the floor.

"She won't, I promise. I'm in charge here for now, and your daddy says that's fine. So why not let's make this place sparkle together! We're a team, the Fantastic Three Pearls!"

"A team! Team!" shouted Pearl B, and we all clapped hands on it.

"OK, girls, here's what we need to do . . ." And I laid out a plan for them to work on dusting the living room windows, while I went upstairs to meet their mother.

"Mrs. Hadley?" I whispered as I entered the room. It was dark as night in there, the curtains drawn, and it stank worse than any manure shed I slept in in my travels. Not a smell you could put a name on, not a smell of this world, I was thinking.

"Mrs. Hadley?"

"Mmmm," the woman in the bed grunted. I inched over toward her and her eyelids fluttered a second. Her whole face was caved in, her cheeks hollow as Alvin's treehouse. Even her eyes seemed burrowed away in a place you couldn't reach; I wished I'd some of the fairy ointment from the Scottish story. I'd rub it on the woman's eyelids, gently. "Missus, I'm here to help you out with your girls. If I can be of any assistance to you, let me know." I was proud of how polite I was sounding. I'd never seen a person look more like a corpse than this, even little Todd after I'd dropped him had looked closer to life. I could see the line of her arm bones under the thin coat of skin. She opened her eyes briefly and I thought I saw her head nodding, but I couldn't be sure.

Downstairs, the girls were scrubbing, or Pearl A was, wiping down the tables, piling dishes in the sink. Pearl B followed her in cautious moves. They were humming a tune, loud, like bees circling a flower, and I joined in though I had no idea what it was. We went on like this, hmm-hm-hmmmming, until the light bursting through the windows faded out to a dim violet sheen. And I spread hard-boiled eggs on some bread slices and set my little workers down to supper with two glasses brimming with milk.

"No, no, no," I yelled at Pearl B. "Don't dip your bread into your drink. It'll get soggy and taste horrible. Just eat it in neat, little bites." The girls ate just like I used to, fast and greedily. Those tangerines on PB's ledge came back to me, and that awful, bloated feeling. Maisie's tea parties at the boardinghouse had taught me to be dainty with my food and drink. In the English manner, she'd said. Not that I enjoyed picking like a bird, but Mais said it was civilized. And surely that was something I should pass on to the girls. "Plus, your food'll last longer that way," I said, but I was really consoling myself.

"Who cares?" Pearl A asked. "We can eat as much as we want. Daddy said so."

"Well, I don't!" I countered, quick as a flash. "Eat only until you feel satisfied, then walk away."

Pearl B looked at me as if I'd just flown in from the full moon. I was beginning to feel like I had.

"OK, OK." I stood up. "Follow me." And I bunched up the paper that had been shielding the living room window, and tossed it into the grate. There were a few odd sticks there already, and I criss-crossed them over the paper. "We're going to have us a fire," I declared, even though there wasn't a log in sight.

The girls sat next to me, mesmerized, as the paper took flame, but it made only a few wisps of smoke, and fizzled out in seconds. No heat in it, no stars winking above us, no marshmallows scenting the night air. I wasn't sure how much of civilized I could take, myself.

I dug out a corner for myself in the tiny rectangle next to the girls' bedroom upstairs. Lucky I had no belongings, or not much anyway, beyond old Ama's special coin. Mais had given me a pair of her old shoes and I kept them as spares at the foot of the bed. The girls' room was knee-deep in junk and old newspapers, but by bed-time, it was all I could manage to lay the girls down and sing them a lullaby before I hopped onto my own mattress. I hadn't been this weary in a long, long time. Tomorrow would take care of every-thing, I thought. Just wait, whatever's next, until tomorrow.

Chapter 15

The following day broke out sunny and warm and the rays beaming in shone all over the dust motes and cobwebs. It felt almost like spring, though we'd a few months to go before the geese returned. And would they return here, I wondered? Maybe they'd headed to the Idle River year on year and not found me lying in wait for them; maybe they'd finally follow me out to Pendleton. The notion, wild as it was, fed hope into my heart.

"More dusting and sweeping for you girls," I announced over breakfast. Best to keep busy.

"Goody!" sang Pearl A, and I showed her how to run the broom in one direction, while Pearl B gleefully hunkered down with the dustpan to catch whatever came her way. Their enthusiasm at such a dull task got me to thinking how everyone in this wide world needs needing, even little girls. Little Pearl delighted in calling me Pearl C, and she never forgot it was our secret. Whenever Bob or anyone was around, she'd mouth my new name, no sound issuing out of her little lips, her eyes full of mischief. Sometimes it was a consolation to be someone else for a while.

I spent the morning with Mrs. Hadley, trying to get pills down her, red ovals, white circles, gold pellets. But she'd wince every time

I tried to slip one between her teeth. She'd spit the water out, letting it dribble down her chin onto her nightgown. Her face'd pucker up into a tight fist.

"Mmmm, uhhmmmm," she'd growl, and I'd just remind myself to stay calm but firm. I persisted with each pill till she swallowed them all and lay back exhausted on her grimy pillow. I knew I'd have to steep her linens and scrub at them for hours to restore any brightness to her bed. My ma could do that in her sleep, I knew, and the thought made me lonesome.

For lunch, we three Pearls wolfed down cheese sandwiches and a pint of milk each, I'd say. Then back to work: I hauled a pail of sudsy water up to Mrs. Hadley's room, and while she dozed, I scrubbed away at the dressers, cupboards, floor, windows, mirror, lampshades, till everything sparkled silver. In the oak closet hung dozens of beautiful dresses, all shimmery and soft. I'd never seen such a selection. I turned to make sure Mrs. Hadley was still sleeping and then, Lord help me, plucked the creamy chiffon one out.

It had tiny rose petals scattered across it, like a summer breeze, I thought, and pressed my cheek against its softness. Had I ever set eyes on something so beautiful? And the seed dropped straight out of the air and into my heart: I would wear this someday. I would waltz down Main Street, aglow with pink petals, and everyone would turn in awe at the undeniable beauty of Pearl C. Maybe even PB would stroll by and catch his breath and hold out his beautiful hand to me, forgetting all about Miss Ruby-Lips Pencil, and I'd forgive him everything and he'd forgive me, and we'd float off together on love wings.

I set the dress back in its place, but slowly, sadly, and took one more glance round the room. It looked good, more like a bedroom now, but still that rotten smell lingered.

When I roused Mrs. Hadley for her mashed food and the next round of pills, her eyes fluttered briefly as she took in the newness of her surroundings. Her gaze swam round the room like a bird's looking for the best pickings, and I could have sworn her face brightened a little, like a light coming on from inside.

Before supper, I marched the girls out for some air again. We went all the way into town, up Emigrant Street, down Mercer's Alley, back along Dover Row. Pearl B was still sullen and holding back, but I held her hand firmly, and while she didn't speak or seem interested in anything, she kept walking. I was nodding to Pearl A as she pointed out this tree or that, when round the corner, who should come pedaling by but kindly Bob. He was whizzing past at a terrific rate and before I could stop my hand, it was waving at him. "Hey, Bob! Bob!"

He turned and broke into a smile when he saw me, but he kept going, and his eyes took in the whole scene, two young girls on either side of me, and his expression changed somehow. He was too far away to see exactly, but something in how he held himself was different. He waved back at us, at me, and shouted, "Can't stop! Sorry!"

"See you tomorrow!" I screamed and let the wind carry my message wherever it would.

When we got home, I realized I was out of sorts. Why had that upset me? I mean, maybe he was in a big hurry. Maybe there'd been a murder in the town or a problem up at the mill he had to sort out. He had his smart uniform on. He could have been late for work. Surely he'd have stopped though. I mean, he was such a friendly type—why wouldn't he take the time to get off his bike for a real hello?

It seemed that men were always hurrying somewhere, dashing after their cowboy dreams, or toward their precious jobs, with hardly a backward look for their loved ones, who had to winter on without them. I let the brimming notions swish round in my head that night as I lay down to rest. It'd been a long, long busy day and soon, I was off in Dreamland, sliding down a well wall straight into a murky mudhole.

Saturday arrived before I could stop it. I was jittery all day. Even the girls seemed to notice it as we sat with a bucket of crayons and butcher paper, making pretty shapes and patterns.

"Are you all right?" Pearl A asked me, finally.

I nodded, but I was circling the same inch of paper for the hundredth time, so that I'd almost bored a hole in it. "I have to go out tonight. I've to meet a new friend."

Pearl B threw her crayon across the room but her face didn't change. Maybe that was her way to say she cared. The notion made me happy for a moment as I strode across the room to pick the crayon up.

"I won't be gone long, but it is my night off," I said. "And I've been invited to a concert." I felt proud as I said it.

"Can I go? Can I go?" Pearl A tugged at my sleeve.

"Sorry, little one. This is just for grownups." And a zing rang through my body. Me, a grownup? When had that happened? I was only fifteen, sixteen at the oldest. Yet all of a sudden, I did feel like an adult, someone with responsibilities and worries and young men on her mind. Then I thought of Ma and how broken she was, and I wondered how long adult feelings lasted, and just how many of them there were.

PB's image was dancing round the closet as I went in to give Mrs. Hadley her afternoon dosage, the one where he'd held me tight in the park, the one where, if I was writing the story, he would never let me go. I tried to concentrate on my work. The bottle with the blue label was empty, and I made a note in my head to tell Hadley when he came over again. It took her ages to swallow the red pills, and the gold one she just spit out into her milk. I pried it out and threw it into the tin we kept for waste. "All right then. If you don't want it, I'm not going to force." My hands were tight on my hips, as I stared right at her, trying to look mad, and I imagined I caught a smile creasing her lips.

I leaned backward, forgetting the closet door was open, and whoosh, I fell against the pile of dresses lined up in rows. When I looked up, that creamy dress was crying out to me, Wear me. I had visions of PB sitting behind me at the concert and wishing he'd had more guts to love me, even if I wasn't a model and the daughter of the foreman. He'd be all crushed in his chest at the sight of me, struggling to breathe. That dress would turn me into a princess, just like the shapeshifters in my pa's folk tales. I couldn't get the vision out of my mind. The girls chattered on over supper in the kitchen, but I hardly heard a word, only the rose petal dress shimmering like a star on my own private horizon.

How could I wear it without the girls noticing? Would they tell their mother? Or worse, their father? Would I end up back in jail for thievery? And I had to laugh at that, Bob the policeman arresting me for dressing up for our date.

While the girls were drying up the last of the dishes, I ran upstairs and straight to the dark closet and out came the dress. In one swish, I had my old rag off me and slid the beautiful thing over my shoulders. I walked slowly toward the mirror and caught my reflection with a gasp. I looked, what was the word, womanly, graceful, and I combed out the tail of my hair so it fell down my back like a pony's. It was as if another person, someone in a newspaper, was staring out at me and she was smiling, a serene smile but wide, wider than the River Idle, and brighter. I felt like the princess in every fairy tale ever written, and I had to remind myself that even though I was going to the ball, it was with the wrong prince.

As I spun round to see the back, I found Mrs. Hadley with her eyes wide open staring at me, her lips moving in and out. And I gasped, terrified, but her head fell onto her chest as if she was nodding, and her eyes closed again. Maybe I dreamed it, but I chose to believe she looked kindly on me that evening as I walked out to meet my cheery policeman.

Chapter 16

Things hardly ever turn out as you hope they will. I knew that, even as I walked toward town with my head high as a swan's, and my heels tap-tapping the sidewalk like any young girl who dated all the time. The rosebuds reminded me of Maisie's mouth and I pretended she'd planted her kisses all over my dress for good luck.

Bob was waiting for me when I got to the Masons' Hall, his hair spruced back with oil or something. It was neat and shiny, just like his face. And he had a white tie on over his shirt. He took a breath in when he saw me and stood up straight, just like in my dream, and held out his hands to catch mine. "You look . . ."

I smiled at him. "Arresting?"

"Forgive me," he missed my joke, his face all flushed. "But I wasn't expecting . . ."

"It's all right," I laughed. "You haven't seen the new me till now." And I realized right then that I hadn't either, or at least not felt it till I saw it reflected back at me.

Bob led me into the hall, his hand at my waist like a sash. "I've saved us the best seats in the house," he said, as we moved into our row on the balcony. So this was how royalty felt, sitting up here on top of the world, beautiful and glowy and powerful. No wonder the kings and queens ruled the world; you owned everything from up here.

Bob slipped a thick piece of paper into my hand. "The program," he said.

I didn't want to ask him what that meant; why spoil the moment? I just nodded and held it in my lap. The whole stage was taken up with chairs and benches and unusual instruments and then a whole army, though I guess it was policemen, marched in slowly and took a seat. Men limping, sad-looking, tired men. Bob whispered that many of them had retired early because of certain disabilities and ailments, and had taken up music instead. Those years of practice had paid off, as far as I could tell. When they held up their gleaming golden trumpets like animals' snouts, and blew sound into and out of them, the sounds they conjured were gleeful. They played light melodies that set my feet tapping as they carried up to us on our heights, and we swayed our shoulders side to side in a soft and easy rhythm and I felt all the cares and pains of the world leak out of me then, down, down, down into the wide, open earth, who I knew loved me and would take it.

Every now and then, Bob would turn toward me and grin his wide grin at me. It felt like basking in the sun.

Afterward, Bob introduced me to half the audience. "This is my new friend, Taffy Stetson, folks," he'd say. "Sweeter than any salt-water taffy, she is. And don't you forget it."

He sounded so proud of me, but I couldn't bear another man using my name, when it felt PB had true purchase on it.

Afterward, Bob announced, "We're going to have us a chocolate malt. And I'll let you guess where!"

My hands shook as he opened the big glass door into the Rainbow Grill. I could still hear the dish smashing against the wall where I'd tossed it. "No, no," I tried, "we can't go in there."

"Of course we can," Bob smiled. "We can go anywhere. Remember, we have this place to thank for us meeting at all. Besides, it's the least we can do to support their new open policy, which you, may I remind you, helped promote."

My breath was ragged as he pulled out a chair for me by the window. What if the waitress showed up and spat on me or something? How could I enjoy a malt thinking she might even poison it, like people did to princesses in fairy tales? I'd have preferred one of Hadley's sherries any day.

But I needn't have worried. A large, rumpled woman I'd never seen before came up to take our order. "One chocolate malt, please," Bob asked. "Two straws."

"That sure was some good music," I said. "Made me want to jump up and dance around, how about you?"

"Sure thing," Bob grinned his whiteness across the table at me. "Yessiree. Yes, ma'am! Foot-stompin' good it was." And then his voice softened, like ice cream melting in the heat. "Say, I wanted to apologize for cycling on by the other day. I had someone waiting for me. Jem, actually, the manager at the tavern . . ."

"It's OK, Bob," I said, wondering if I meant it. What could he have to say to that mean old coot that couldn't wait? "Just wanted you to meet my new employers is all."

"Those young girls?" His voice sounded like he wanted to make a joke, but it came out serious.

"Yeah, I'm taking care of them for a while, seeing as their mom's ill and all. House out toward Reith. I got room and board."

"It's the Hadley twins, isn't it?" And for a second, Bob's face turned grim. It was the first time I'd seen it like that.

"How'd you know? I thought it was a big secret."

"They'd like to keep it that way." A strange look flashed across Bob's eyes. "I didn't intend that to sound the way it did. I mean, I understand they need their privacy and such."

I hadn't thought about how much I'd tell Bob, but it seemed he knew plenty already. Maybe the police just know everything, I thought, and it unsettled me a little.

"Shame what happened to Missus." He hung his head down so low, it almost hit the malt glass.

"Shame for the children too. The little one's off in her own world; breathing's the only thing keeps her alive."

"It's a tragedy all round."

And I wondered if he knew about Hadley and how he'd pasted paper all over the windows and tied scarves round the girls' mouths, and how filthy the house had been inside. I wondered if he'd call it a tragedy or a sin or maybe illegal. It was too much to weigh up in my head right then, what with me in my pretty borrowed dress and a giant chocolate malt plopped between us like a dare.

Bob cheered a bit, lunging for the straw on his side. "You get first taste," he smiled. "But hurry, this looks too good to wait long."

And so I leaned forward and set the straw between my lips and Bob did the same with his straw, so that we were eye to eye, slurping away, and I could see kindness and heat in the brown circles, and it was like a blanket warming me. When I pulled back, my mouth moist with the taste of chocolate, half of my hair had fallen into the glass and before I could remove it, Bob put his hand in and lifted it out gentle as a jewel and I sat watching as he ran the strands through his mouth, licking each one like they were a dozen straws. The sight made me gooey inside and I was trying to ease back into my seat softly when I saw it.

Maybe I heard it first, a thump, or was it a gasp. Anyway, it was some kind of noise from outside, and there in the glow of the street lamp stood PB, like an apparition at Hallowe'en. He stood, solid as a tree, only his eyes riveted on something, not me, not Bob, but somewhere in between, the malt glass maybe. Then, just as quick as I'd spied him, he turned and was gone. I sat for a second, just sat, then all I could think of to do was ease my hair out of Bob's hand.

"You have such beautiful hair, like a real fine sunset," Bob was saying, and my heart all of a sudden riddled with arrows, and PB, my own love, buried under them.

As Bob walked me back up Main Street, I got to thinking how I ought to be careful wishing for things, because even if they happened, they always had a way of surprising you. Maybe PB thought I was a traitor, going back to the place that had rejected him. Maybe he knew nothing about that smashed dish. Maybe he thought I was in love with Bob now.

As I crawled into bed, after Bob had given me a cozy bear hug at the door, I told my pillow how hard it seemed to be an adult. I didn't know of a single one who was entirely satisfied. Mr. D, maybe, came closest. He had a job he loved, a woman he loved, but he was just as far from home as I was, and probably even he had troubles of his own. Maybe my dad had become a cowboy, but what if even he wasn't happy at that? How could he be, really, when he'd had to leave his own family behind to do it?

PB came to me in my dreams that night. He was in the water all tangled up in river weed and I was trying to pull him out only I couldn't even get near, and he kept changing into a seal. Even when I shouted loud as I could at him, he didn't budge or look my way.

I woke in the pitch dark of night, feeling hoarse, my throat dry and rough. And it came to me: Don't see Bob again. It isn't fair to PB. Even if he is seeing Pencilla Hadley, even if he wants to buy that stupid house, well, that doesn't mean I have to hurt him, does it? He must care a little bit surely, running away from the window like that. One day, one day—weren't those his last words to me after all? Surely I could teach myself to be patient. Even though Ma used to say I lived and breathed by impulse, surely I could learn to be otherwise, especially if it led me back to my own love.

And that all would have been fine maybe, except the time never seemed right. Bob showed up on the doorstep three days later, all bashful, and just as I was about to tell him, he handed me a letter. "This came for you," he said, standing there. I didn't ask him in, but the girls were peering round my skirt to watch him.

"Me? A letter for me?" I could hardly believe it. Who even knew I was here? Must be from Hadley, I thought, or Mais, but no, there was a red stamp right across it that read, Marlow County, December 1918. That was almost two months back. In the bottom corner of the envelope, it said, Please forward.

"How'd you get hold of this?" I asked, trying to catch my breath.

"A man, Timmy, from next state over. He said he'd given you a ride out here a while back, and somebody near Milton-Freewater, Bessie, I think, handed him this for you. Heard him asking the post-master if he knew your whereabouts."

"But . . . but," I could feel the tears welling up in me as I stared at the white square between my hands. This came from the Idle River, I knew it. It could say anything. Could I bear whatever it was?

"Pearls, Pearls," I said, out of nervousness. "Go outside and play. Now!"

Bob opened his wide smile in an instant and said, "I'll play with you girls. Your pal here needs some time to herself." And off the three of them went, chasing a ball in a blur as I moved back into the darkness of the living room and sat down.

"Dear child," it said in the pencil scrawl I knew to be Ma's. "Dear child, thank you for your letter in Idaho. The boys miss you. Todd out of hospital. Hank gone to Granite for work, he lost the driving job. I miss you also. Look after you now. Your mother."

Todd was alive. After all this time, he was still alive, so how come he'd been floating like the ghost of a boy round my head? And oh, they missed me! I clutched that letter to my chest to soothe the heaving, but nothing could stop it, the streams of tears floating out of my eyes and all the way home to the Idle River.

God knows how long I sat there, bawling away, it might have been days. All I know is that at some point Pearl A came running in, tugging at me, "Come on and chase us."

"Let me alone, girl," I said, wanting to stay there with my old friend, Sorrow, where I always had a home.

"Don't be a spoilsport!" Pearl's voice had an irritation in it. "You're the one always tells us to play. Now you won't even do it yourself."

That stung me all right, so I let her lead me out to the bright light of the garden, and there, under the scrawny pear tree sat Pearl B, right in Bob's lap, and she was pulling at his ear like it was a bell. It may have been the first glimmer I'd caught of interest, even curiosity, in her. She was pull-pulling away and Bob beaming like the sun itself down at her. "BobBobBob," she was almost singing.

"Ah, there she is," he turned toward me. "Are you all right?"

"I . . ."

"Sit down here beside us, and tell us all," he said so kindly that I plonked my shivering body next to his on the grass and poured out the sour milk of my life to everyone. On and on I went, telling them about Todd and the accident that day, about Hank and his meanness, about Ma and her fears, about the long, lonely road that had led me to here, and I wasn't even done yet. I still had to find my dad, and would I ever make it to the Wallowas at all and what if he wasn't there anyway, or what if he was, would he even know me or care to know me, and who was I really, only the child of two far-apart people who never saw each other one year to the next, on and on, I rambled, and no one said a word the whole time, not even the girls, and then I read them Ma's letter, twice, maybe three times, and I kept stopping at the part where she said, "I miss you also. I miss you also. I miss you also."

"Mom, she misses you," Pearl B said, as if everyone in the world knew that much. "I miss you, also." And she pushed herself up out of Bob's lap and pressed the sleeve of her dress against my dampened cheek, one gentle stroke after the next, until she'd sopped it bone dry.

"Well, to my ears," Bob said, standing up, "that's reason to celebrate!" And he picked up Pearl B and swung her round in dizzying circles till the sound coming from her throat was like church bells, fine and clear. It was music, pure, fresh, wide-open music we heard that morning out on the lawn of our ramshackle house; it was a slice of God's joy come down for a visit, and we all, each one of us, got to taste it.

Chapter 17

After that day, Bob took to stopping by our house every so often, and somehow it didn't feel right to say, Don't come. Pearl B would dash out to greet him, and he'd draw her up into his big arms and rain her face with squishy kisses till her eyes shone. She still didn't speak much, just "BobBobBob," like a chant or something, but you could see how her sore little heart was mending and a flower budding over it. It did my own heart good to watch the pair of them hamming it up in the garden, for I could see Bob was enjoying himself too. He said he had a big family over in Monument, where he grew up, five brothers, but not a single girl among them.

I never told him that I carried Ma's letter to bed with me every night and cried, nor that it opened up a new place in me, a dark, grieving place, like a little altar that Ma and I could share. For I got to thinking that we may have had our differences—like chalk and cheese we were—but we shared that same deep thing you can't ever put a name on: we both had lost the men we loved to other dreams. And in the long, black hours before sunrise, I'd cling to that awful place inside me, a bird fumbling in a cave, and the only thing that kept me breathing at all was the thought that Ma came here too. It was home of a kind, I suppose, and we went there because where else would have us?

One rainy afternoon in spring, Bob came pedaling up the footpath, out of breath. "Say, I just saw Maisie down at Grave's and she's sure upset with you. Says you had a rehearsal last Sunday and you never showed . . ."

"Oh no!" I yelled. In all the turmoil over Ma's letter, I forgot all about our music plans.

"Once she found out you were OK . . . She was worried you might be mad with her." And he looked puzzled. "But I told her no, I didn't think so, that you were busy and all."

"True, true. Thank you for that, Bob. But I better get on down there now and apologize."

"You surely had." Bob sat back on the seat of his bicycle, sweeping his arm toward the gate like a person conducting a show. "Go now, girl, 'cos Maisie has some good news for you . . ."

"Tell me," I begged. My heart was leaping round inside like a wild frog's. Was she getting engaged, was that it?

"BobBobBob," Pearl B came running over.

"Well . . . see, she's got you three a musical engagement at the tavern."

"No!"

"Yes, ma'am. The Pendleton Trio will be performing at 3 P.M. on Sunday, August 24, to the delight of local patrons." Bob beamed at us. "It's all set!"

"But we've hardly practiced at all. And the manager was rude last time."

"All set, honeyboo. Jem and I had a good talk a while back. They're giving you the afternoon spot as a tryout. If it works, they'll start a series. They even came up with a name: Amateur Afternoons. The whole town should be out there cheering you on. Me included!"

Honeyboo, that's what Bob had taken to calling me, though Lord knows where he dreamed it up. I'd definitely have to tell him soon.

"Can I go?" Pearl A was now at the door, jumping up and down like a bean.

"We'll have to see about that, won't we?" Bob grinned his apple face on her and I sat down on the stoop, to catch my runaway breath.

"If you let us go," Pearl B pulled Bob's ear down to her mouth, "I'll tell you a special secret."

"Well, in that case . . ." Bob lowered his head and listened, and when he sat back up, he said, "Well, well, well."

We had almost nine weeks to put together a classy act, Maisie told me when I got down to the store that evening. And Mr. D would be on the road some of that time, so we had to move quickly. She had a plan in mind: we were to meet twice a week, on Tuesdays and Sundays, if I'd remember, and our rehearsal space would be the lunchroom at the county jail! It was all worked out, she said. Bob had talked to Sergeant O'Connor and they were behind the idea of adding more culture to the town. "More culture, less trouble," is what he said to her. And they had my tambourine ready and waiting.

"Write it on your forehead if you have to, Sunday at three, just don't forget!" Maisie smiled and circled me in her arms. "Plus it'll be an excuse to see you more. With that new job of yours, you're fairly becoming a stranger. I predict one day you'll just up and abandon us, and me and Mr. D'll have to elope to England in sorrow." There was that stupid word again, Ama had put in my head all those months ago. Why wouldn't sorrow just walk out the door, and keep on going?

Bob did his best to keep a distance between me and that dreaded word, though he probably didn't know it. One payday, he arrived with a bucket of oysters, said they came from a cannery in Oysterville, where his oldest brother worked. And he sat us girls down on the lawn and had us pry each one out of the ice. "You find a pearl," he declared, as we gobbled our juicy treasures, "any pearl, as fine as the three sitting right next to me, you just let me know, I'll trade you."

Our first, let's call it, official rehearsal started out with a heap of laughter. At least, everyone else laughed and I watched them. "What's so funny?" I wanted to know, and Mais would throw her head back like a horse while Mr. D smirked like one of those Cheshire cats he'd told me about.

"Let me in on the joke, would you?" I asked, frustrated.

"Sorry, love," Mr. D. said, "it's just . . ."

Finally, Mais hauled a mirror out of her purse and handed it to me. "Here, take a look for yourself."

And there, scrawled across my forehead in bright red crayon, were the words Ree-hurcill, 3 clok.

"The girls! It must've been Pearl B up to her tricks." With a little help from Bob, I'd wager, who'd been teaching them to write. I could just see her bent over me, scribbling away while I was sleeping.

I kept the reminder on all afternoon, for good luck, so that when we got stuck or I played too hard or not hard enough or at the wrong time, I could call up the memory of my two sweet girls, who wanted me to be here with all their might. And in spite of my fears about ever getting it right, I drew strength from knowing I was doing something not just for me, but for them.

"A little softer, love," Mr. D. cautioned me, as Mais sank into her soft voice. "There. You're getting it."

He was kind. I was a long, very long time getting it. I could have used maybe another year to get my part down, but the pair of them egged me on and hugged me when I got it close to right, and after a few weeks, well, it felt good to be part of the team. It made me warm inside to think I was doing something with other folks, not struggling forward all by myself, like I was used to.

The next months passed in a hazy blur. Spring, then summer. I heard the geese sometimes high overhead on their way somewhere beyond our little town. I'd wave up at the heavens that held them, and their wings seemed to wave too, though it wasn't at me. Their beaks were pointed way beyond Pendleton.

I thought about my dad galloping across the Wallowas, and my ma waiting for a letter back. And the wishes that lay like dust in back alleys, wasting. If only we all had the same wishes, that might help, but I knew I was only fooling myself.

Mr. Hadley came round only once in a while, usually with a wad of cash and crayons or chocolates for the children. He always looked dazed when he came in, as if he'd just stepped into another century. He spent most of his time upstairs, sitting at his wife's bedside. One time, I heard him whispering to her as she lay resting, and I imagined his hand resting on hers, all of his frustrated love pouring out of his crow's chest.

The girls seemed to frighten him. He'd look at them as if they were strange animals somehow caught in his house, and there was nothing he could do about it. He'd give them an awkward hug when he was backing out the door, and pass a weak smile to whatever they said to him. But mostly, he was a ghost in that house, ill at ease, doomed to wander the rooms.

I think he was pleased at how the house was shaping up and how the girls were brightening little by little, but if he was, he never said so. Just "You're doing a fine job, keep up the good work." And then he'd be gone. Like that, whoosh, out the door, see ya!

It didn't bother me. I liked having the run of the place without his odd presence lurking round us. And Mrs. Hadley, well, she was back to her regular medications because her husband said it was "imperative," though on the rare day she got stubborn and spit them out like bullets, I let her be. Surely your own body knew best what to accept or refuse. She slept most of the time, so she hardly noticed him when he did come. But the girls, it was them I ached for, their sorry eyes fixed on their own father disappearing down the street from them, and nothing in the world they could do but watch.

Between house chores and Bob's visits and the music rehearsals, I hardly felt the time flashing by. And though I still carried PB like a blossom in my heart, I let it brown over, or maybe that's just what time did to it. He still throbbed inside me like an ache at night, but the days were too busy to be pining for something that might never be mine. I had other people to think of now, and I knew I had to put them first. I tried to cheer all three of us with my pa's ballads, though I'd only sing the good parts, *And it shall come to pass, on a summer's day, when the sun shines hot on every stone, that I shall fetch my little wee son, and teach him for to swim in the foam.*

Chapter 18

One June evening, while the girls were out sitting under the tree stranding daisy chains for each other, I happened to glance out the window and there was Bob kneeling down between them and they were strewing daisies all over him till it looked like snow. "BobBobBob!" rang through the trees. And I smiled to myself, thinking how lucky my life had turned lately.

But when Bob came inside, he looked serious and my skin prickled, just for a moment. It felt cold and snaky, and it sent a memory of winter shivering through me. "What's wrong?" I asked.

"We need to talk," he said to me, his hands gently guiding me to a chair in the living room, and his voice sounding deeper than I'd ever heard.

"OK," was all I could say, though I had the feeling it was him who needed to speak, not me.

"Honey," he said, and that was a clue, for he usually called me Honeyboo. I knew he had serious things on his mind. "Honey, it's about, well, several things. . . . But first, the girls."

"What of them?"

"They're getting on, almost six now."

"You don't know!" I was shocked, for Mr. Hadley had never even told me their ages. I just had it set in my head they were children and they'd stay children forever, the way Todd and Joey were still babies back in Marlow County. I watched the girls spiral hand in hand round the pear tree.

"I'm afraid I do." Bob let out a sigh I'd never, ever heard from him in all my days of his acquaintance. "I'm afraid so, yes. The girls were born between 2 and 4 P.M. on November 11, 1913, at the Umatilla County Mental Facility."

"What are you telling me?" I was up off my chair, pacing round the room now.

"Sit, sit down please. These are some hard facts I'm having to share with you. It's not easy."

"What?"

"Being in the profession I am, sometimes you learn things you wish you hadn't. I knew about these girls before ever I set eyes on you with them."

"What else d'you know? Tell me." I slumped back onto the chair.

"They, they were born to Mrs. Hadley all right, when she was in the home, but Mr. Hadley is not their real father."

"Hang on, you've lost me here. Hadley not their dad?"

Bob looked down at the carpet. "Mrs. Hadley was, was impregnated by someone in the home."

I had my hands cupped over my ears, because there was an ocean roaring through them.

"Please, honey," Bob gently pried my fingers away. "I'm so sorry to have to be telling you this, but it's important. The word they use for that, that sexual attack is molestation."

"Molestation," I said, nodding. It was a word I'd heard before, a horrible word, hard and rough-edged, like a curse.

"They never caught the attacker, no evidence, except, of course, her swelling belly."

"Stop! I don't . . ."

"It's OK now, shush," and Bob put his arms round me. "It's OK. See, the girls have a home and two mothers now."

"And Missus?"

"Ah, dear Mrs. Hadley, she had to be heavily sedated. Has been ever since, as you can see."

"But she hates taking those pills, and once when she spat them out, I just tossed them, and she seemed more lively."

"Yes, but that's only a brief blessing. If she doesn't take them for a while, she gets so nervous, she's out on the streets screaming and wrenching her own hair out."

"Does she remember . . . ?" I let the sentence fall out into the air.

"Who knows," Bob said, and then, seeing how upset I was, said, "Probably not. Those drugs help ease her of her memory."

"OhGodohGodohGod."

"I know. . . . They could've taken it to court, probably had the home shut down, but Mr. Hadley wanted it hushed up. He said his wife didn't need any more intrusions in her life; just let her rest."

"So he shoved her off to the outskirts."

"No, honey, from what I hear, and I was only a boy at the time, his eldest daughter, Lara, had a fit. She's like her mother, very fragile, and she almost ended up in a home herself when she found out. So Hadley did the only thing he could think of, and bought a place for Missus and the girls here."

I thought how odd life is, the way it comes round at you from the back and sneaks in and stabs you, only it waits till you're good and settled and then it pounces. It dawned on me that PB was hooked up with the girl who had rejected my little Pearls.

"Besides," Bob was going on, but I could barely hear him, "he thought it best to keep her out of the public eye. You know how small towns are. People can be cruel."

"Ain't that the truth!" I said, that old bitter tone cracking through my voice again.

"But I'm telling you this, honey, because the girls will have to start going to school soon, even this fall. They can't stay home forever."

This was all too much news to take in at once.

"School? How?" I hadn't even thought about that.

"Well, that's the question. How? People know Mrs. Hadley is convalescing, but not everyone is aware of her young daughters. It's just we can't hide them away here forever."

"Well, we'll just march right down to the local school and sign them right up. What can they say?"

"They'll need legal guardians, people who can look after them fully. If we just take them down there now, they'll be taken off to a foster home, I promise you. I've seen it happen before."

"What'll we do?" I was almost screaming now, trying to shout above the ocean in my head. Hadn't Hadley himself mentioned his fear of foster homes once?

"I had an idea . . ."

"Tell me, anything, anything."

"I will tell you, but only if you'll promise to listen without saying a word, and think about it."

"Yes, hurry, what?"

Then Bob tightened his big hands round mine and his voice got lower, back to the old Bob I was used to. "Well . . ." and he coughed. "Well, here's what I was . . . I love you, and you love the kids and they both love me, and well, I was wondering if, if, if . . ." and his face was red again, "if you'd marry me and we could adopt them for ourselves!" And he held his breath in so long I thought he'd burst.

I sat, my head teeming with waves, one crashing over the other, boom smash boom. Isn't that how the ocean worked, never could settle itself once and for all. Tell me I'm dreaming, someone, I prayed. How could I marry Bob, he was my friend, my friend. Didn't he know my heart still cleaved to PB's? I should have told him long ago. But what about the girls? PB hadn't wanted them, at least not yet. I couldn't bear the thought of them in a foster home.

"You don't have to answer now, just think . . ."

And the girls burst through the door, and laid daisy chains round each of our necks, like funeral wreaths.

Chapter 19

Bob didn't come round for a while after that, just let me sit and ponder. Every time I'd watch the girls drawing or playing ring-a-rosy together, my heart would tumble like chipped rocks down a cliff inside me.

I knew I had to see PB, talk to him, before I made any rash decisions. Maybe he'd decide that love was better than a picket fence. Maybe he'd already grown weary of Pencilla Hadley, and was secretly pining away for me day after day. He'd have had time to consider things, at least. And if I told him how the Pearls were in danger, surely he'd figure out a plan. He seemed good with plans.

On my afternoon off, I went up to his cabin, and was surprised how calm I felt as I walked up the hill. Even though I knew what he said could redirect my life forever, I wasn't nervous. I wanted answers; I needed clear signs about what next step to take. And it wasn't just my life that depended on it. It was too late in the season for camas, so I plucked a bunch of speckled forget-me-nots from a field along the way, a peace offering for his shrine.

But when I got there, the cabin door was ajar. I nudged it just a little and it echoed as it swung open. There was a grimy dish on the kitchen floor, and a spider crawling round in it. The mattress I had slept so sweetly on was gone. And a tray of beads that usually sat on a stool, where PB could pluck and stitch with ease, was empty. "PB!" I shouted, "Clem!" But I knew I was shouting to no one. I tossed the flowers in the bowl and set off for the mills.

There was a man at a desk inside the door now, in a uniform. "Sorry, nobody allowed past without a permit."

"Since when?"

"Since I said so."

When I told him who I was looking for, he shook his head. "You won't find him here." And his next words seemed to come from another country. "PickingBones is gone. He and Miss Hadley're off Portland, showing off our best Pendleton wares."

"It can't be!" I had to lean against the door.

"It can, young lady, and it is. They'll be in Hood River, I'd wager, by now, what with that brand new highway. Left day before yesterday."

I took the long road back, my feet heavy as my head. Maybe PB thought I was dating Bob when he saw us that time. Maybe that was when he gave up on me. He had been going to tell me something in the park that day. Why oh why didn't I listen? He could have been about to tell me something important. I shouldn't have walked away. I shouldn't have been so impatient.

I'd no sooner drawn my conclusions than I turned around and ran back fast as I could to the mills. "When?" My breath came in spurts. "When will they be back?"

"Oh, depends on the response they get. Mighty popular Miss Lara, if I may call her, Miss Lara's shows. And I can see why."

"WHEN?" I couldn't steady myself.

"Easy, easy now." He spoke to me as if I were a high-strung horse. "Another couple weeks, maybe less."

I let the night sky drape over me as I turned back toward home again, busy forging my own plans. Soon as he returned, I'd tell PB how much I loved him. He mightn't have figured that out, by the way I'd behaved. And he deserved to know that much. But what if I was too late, if he and Lara were—but I couldn't allow those notions in.

Then one evening, I was in the kitchen skinning carrots into the sink. The girls were upstairs tidying their room, and I heard the front door open. I didn't move, but felt two hands slowly easing round my waist, and a chin resting in the bed of my shoulder and as I turned my head to the side, I could see my hair covering Bob's face like a veil, and he was inhaling real good. "Mmmm," he was saying, "your scent, it's like a wet forest. I love it."

I tried to shrug him off, but he whisked me round in a fast twirl till I stood facing him, the knife still in my hand, and he looked me straight in the eyes, like he was searching to see behind them, and he said, "I love you."

I looked back at him, dumb, my head all fuzzy clouds. Not a word would come to me, though I tried to make some sound and that was when he leaned in toward my mouth and planted his own right on top of it, and he was stroking my hair and parting my lips all at the same time and this wet tongue leaping all over mine like a lizard's. And I could feel his chest thumping right up against my own and the heat of him, so hot, he might have been smoking. And he kept on like that, stroking, and swirling his tongue round the inside of my mouth like a cave explorer. And I just stood, a mound of cotton wool.

However long this went on, I'm not sure, only when he'd done, he cupped my head in his hands and kissed my forehead.

It was all too much for me, the news about the girls, Bob's proposal, PB's departure, everything unraveling so fast, I couldn't keep up. "Bob, PickingBones . . ."

But whatever it was I was intending to say, I never said it, for he had turned on his heels in an instant and was gone.

It wasn't as much fun playing with the girls without Bob; it was like a spark had gone out of our lives, and even though I loved them with a fierceness that surprised me, I knew it wasn't the same, or wasn't enough. I tried to keep us busy, but I could almost feel the old gray cloud moving in over us and hanging there, threatening. I wondered about Todd in the hospital. How badly injured was he? Did he remember that awful crack when I dropped him? Had Joey been lonely without him? Without me? When I finally sent an envelope stuffed with dollar bills to Ma, I never put in a note or an address. Just wrote on the top bill, With love, Your daughter who misses you too.

I used to lie awake, pretending blind Ama in Idaho had promised a different future, like how she'd seen the boys grow up strong and healthy, and how I'd introduce them to the two Pearls and how they'd all fall in love and I'd be waving a rainbow of balloons at their wedding. I knew it was ridiculous to be dreaming up these stories, but once I got going, the visions took over. Ma'd be there too, at the wedding, smiling and radiant; Hank'd be gone, but Ma wouldn't care 'cos I'd have brought Pa back to her and she'd be so happy to have her family again. And maybe she'd meet PB and ask him to make a glittering shirt for her, so she could move out to Pendleton and fit right in. Oh, and Mr. D and Mais of course would be there. Why, we'd have four weddings happening all at once, or five even, Ma and Pa repeating their vows, and the only air in the whole room would be love, easy and free. The kind that forgives everyone's mistakes, because no matter how hard I tried, I couldn't find a place in that dream for Bob.

Chapter 20

I took to walking by the Hawthorne School playground on my way into town, just to get a feel for it. You'd see little kids dancing and skipping and playing ball in the yard at recess, and at three o'clock, there'd be motorcars parked and bicycles propped up against the wall and a stream of parents wandering in to scoop up their little ones and take them safely home to their real family. And my heart fought itself with worrying whether my little ones could fit in there or if they'd be washed away under the weight of their history.

I didn't say anything to Mais, didn't want to worry her, what with her big musical debut coming up, and her new romance. Mr. D wasn't what you'd call handsome, in the strict sense of the word. He was bald as an eagle, with only a tuft of gray sprigs standing up on his crown, and his nose was broken, like a boxer's, yet Mais loved him like he was the king of England. And I felt mad at myself that I couldn't see Bob in that same way. Sure I loved him, and his gaiety and his warmth. Sure, I did. But he wasn't PB, who had the arrow of my true love wedged in his heart, and whether he wanted it there or not, I couldn't pry it out.

I kept hoping for and dreading Mr. Hadley coming around, 'cos I had in my mind to ask him about school and the girls. And if he'd any news of Lara's whereabouts. But weeks drifted by and no Mr. Hadley and no Bob. Nor any sign of PB's return. The house seemed to shrivel in on itself. I'd sit at the foot of Mrs. Hadley's bed, just watching her as she rested, her face sunken like a ship that had given up on its harbor. I'd talk to her sometimes, just words, soft words about anything, to comfort her. Mrs. Hadley, I know how you've suffered in your life. And I'm awful sorry, I'd say. Or you know, I've seen some hard times myself in these past years. You and me both. Or I'd launch into some tale from my childhood to cheer her, like the time I hid from Hank in the alder tree and the branches snapped and I came sailing down straight into the swamp and Hank got his body wedged into the mud right up to his thighs, trying to get me.

Or once, when I went to town for Ma's cigarettes, how I borrowed a slab of berry ice cream from the grocery, and hid it under my dress, till I wanted to scream with the cold. My lips were chattering when I went up to the counter to pay for the cigarettes. But it was Ma's birthday coming up and I wanted to get her something. Only walking home, the ice cream melted all over my skin and scarcely a dribble left in the tub when I got there. The rest was all caked in pink smudges on my body. So you see, Mrs. Hadley, my life wasn't that smooth either. And now Bob says he loves me and wants to get married and I happen to love PB, this Chinese Indian, who happens to love your own daughter Lara, and Mr. Hadley loves you and you probably love him too and yet you live with me and he lives with Lara, and so no one's happy. Why did God make life so confusing, I wonder? Do you?

At rehearsals, I'd watch how Mr. D would lay his hand, gently, on Mais's arm, or his eyes'd be peeled on her as she sang, as if she might dart away if he took his gaze off her. Unless I went to the store, I hardly ever saw Mais without him. But once, when he went to the bathroom, Maisie drew me into her, and said, "Ain't I struck gold?

If I can't make it to the British Isles, well, then the British Isles have come to me. And how. Wheeee-ooh!" And she swiped her arm across her forehead like a cowgirl. I had to smile, though inside me was an echoing cave, full of air and memory.

"Say, where's loverboy from the jailhouse? Seen him lately?"

"Nah, he's not been round for a while."

"You cooling off on him, are you, girl?"

"Not sure, Mais. I like him and all, but he's getting mighty serious for a boy I've only known a few months."

"Been more like a year. You don't know what's good for you, that's my five cents worth!"

"Maisie love," Mr. D walked back into the room. "On matters of the heart, young ladies need to follow their intuition."

"And see where that has landed me!" smirked Mais.

"Precisely!" Mr. D smirked back so you'd swear you were looking at two sides of a mirror.

"OK, OK, let's get on with the music now," I said, slapping my tambourine against my thigh. "No time to waste."

And we launched into what Mr. D called our "medley" of tunes. I was learning all these new words, debut, medley, official program. My head was full of them. I only played background on about three of the songs, which was all right with me. Mais was the star, her voice like honey and glass all at once, and Mr. D's fiddle moving along like a third arm beside her. My all-round favorite song was the duet they sang together, *Ol' Candy Blue Eyes*. Mais said she wrote it for Mr. D and my oh my, if you could just hear them crooning back and forth like cats in heat, soft then loud then all gooey mushy and their eyes fixed like glue on each other. It was something to witness.

And it always made me long for PB. Every single time I'd hear it, my heart'd waltz back to that night in the candle's glow when he had lit a flame in me. And no amount of crying or wrestling with it or just plain ignoring it could tamp it out. I'd be walking up Main

Street, minding my own business, and something, who knows what, would set the thing firing up inside me, till I'd have to chase down a tall glass of cool water or stick my face into the fountain in Leonard's Park. The heat was always there.

Where was he now? I could see him fanning Lara's flaxen hair between his nimble fingers, and her ample ruby lips lapping it up. Sometimes they were on our mattress, sometimes in the woods, next to a tree, even though I wasn't sure she'd be a girl who'd fancy fresh air. There was a war inside me, trying to fight back such scenes.

"Mr. D," my voice sounded like a squeak. "You haven't heard how Lara Hadley's tour is going?"

"You mean PB's?" Maisie cut in. "Darlin', he ain't here. And your policeman is. In some cases of love, logic fares better than intuition. Am I right, Donald?"

Mr. D patted my arm. "Dear, Officer Dixie's a solid chap, and he cares for you. PB is too, of course. But we need to exercise caution here. If we are to believe the *Oregonian*, the Pendleton tour is making a big splash in the city. And Miss Hadley, in my experience, is a young lady who tends to get what she wants."

The ceiling and the floor seemed to crash together then, like night and day, like stars and moons, everything colliding inside me. Mais was so taken with her Welsh beau and her concert, she couldn't know the misery seeping through me. And she didn't have to; I called on Taffy Hero in a way I'd never thought I would, and donned a brave, accepting countenance. And waited till I could go home, to my own mattress, to give in to my hovering darknesses.

Chapter 21

Maisie roped in Ted Begley, a scrawny boy who worked at Hardacre Stationers, to do up advertisements for our show. She even paid him a dollar to draw a picture of our likenesses, the Pendleton Trio, bunched together like petals in a flower, waving our fiddle and tambourine like they were trophies. Young Begley fashioned them on bright yellow paper so that you couldn't miss us.

The four of us spent the whole of a July Sunday nailing the things up around town on the doors of every store that'd let us. Mais put a gigantic one up right in the front window of Grave's Trading. I even heard that Mr. D had them up on every spare inch of the staff room at the mills. I could just see PB wandering in there for a cool glass of milk upon his return, and finding my face grinning down at him, and his heart all sore that he'd ditched me for a pencil stick of a girl and a house with a picket fence.

Then I caught myself. Who was I to talk about strange choices? Besides, I was starting to realize that you don't exactly have control over your heart like you do over your hands, say. It just goes ahead and loves what it wants to and there's nothing on earth you can do about it. I should have asked Mais to write a song about that.

Only once did Mais and Mr. D come round to where I lived. It was July 4th, Independence Day, and Maisie had a great big flag pinned to her chest. Mr. D was even wearing a stars-and-stripes bowler, which made me laugh out loud, him being Welsh. Everyone was still heady in the wake of the armistice. They brought six thick buffalo steaks from the store and after I'd got them cooked and juicy, I brought out the little living room table to the front stoop. And we sat on the steps and the lawn, milking the sun, as if we were lords of the manor. I'd never seen the girls dig into a piece of meat before—we rarely ate it, it being so costly—but they wolfed theirs down in no time, like it was ice cream. One extra slab sat on the plate cooling, and I couldn't tell if it was Bob's or PB's face rising up in the steam from it.

"I'll have seconds, please, Lady of the House," Mr. D announced gleefully after he'd slurped the dregs of the juice off his plate.

"Wait up there, buster," Mais joked. "We still have strawberry shortcake to come."

I got up to clear the dishes away, but my skin was tingling all of a sudden. Was it the oddness of being called lady of the house? Since when had I been playing that role? What about poor Mrs. Hadley upstairs? I was about to bring her her pills, but something, a cool draft through the door, something, kept me from walking up those stairs. Instead, I made piles of washing-up on the sideboard.

Lady of the house indeed. No, it wasn't the matter of household chores that bothered me, for I seemed to end up doing that wherever I was, but it was more the awful notion that I might actually be settling down. How long had I been here now? Longer than any place since I left the Idle River. Going on a year. Lady of the house. No, that was never a label intended for me. It surely wasn't, though PB had his heart set on a house, and I ached when I considered who might be his lady. I reminded myself as I sliced pieces of shortcake for folks, I had only intended to stay in Pendleton overnight; it was

Timmy the mailman forced me to stay longer. I still wanted to find my dad in the Wallowas, bring him back home to Ma. Let her be lady of the house.

That night, after Mr. D and Mais had sauntered off into the twilight, arms wrapped tight round each other's waists, I slipped up to Mrs. Hadley's room, with a fistful of pills and a spoon of fresh cream, feeling badly for neglecting her all day. I could hardly believe what I saw there: a woman sitting up straight in bed, her eyes glittering wildly, a huge half-moon of a smile on her mouth. I called to the girls and they came up in a flash, and we sat, all three of us in a ring round her. "Pearl. Pearl." She opened her lips into a generous circle. "Pearl." I set her pills on the carpet, while we sat there, silenced, and let her dazzling brightness flood the room.

"That was the best July 4th ever," Pearl A announced next morning when she woke in the nest of her mother's arm. We had fallen sound asleep within minutes, three lost birds on a blue counterpane, Mrs. Hadley, it seemed, watching over us with her dazed smile till dawn.

The weeks slid by, as we busied ourselves preparing for our big concert, and though I checked the *Examiner* for news of the Pendleton tour, I found nothing. Maisie made us practice—rehearse, she called it—till we were nearly numb from the same old tunes over and over. I never thought I could play *Sweetheart, that thang you left me with ain't love* one hundred and fifty times without keeling over of exhaustion. But Mais said it would all pay off on August 24th.

What we hadn't counted on, none of us, was that folks in town were gearing up for the big Pendleton Roundup. Mais said it was only five years old, but it was the biggest rodeo for miles around and people came from as far as Texas to witness it. "Holy Mo," she screamed, when Mr. D mentioned that the Regal Hotel was fully booked through the end of August. "We're being invaded." But then her eyes lit up into two big silver sparklers, setting her glasses on fire. "Hey, this could be our big chance. We may have a bigger audience than we ever dreamed of! We gotta be perfect!" That made me swallow hard for a while.

Suddenly every store in town was chockablock with new faces. I couldn't take my eyes off them, kids with big eyes and round faces, tall, skinny cowboys in narrow boots with silver things sticking out the back. And Indians, lots of them. They looked so beautiful to me beside the scrap leathery skin on cowboys. The Indians' skin was a soft sun shade and the women carried their little ones like packages on their backs. I followed one the whole way down Main Street, cooing and smiling at the little boy and his tuft of black hair. He looked like a blackbird glued to his mother's back. The street was so crowded that the mother had to stop before she could cross it, and I couldn't help stroking the pack around her shoulders. It was the oddest-looking baby carriage I'd ever seen. "Papoose," the woman turned to me and smiled, her eyes like two slivered almonds.

"Papoose," I repeated. And then my eyes must have gazed down at her feet to the two yellow cushiony slippers she was wearing. "Moccasin," she said.

I swirled the words round on my tongue, papoose, moccasin, beautiful gentle words like feather pillows I wanted to ease right down into and cuddle. And as the woman glided across the street, it was me I saw there, floating in my cozy moccasins, my little papoose full to brimming with a bright cherub, a love gift delivered specially to PB and me. I was deep in that reverie when I ran smack into a black pole that smelled of smoke. After I reeled backward, I realized that no, this wasn't a pole at all but a giant from a dark fairy tale. I craned my neck back so I could follow it up to its huge height, and saw before me the tallest cowboy ever born. His thin body seemed to just go on and on. You could hardly see his face for the rivers of lines on it. It was like Grandma's bed quilt before she died, patchy and worn, but still working.

"Howdy, ma'am." The cowboy leaned down toward me and a billow of smoke trailed straight into my face. "Crazy Bill Locum," with a swing of his hat in a bow. "Mighty pleased to make yer acquaintance."

"Well, Bill," I tried to smile up at him. You ought to be friendly to outsiders, that was my theory anyway, being one most of my life myself.

"Crazy Bill," he corrected me. "They call me crazy out in Wallowa, 'counta the poor shots I have with my gun. One time . . ."

"Wallowa! Did you say Wallowa?"

"You got that right, ma'am. I comes from three generationsa Wallowa folks, and 'fore that . . ."

"Wallowa." I could hardly keep my feet quiet under me. Hearing the word from a stranger's mouth made me dithery and suddenly a swell of excitement took over my throat. "You just come from there?"

"Swear on my Stetson, ma'am." And he swept his hat down in one stroke to his chest. It was badly dented round the rim. "Blue Mountain Creamery of Enterprise brought me out along with their butter."

"Say . . ." my heart all bouncing around inside me. "You, um, you wouldn't happen to have . . . made the, um, acquaintance of . . . ?"

"Wallowa County's the one for me, ma'am. You ask anyone." And the smoky cowboy burst into a wild song that nearly destroyed my ears. "And . . ." he sang, as he danced off down the street. "Happy birthday to you too!"

I stood on the sidewalk, my heart panting, people swirling past me in clouds. I had met a man, I told myself then, who just might have met my very own father. My own father, the whole reason I came out this way. It was on account of my father, I realized, that I was standing still as a graveyard in the middle of a busy street in downtown Pendleton, Oregon. It was on account of him that I'd met PB and fallen in love and gotten jobs and found friends like Maisie. And for a while, Bob. But still I hadn't found the man himself. And I was beginning to wonder would I ever? How far could Wallowa be if a crazy cowboy could get all the way from there to Pendleton? Finally, someone jabbed me in the ribs as they passed and I set one foot ahead of the other and started walking in the direction Crazy Bill had taken.

I didn't find old Bill for two days and then it was in the back den of the tavern and he was bent over a card table snoring away, a tipped-over ashtray resting on his arm. I shook him awake, and the cigarette butts crawled all over the table like worms. He shivered as he sat up, blinking his red eyes. "Worst game I ever played. Used be a tiptop poker player. You jes ask anyone in Wallowa County. I had them beat, ever single one of 'em."

"Say, Crazy Bill . . ." But he was busy talking to the air.

"Lady, if I ever played a round poorer than this one tonight, I'd appreciate knowin' 'bout it."

"Nah, that was a fair game you played all right," I smiled at him. "Bet you even beat that man from the Idle River."

"Him too." Then he paused a minute and screwed his eyes into fists. "Idle River?" And he took a breath as he ransacked through his memories. "Can't say I ever beat him, no, but I had him, almost, in the last round. The dice was rigged, I swear it, but who would believe me over a Johnny-come-lately?"

Oh, it was maddening, not knowing if he was truthful about anything or if he was just fooling me round. When I tried to press him, he just laid his head back down and snored. But oh jeepers, as Mr. D used to say, it sure got my feet scratching again to head on out to Wallowa country. Once PB came back. Once I'd sorted out school for the girls. It was barely noon, but I ordered a tall glass of beer to calm me.

When I told Maisie, she said, "Honey, your daddy might be here in lil ol' Pendleton. If he's a cowboy for real, he won't miss the roundup, believe you me."

I started looking for my father in every nook and cranny of that small town, the way I'd searched through Alvin's ancient books. I sat in the lobby of both the Hargrave Motel and the Slink Inn for two whole afternoons, watching cowboys of every stripe pass by. But none of them had the look of the man I wanted. They were too tall, too wide, not scarred enough, or not in the right places, their boots were too scuffed, they walked funny. And you couldn't even see their hair. I knew my daddy's hair would be red as my own, if he still had it. I studied each face that passed me as I moved from street to alley to town square. I must have covered every inch of that town.

But no one matched my cowboy dad: I peered into so many faces that I grew dizzy and forgot what I was really looking for. If this had been a fairy tale, my dad would have left a trail behind him, but there were no crumbs or clues to follow. All I had was a page from a book he'd probably forgotten. And his dauntless girl ended up long after dark, sitting on the church wall, feet torn up and throbbing, and not one step closer to a happy ending.

I sat there, considering what a sad world this was, what with disappearing fathers and molested mothers and orphan children and jolly policemen who loved girls with gypsy hearts. And I wished right then I could just take the world and wrap it up in a warm blanket, with my own family in the center, and give it a great big hug.

Instead, I went up to the park, slid off my battered shoes, and eased my toes into the cooling waters of the fountain. They dabbled there like ten baby sausages, burnt and sizzling.

Chapter 22

The girls were asleep on the rug in the living room when I got home, curled up like two little bears in the woods. I bent down and kissed their pale eyelids and covered them with the quilt from my bed. Pearl B blinked and turned her face up to mine. She looked like she was still sleeping, but her voice said, "Todd."

"What did you say?" I thought I must be dreaming.

"Todd. Is Todd broken?"

My heart skipped a beat. Little Pearl must have been listening real careful when I poured out my past that time to Bob in the garden. How could I have been so careless? I sat on the carpet so my face was right close to hers. "Sweetie, Todd's not broken. He's just hurt is all. Don't you fret, he's probably all mended by now." But even as I said it and Pearl's eyes slowly closed, I wondered how true that really was. Broken, broken, I let the word float there out in the bedroom—not just people, but families too; Bess had lost Lourdes, Maisie's mother was divorced, and even Mr. D got separated from his sheepherding kin. Stroking the thin curve of Pearl's chin, I watched her snuggle up to her sister. I'd hardly been home lately, and now, with only three days to the show, I knew it'd get worse before it improved. I went to bed wondering just how many folks got through life without being broken.

Next morning as I woke, the sun danced through the window on my quilt and I was glad of it. The girls were cheerful at breakfast and eagerly helped me set up a tray for their mother. The three of us sat on Mrs. Hadley's bed and took turns feeding her baby mash. Since the Independence Day miracle, I'd been easing off her medications, despite her husband's warnings, and for all the world, she seemed more lively. She didn't speak so much as motion with her eyes. Pearl B had gotten quiet again since Bob had stopped coming round, though maybe that was worry about Todd; she sat still as mice on the bed, staring. Pearl A was stroking her mom's hand gently, gently. It was a soothing sight, four girls cozy on a bed, drawing all the sadness out of each other just by being there.

Maisie had an appointment with the hairdresser at two that afternoon and then we were supposed to dress rehearse, she said, which meant I had to find an outfit pretty soon. Otherwise, I knew Mais would try to throw one of her creations on me, including that sticky old brassiere, and the last thing I wanted was to feel uncomfy on our big day.

"Girls," I said, to my three companions on the quilt. I was having difficulty getting excited about the show, with so much uncertainty floating about. But it was so important to Mais that I needed a way to stoke up my enthusiasm. "Girls, I think I need some help . . ."

They listened thoughtfully, all of them, as I explained my situation. And no sooner had I stopped speaking than lo, Mrs. Hadley lifted her free hand just a fraction and pointed a finger toward her wardrobe.

"Closet." Pearl A leaped up and opened the fine wood door. I couldn't move for a moment, stunned at the first real motion from this tired woman. And now, she was opening her heart to me. She was taking in more than I'd ever realized, maybe she'd actually heard everything I'd said to her over the months. Yes, she probably had, and maybe I'd known it all along too or I'd never have opened my mouth. I felt comforted, knowing how Mrs. Hadley had plenty sorrows of her own, and yet she was on my side.

"C'mon!" Pearl A was picking through the dresses. "How about this one?"

"This." Pearl B walked over and pulled out the hem of a pale blue dress, the color of cornflowers, and soft as air. It had a scooped neck and no sleeves and it fountained down into a sheaf of folds at the feet.

"Oh!" The beauty of it took my breath away. Why hadn't I seen that one before? "Yes, yes."

"Try it on!" Pearl A was tugging at my sleeve.

And so I waltzed round the bedroom, in my flowing blue gown, my body feeling lighter with each twirl, as if the sheer loveliness of it could sweep all of my cares far, far away.

And they almost did, for a while anyway. Those three days leading up to the show were happy: the girls helping me with the chores, Mrs. Hadley starting to eat a little more, and even Bob came round to offer his help. I was surprised to see him in the lintel, after a whole summer. His usual smile was nowhere to be seen, and he spoke firmly, as if he'd thought his words through beforehand. "I thought you might need some time to get ready and all, so I'll take care of the girls till Sunday. I've a few days off."

"Oh no, I couldn't ask you."

"Also, you should know there may be some trouble . . ."

I never got to ask what Bob was going to say for the girls stormed in, and everything else was forgotten.

"BobBobBob!" The girls danced around him like he was a Maypole. And he swung them out to the garden, where I left them, "BobBobBob!" shrieks of laughter dancing out on the air, as I closed the gate behind me, thankful, and headed toward town.

Mais's hair had been curled in tiny little ringlets, which she said was the real thing over in England, and she had on a dress that startled my eyes. It was navy and red and had a mess of silver stars across the chest. "It's a combination of the Union Jack and the American flag," she announced proudly.

"Union who?"

"The English flag, silly. I'm a, what's the word, Donald?"

"Hybrid, dear, hybrid," Mr. D said, as he polished his fiddle. Even he looked dapper in his pale suit and colorful tie. "She's more English than me, I think sometimes."

"You catch sight of your old daddio?" Mais asked me, as she applied her makeup.

"Nah," I tried to sound casual.

"Beats me why you insist on pining after folks who aren't here, when there are plenty of us who are." Maisie meant to be kind, but her words stung like nettles. It was easy for her to say, when no one had ever left her high and dry. "Maybe you just didn't look in the right places?"

I didn't want to tell her how foolish I'd been, hunting him down in every nook of Pendleton. "Yeah, maybe," I muttered, and pulled out my blue dress from a paper bag.

Maisie whistled soon as she saw it. "Slip it on, girl. That thing's a winner."

And it was, I could see it in her eyes and Mr. D's look, and that cheered me some. "All you need's a flower for your hair. Something soft," Maisie said. "I'll try to remember to bring a fresh one on Sunday. We just got a new shipment of dahlias in the store today."

We sang that evening till our throats were dry. It felt good to be wearing Mrs. Hadley's dress, with her blessing. I could sing and swing my tambourine for her. It was as if she was right there with me, saying, We may have suffered, we two, but we're not knocked out yet.

Chapter 23

By Sunday morning, the nerves I hadn't been feeling descended on me all at once. I was all atwitter, washing my hair in the vinegar solution Mais gave me, to bring out the chestnut highlights, she said. She read about it in an English magazine. I had been up and down the stairs to tend to Mrs. Hadley at least four times. I'd laid out three meals for the girls in the icebox, cleaned the living room, scrubbed the windows and floors. I'd polished Ama's coin till it gleamed. And it was still only 9 A.M. I kept thinking there'd never be enough time to get everything done. My hair was dripping over my head and into the sink, the faucet running mild water over it, when I heard a sound in the hallway.

"Hi," I heard Bob's voice behind me. "The door was open."

"Come in, come in."

"I am!" said Bob, and that was the closest to the old happy Bob I'd heard in a long while.

"Could you pass me a towel?" I asked from under my sheet of wet hair.

When he slid a towel into my hand, his fingers lingered there a second, but enough to figure he still cared for me in that special way I couldn't return. It set my heart crazy, wishing it could be my dad,

or PB, or even my ma, to see me in my finest hour. And then I felt
bad for Bob, who probably wondered why I couldn't just love him
back, easy as pie.

"I know this is your big day and all." Bob stood up tall, like he
was going to make a solemn declaration. "But there's some talk of
the temperance folk having their way."

"Bobbie! Bobbie's here!" Pearl A came charging into the kitchen.
"Can we go? Please please please!"

"You won't be allowed in, girls," I said, as I wrapped the tea towel
round my head in spirals. "The tavern's for grown folks."

"There may not be any taverns soon is what I'm trying to say."

I wondered if Bob had had too much to drink. I'd never known
him not make sense before. Only I hadn't seen him swallow a drop
of anything beyond milk or lemonade.

"There's talk of closing down Grave's."

That news stopped me cold. I looked at Bob, hoping he'd break
into a smile and say, "April Fool three months late!"

"Our local women have been trying to outlaw alcohol for years
now. They got some places closed down. Looks like they're working
on Grave's too. From what I can tell, the government's about to put
a lid on drinking all over the country."

"Why on earth."

Bob nodded while Pearl A tugged at his sleeve. "I don't mean to
spoil . . ."

"You are spoiling things." I felt annoyed at such news. Surely if
these women had been trying for years, it could be another decade
before they succeeded. "Can't you see this is a special day? Can't
you see nothing's going to spoil this for Mais?"

Bob sighed and winked down at Pearl, his eyes still cloudy even
as he smiled at her. "Who wants trouble? Let's stay here and play
ring-a-fling."

"No one wants us to go, do they?" Pearl's lower lip was all stuck out in a pout.

"I do, sweetheart, I do." And a wave ran over me, a wave of remembering, Ma always shutting the door on me, sealing off her world from mine. How could I do the same to my little ones? "OK then, if you don't mind being trampled by the roundup crowd, why don't you just come along and listen from outside? You know what I look like, so there's no mystery there!"

Pearl brightened and ran off to get Pearl B.

"There's talk of riots. Usually they happen at night, but you need to know it may not be safe."

"I need to get dressed." Who was this Bob barging in and saying these things? Surely he wouldn't get mean just because I didn't say I'd marry him. And if he was right, well, it was too late to cancel everything now. I let out a long breath, and with it all dark thoughts. "Excuse me."

He nodded, as I walked up the stairs. Mrs. Hadley was sleeping when I went in. She looked more peaceful than I'd seen her in a long time, her face smoothed out and calm, though her bedclothes were scrunched up in a heap. But she started to twitch, restless as a hungry bobcat, as I smoothed each sheet out carefully over her.

When I thought she'd settled, I slid on the blue dress and it felt like pure silk on my bare skin. There was a pot of lipstick sitting on a silver tray, with all kinds of perfume jars and little creams. In a fit of daring, I smeared a bit of the pink gloss across my lips, just a touch. And tied my lucky charm around my neck. Then I combed out my hair so that it hung loose down my back. It was sure getting long, trailing below my waist now. I felt womanly and warm and as I kissed Mrs. Hadley gently on the forehead, I imagined her swanning about in this beautiful thing, young and comely herself once.

I came down the stairs like a bride, step by step, slowly and with a sureness I didn't often feel. It was as if a new person was growing inside me, an older, wiser person I wasn't quite ready to meet yet. But what could I do, only try to welcome her? I'd a feeling she wasn't going anywhere else.

Bob took in a breath as he watched me, I could see his chest heave up and down, and that made me glad and sad all at once. Who knew what he was thinking? The girls were clapping at the foot of the stairs and Pearl A was trying to whistle. Then an unmerciful shriek rang out above us, and shivers, the kind you'd get in the ice of winter, coursed up my arms. A shriek like a dying bird. "Mrs. Hadley." Bob and I darted back up the stairs two at a time, and charged into the bedroom to find the woman who'd been resting easily minutes before standing on her bed, tugging at clumps of her hair. Wisps of it drifted down on the air like lost feathers.

"Mrs. Hadley . . . Violet," I tried. "What's wrong? What do you need?"

"Ar . . . thur." She seemed to be saying, the sounds issuing out through some hollow cave. "Get . . . thur."

Bob was next to her, quick as a lynx. "We'll get your husband. Sure we will, just you sit yourself down now and everything's gonna be fine."

I watched as Bob eased this delicate instrument of pale skin and bones back to bed. "Medication?" He turned to me.

"Um, no, she hasn't wanted any for a while now, and was faring well, I thought."

"Where are her pills?" He looked desperate.

"In the bathroom cabinet." I turned to get them, and ran straight into the two Pearls in the doorway. "Things'll be just fine," I said, echoing Bob's calm assurances, though I wasn't feeling them at all.

Violet Hadley wouldn't take a pill, nor a bit of a pill. She spat and twisted her head every time we moved toward her mouth.

"Hush, hush now," Bob was saying to her, and motioning the girls to sit next to them on the bed. "Taf, you're going into town. Call Hadley from the station, will you?"

I nodded.

"Tell him to come over at once."

"But I can't go now." I was feeling mixed up and frightened and nowhere near wanting to sing in public.

"Of course you can," Bob said, "and you'll have a good time. Won't she, Mrs. Hadley?"

"Mmmph, mmm." I watched her lips purse together; they were a shade close to my dress.

"Before you go, there's something for you. Have a look on the dresser downstairs."

I remained there, stuck to the floor.

"Go!" He raised his voice so it was calm but firm.

I edged back downstairs, my heart a galaxy of hurts and worries and doubts, and found, at the foot of the staircase, a great big bouquet of golden roses. I whisked them up, burying my nose in them, and ran back up to the bedroom.

"They're gorgeous," I whispered.

"Gorgeous flowers for a gorgeous woman," Bob said, and I could see his big brown eyes bubbling with love and I couldn't stop myself from hugging him tight as I could. I even plopped a kiss on his cheek, and it left a bright pink line there. Pearl A laughed, Bob looked startled even though he had that old grin on him again, and Pearl B pointed at his face. "BobBob's got red crayon on him."

"That's lipstick, dummy!" her sister said.

"Mmmmph, mmmm," sang Mrs. Hadley, and I kissed her too.

And Bob reached his hand up to where my mouth had been and he just held his palm against it, not rubbing it away. "I think I'll just let it sit awhile," he said. "Now girls, let's go get ready. We've a big concert to catch this afternoon."

I searched his face, looking for hope, but his eyes were narrow as he whispered, "Please, be careful."

The girls went streaking toward their rooms, Bob fast on their hides. "Let's go, go, go!" he said, and I thought I heard that rivery cheeriness back in his voice. "Don't worry, Taf. I'll take care of this end. I promise."

I took his place briefly on the quilt—it was warm from his body—and I set Mrs. Hadley's hand in mine. "I'm sorry, Violet. I thought . . ."

"Mmm, mmm," she pressed my fingers and her head became a spinning top. Yet it seemed there was a smile long buried in her face, fighting its way out.

I carried the roses with me into town, just as if it was my wedding day, only inside I was all tumbling rocks. I could see people sneaking a sideways look as I sauntered along Main Street, for I was a bit more dressed up, I suppose, than the cowboys in their scuffed boots and creased shirts. Not everyone went round town wearing evening dresses, as Mais called them, in broad daylight.

"Can't keep you out of here, can we?" Sergeant O'Connor got the telephone exchange for me, and asked for Mr. Hadley. "Here," he said. It was the first time I had held a telephone to my ear, and it took a minute before I understood the pip-pip meant my call was ringing through. It was a magical sound, almost like hearing air or touching the sun, something you could hardly imagine, numbers running along a wire and landing at the place of your choice. And I sighed, for even though I felt grown-up using such a new contraption, that seemed to be a more challenging state than I'd reckoned on. Hadley picked up on the third ring.

"Foolish, that's what," he raged when he heard about his wife. "I told you, I begged you, did I not, to keep her on her medication? Now, see!" I was in tears by the time he hung up.

"I'm sorry, I'm sorry," I screamed into the phone line. "She was doing so well. She was alive." But it was thin air that caught my words and carried them off to nowhere.

I went on down to Mais's place, where we'd agreed to meet at noon, and tried hard to put on a cheery face. I was careful this time to cough loud and alert her I was coming. I didn't fancy catching anyone in the act of whatever it was today.

But Mais was pacing round her room like a lion, ready to spring. Her door was open and she was talking to herself. "Deep breaths, girl, calm yourself, in, out, in, out . . . Oh child, there you are. Don't you look pretty. Look at those flowers. Where'd you get them? Why, isn't that a pure miracle, 'cos I clean forgot to bring the dahlias for your hair. You can just go ahead and wear the roses."

"Calm down, Maisie darling, take it easy now." Mr. D was standing by the window, and he came over to put his arms round Mais's shoulders. But even he looked a tad nervous; I could see it in the twitch of his brow and the slight band of sweat collected on either side of his nose.

Mais sank onto the bed. She took in a long, deep breath and then let it all out in a rush and a whole stream of tears came out along with it.

"Maisie!" I ran to her. "Why on earth are you crying on your big day?"

"'Cos, hoo, it is my big day and what if, what if . . ."

Mr. D dabbed at his own eyes. And we both watched Mais as she wept for the three of us. She wept, it seemed, for all the heartaches and hopes fanning out from that small room. I imagined her crying for Mrs. Hadley; for Bob, who I wanted to and couldn't love the way he wanted; for the little Pearls who loved him. For all the dead soldiers, PB, my pa. We watched Maisie's tears as if it were our own private concert.

By two o'clock, we managed to pull ourselves together. We didn't do a last run-through, because Mr. D said Mais might get hoarse. Instead, we hugged each other and went over the order of songs, and Mais fixed her makeup so you'd never know she'd been crying. And she clipped a gold rosebud to the side of my hair and tried to talk me into a bit more lipstick and Mr. D patted down his good tie and kissed us both on the forehead, for luck, he said, it's a Welsh thing, and we walked out into the heat and dust of that August afternoon.

Chapter 24

The door to the tavern was held open by two huge barrels and you could see the swarms of folks hanging round outside, drinking cool beers and wiping their faces with their shirt cuffs. The flies were buzzing round, bees too, which loaned color to the air outside. I wondered if they'd make a go for my rose, but they seemed to ignore us. Just like everyone else. No one gave more than a passing glance at our odd attire as we pushed our way inside and moved toward the stage. The feel of the place was much different in daylight. It was like walking into a cave after that hot bright sun outside. The red lampshades still hung down and shone their pale light, but it seemed weaker than before. No wonder the place was deserted, only a few men holding up the bar, and a couple or two scattered round the tables. Sergeant O'Connor at least was standing at the door, elbows crossed firm on his chest until he held out his hand to Mr. D and they shook heartily. There were no announcements for Amateur Afternoons or anything else.

"You're here, good," the barman yelled at us. "Make yourselves at home up there." The manager who'd almost thrown us out the last time was nowhere to be seen. I'd thought to ask him for a glass of something to get us warmed up. But then Mr. D asked where every-one was.

"Could be at the fairgrounds. First bull-dogging trials start today."

"What about all the folks outside?" asked Mr. D.

"Nice day, I guess. But don't you worry," the barman said, as if it was any comfort. "They'll be all down here like bats tonight. You won't find an empty table anywhere."

So that was why they'd let us have our show in the afternoon. Nobody here, so there was no risk. I was so angry, thinking about all our hard work and all of Maisie's grand hopes, that I forgot about my thirst and might have even made some comment on this luckless place through the loudspeaker, only I took a look at Mais and she had the gleam in her eye. She was excited as a child, I could see. This was going to be her Big Day, whether anyone showed up or not. She was going to do what she'd always dreamed of, sing on a stage in public.

And so I kept my mouth sealed tight, and polished my tambourine with Mr. D's handkerchief.

"Anyone here do anything about the lights?" Mr. D shouted to the barman. "It's dark as midnight up here."

"Johnny!" the barman yelled. "Turn on the stage lights back there, would you?"

And suddenly the air flashed, like lightning or something, and the whole stage lit up. It felt as if we were in the lap of the sun itself. The best part was that it was so bright, you couldn't see anything more than a foot beyond the stage. Maybe less for Maisie, who carefully lifted off her glasses and set them at her feet. We could all pretend there was a great big cheering crowd out there, loving every minute.

We tested the speaker, as Mr. D called it, "Testing 1-2-3." He said it first, and it echoed round the whole room. Then Maisie tried it, and it came out a bit softer. Then I spoke in, "Testing Pearl A, Pearl

B, Pearl C," just in case my little pals were listening outside. I knew they kept a loudspeaker by the door, and sometimes it was turned on so you'd hear music belting out of it as you walked up Main Street.

When Mr. D felt the pitch, I think he said, was right, we all moved toward the front of the stage, and Mr. D struck up a dandy note on his fiddle, so light and airy, you'd be helpless but to swing your hips. At least, it got me going; I was swaying like a tree leaf in a breeze, my eyes closed, just letting the tune carry me, and then Maisie took up her part, and sang out, *Summer's a good time for lovin', and you've really got me cookin'.*

And oh, the drift of her voice, so throaty and full that you'd be hard pressed not to lean toward it and bob your head along with the rhythm. I kept my own eyes closed for the first three songs. I told myself it was so I could concentrate, or to shut out the blinding light, but it was maybe my own form of nerves, a way to tune into the heart of the music instead of the musty, listless dark of the tavern.

Maisie carried on with a second cheerful tune and then eased back into her silky creamy voice for *My man, all those times he done me wrong, but I ain't countin'*, and you would've heard even a heel scrape across the floor, had there been one. It was still as October, only her notes skimming the air like wet kisses and my heart was a-tumble at the beauty and the fact that she was actually on stage. I was so glad for her, for us, that my eyes burst open all of a sudden. I kept hmm-hmmming in the background, but I almost lost my place when I looked down below us, and saw through the haze a crowd gathering, people wandering forward, elbows leaning against the stage, others pressing in behind them, and all eyes fixed tight on Maisie, as if she were a goddess or a foreign queen. Mr. D caught my eye and winked, and I smiled so wide I left out one of my hmmms. No one seemed to notice; they were all drifting along with Mais and the golden river of her voice.

When she trilled out that final note, it hung in the air for a brief moment before everyone broke into a gigantic roar. You'd be almost deafened by it. And suddenly, flowers and money and who knows what else started landing at Maisie's feet. "More! More!" people were cheering and Mais stood there, her feet circled by silver coins and petals, her face beaming.

I could hardly stand still for the glad thumping of my heart. "Keep on singing, lady!" someone shouted, or we might have just stared back forever.

And so Maisie sank into her next song, not missing a beat, another mournful ballad about love betrayed, and for a flash, I wondered if those songs had been written with me in mind. All those people I had loved and let down, not even meaning to. I was wondering if Mrs. Hadley had gotten her medication when Mais livened things up with a trio of dance tunes. People were staring at her, awestruck. Mr. D got into the rhythm, and I followed as best I could, and everyone clapped along like it was one great big party. We sang and swayed and clapped and played until Maisie's voice started to crack on the high notes. And we realized it was time to take a break.

Before we could even set down our instruments, the barman was on top of Mais with a tall glass of water, and he was almost bowing to her, asking her did she want this or that and could he get her anything else, please? "I've had to call in two more workers, the place is getting so filled up," he said to us, his eyes wide. "Old Jem the manager'll be amazed. We ain't never had a crowd this big on a Sunday afternoon, ever."

People were flocking round the stage by now to get a word in with Maisie, and the barman had to sneak us back to the resting room, pushing everyone away. "Our own personal bodyguard, what d'you know!" Mr. D chuckled, as we flopped down, all three of us, onto the dingy leather couch, and Maisie collapsed into a giggling fit. "Where are my glasses? My glasses! I can't see a thing!"

Soon as she recovered, Mr. D cupped his beloved's face between his thin hands, and plopped a juicy kiss right on her lips. "You're a winner, m'dear," and you could hear the proudness in his voice. I'd never seen him so wildly happy.

And Maisie, dear Maisie, sat in a daze, drinking it all in. The crowd had started up a chant now, "We want more! We want more!" and the barman peeped his head round the door, his face all worried. "I'm afraid they'll do damage out there if you don't get back to the singing soon," he said.

"Fine, fine," Maisie said, rising first, and downing a full glass of lemonade. "Let's give it to 'em!" she announced, her head held high, as if we were marching out to battle.

We must have played another half dozen tunes, and I could see Mr. D was tiring. He kept wringing his hands out, and even I had an aching wrist from swinging the tambourine. But one look at Maisie and you saw she could go on all evening. "This next one's for Officer Robert Dixie," she growled into the speaker. "If you're out there, Bob, here's to you for getting us where we are today."

I stood beside her, stunned. What had Bob got to do with our success? Sure, he'd helped me with the girls, but how else had he played a part? Then suddenly, I caught sight of Jem the manager approaching us quickly, and it all clicked into place. Of course! Bob had been going to talk to him that day he'd cycled right past me and the girls. A man with a mission, yes, that's what he'd looked like. Had that something to do with the trouble he'd hinted at?

Someone shouted, "Cancel the Heppner Hicks tonight. Let Maisie keep on singing!" Jem the manager probably knew what a good thing he was onto, and he wasn't going to give it away all at once. He came onstage, polite and gentlemanly; you'd never guess he was the same toad who almost kicked us out of his establishment a few months back.

But I tried to let that go and smile as he held Maisie's arm up in the air. "Our local singing champ!" he roared, and everyone cheered till the building nearly rocked itself over.

I only half saw Mr. D bend down to rescue something sitting close to the edge of the stage. And barely felt him set it in my hands. "From an admirer," I thought he said. It took me a minute to figure out what it was: a container of fresh berries, it looked like, all colors, red, black, green, blue, and they were all shapes too, oval and round and flat and thick; I thought it was the most beautiful arrangement I'd ever seen. But no, it was not a bowl after all, but a bird's nest. The berries of summer clustered together in a nest of twigs and mud and leaves. And my mind flashed back to that first summer on the road, and how I lived off these juicy fruits of the land. A feeling ran through me then like a telegram: I could love the person who knew the exact gift that would charm my heart.

So I almost didn't hear with the screaming at first; it could have been a train whistle, a few sharp *pfffffs* into the air, but then there was plaster falling off the ceiling and smoke everywhere until you felt it could be Hallowe'en. Then a lady screaming "Drink is the Devil's work!" and a man's gruff voice, "Get yer hands offa me!" And another shot, yes, that's what it was, bullet holes through the wall, and gunsmoke. Oh no, Bob's warnings had been right. And then hands in the air, and people coughing and scrambling toward the door, so many they got wedged in the archway, like sheep too anxious to get home.

Mr. D had set down his instruments and was trying to pull Maisie back from the stage. But she wouldn't budge, just kept singing, one note after the next, mist gathering round her like a shawl. "Ain't no two-bit loser with a holster gonna spoil my big night." And on she went, pushing Mr. D and me aside and coughing into the speaker. I don't know how she kept singing as long as she did; the stench of gunsmoke filled my nose so I could hardly breathe. For a moment, I thought we must have died, and half expected to see Lourdes float down from the rafters.

Then out of the din rose a sound, faint as a distant whistle at first, and slowly it grew louder, an unearthly sound, like sorrow floating through all the empty spaces in that room, a dark and haunting sound, but so smooth, so dreamlike, it stopped me. I stood and listened as the rising and falling notes drifted above the heads of the milling crowd and seared their way into my heart. And then I saw him: like a ghost moving toward me, a golden boy with a flute in his mouth, and he was playing it just for me. Moving closer, he fell into the glare of the spotlights and I could see, clear as snowfall, that I was staring straight down into the lemon-drop eyes of PB.

One day, one day, hadn't my own love said that, and now here he was. My heart seemed to burst straight out of my chest then, boom-boomboom, as I hunkered down toward his face. He looked strained, not happy, as if he wondered whether I'd even speak to him at all. There was no sign of Lara Hadley. I remembered that time we'd quarreled in the park, and the time he saw me sharing a malt with Bob, but that was months ago, that was in another dark story featuring a pencil-shaped girl. In this one, here and now, PB's heart was beating with me, thumpathumpathump, I knew it, and so I reached my hand down from the stage and softly stroked the blackness of his hair. "Thank you," I mouthed and his fingers found mine, his hands the texture of long-ago love. Someone, a woman in a hurry, ripped right through them and knocked the berry nest straight into my chest. Still I reached out through the thickening smoke for those hands, the only ones that would ever fit mine, and soon as they found me I didn't even hesitate, but just glided straight out on the air and into the bustling crowd.

As I came down, PB's flute scraped against my face and drew blood; I could smell its sweetness. My feet buckled under somebody else's, and I tilted backward, but if the entire tavern had fallen on me just then, I'd hardly have noticed. I could think of no one but PB, and the lure of his arms.

I clung fiercely onto my nest, the berry juice dribbling out and down onto our fronts when we hugged, leaving big red hearts smeared across us. What other sign could I need, even as I gasped at the red stains coursing down the blue of my borrowed dress, even as I struggled to breathe through the gunsmoke and screams? PB and I were imprinted with the blazon of love, geese whose eyes could fix on no one else once they'd met, just as I'd always known.

Even as PB took my hand and led me out through the crowd, I followed, even as we soared right past Bob, with Pearl A and Pearl B seated squarely on either shoulder, and Sergeant O'Connor wielding a club and shouting, "Get back! Get back!" The girls didn't see me, and who knows if one look might have stopped the course I seemed set on taking. All I knew for sure was my legs were running and I was going with them. And the moods I caught sweeping across Bob's face as I passed, first bright like sunshine and smiling, then dark and heavy as March skies, and I pulled the rosebud from my hair and, don't ask me why, tossed it toward him. Did his hand rise to meet it?

And then I was gone, gone before the huge burst of rain, I was lighting after my own heart, a helpless crumb in PB's wake.

Part 3

Chapter 25

"PB! PB!" I shouted, between gasps for breath. "Where . . . ?"

"Come, I'll show you." And we ran all the way down Main Street, hand in hand, people turning to stare at us, and some even throwing coins our way. I pretended it was confetti, that this was our wedding day, and I watched the bright spin of silver arcing through the air and laughed out loud as we outran it. My dress trailed in a blue wing behind us. Then we turned onto Emigrant Street and down an alley to Frazier, Clem at our heels. And all at once, PB came to a halt so that I thudded against him.

"Clem, we have to be real quiet now." PB led us on tiptoe round the side of the Temple Hotel. I'd only looked through the window once, straining for a sight of my dad. I'd heard it was fancy; it was where the extra-rich folks stayed when they came to town. "In here, quick!" And we snuck through a narrow door and down a long corridor. I couldn't get over the carpet, it was so thick, it almost curled up round my ankles as I moved. "Look!" PB guided my eyes toward an open door across a hallway. Women in frilly dresses and necks choked with jewelry were sitting at tables, picking at food. One woman had a cup to her lips, and it was so tiny, I thought it was a toy. But PB said no, these ladies came every Sunday at 4 P.M. for high tea.

"High tea for high society," he said. "One day, that'll be us!" I nodded, only because I liked the thought of us together in some far-off future. It didn't look like there was much on the women's plates. I hoped this wasn't Maisie's idea of civilized. Give me sausage and grits any day. But I watched anyway, helpless, for the glittery sheen of the room, the lamps hung down from the ceiling in great clumps that looked like pearls, it all made my head dizzy. And the seats and couches, they seemed to be made of velvet, the same kind you'd ache for a few yards of to make a dress. They were the deepest shade of rose I'd ever set my eyes on, and it was hard to look away, but PB was already dragging me somewhere else.

Up a wide staircase we went, PB taking the steps in twos, leaping from one to another like a cat. "Wait till you see what's up here." At the top, we turned a corner, and lo, it looked as if a lake had edged its way right into the room. I just stared at it, its blue quietness and beauty. There were leafy fronds all round, like you might see on a summer's afternoon in the woods.

"What's that doing here?" I asked PB.

"It's a swimming pool. Clem, come back here!"

The dog was about to slurp a tongueful out of the big bathtub.

"A what?"

"For swimming in."

"But how did they get all that water up here?"

"Easy," his voice still a whisper. "When you have money, you can do anything."

I'd never thought about money in that way before. All I ever saw it do was distress folks, but I loved PB, I loved him with all the vast acres of my heart and I listened to him then, half dreaming, and nodded.

We heard someone move, footsteps getting louder, and PB rushed me back down the stairs, only we didn't take the corridor the way we had come. No, we went belting down another staircase, but this one had no carpet, and on through a small door, so short we had to bend down to get past, and then it got dark, only a chink of light from a crack in the doorway, and still further down. But the steps now were concrete and cracked, and we knocked stones loose with our footsteps and they skimmed down ahead of us in piles. I could hardly believe this was the same Temple Hotel we'd been eyeing. PB hooked his flute into the folds of his pants and cupped his free arm round my bird's nest. "I'll carry this for you."

"Where are we?" This place didn't feel too inviting. I was shivering with the coldness of it, and I had to feel my way along the edge of the wall. Feathery things, maybe cobwebs, brushed over my hands. "Was that the temperance women firing up there?"

"Just a scare tactic. Sadie Crank, up to her usual tricks. Her husband drank himself to death, so now she goes round with her hatchet and gun, swiping drinks off tables, beating the drink to the punch."

"I never heard of her."

"Count yourself lucky." PB placed his arm carefully round my shoulder, like half a hug, and I settled against it. "Now she has the law behind her, there could be big trouble." So had Bob known what he was talking about?

PB pushed ahead of me, and if I hadn't been holding onto the heat of his hand, I might not have kept going at all. My heart was still jigging from all the excitement, and I longed to sit and rest. PB must have sensed it, for he stopped in that instant, and turned toward me, and slowly, gently, set his two lips over mine. I felt a jolt inside me, and the sizzle of his tongue as it sought out its match. And nothing, not even an avalanche, not even the world collapsing, nothing could have budged me then.

When he finally pried away, he stroked his fingers down over my eyelids and said, "Keep them closed. I have a surprise for you." And as I followed the pull of his hand, I wondered just how many more surprises my body could take.

We'd walked maybe a dozen or so steps on level ground, when PB said, "OK, you can look now. Ta-daa!!!"

And my eyes opened onto, how else to say this, onto a whole other street full of cobblestones. Clem ran in circles as if he was chasing his own tail. We seemed to be in a tunnel, yet there was light flooding in from above, and this tunnel had storefronts with weird-looking signs on them and little doors that ran in zigzag patterns along a wall. A big hole on one side had a musty blanket draped down it. Little oil lanterns jutted out from hooks at odd angles.

I thought I must be dreaming and wandering through a folk tale where people lived whole lives in caves. This was definitely not the same place as the Temple Hotel.

PB didn't say anything for a while, just let my eyes drink it all in.

"Where is this?" I finally asked, my mind teeming with questions, so many I didn't know where to begin.

"China." PB hunkered down into the brightest place there was, and I sat next to him. "Look up," he said, and there above us was a square of glass, loads of tiny purple squares, and it looked like daylight seeping through. I was staring at it when this black clickclickclick drummed against the other side of it. "That's someone walking by!" PB announced, cheerfully. "That's Main Street above us, and no one knows we're down here. We're safe, you and me."

I just hoped the Pearls were safe. What if they needed me? I should have listened to Bob. "Let's rest a while and then I'll give you a grand tour."

"I thought you said China was overseas." I'd never heard of a country underground.

PB's laugh rang hollow through the cavern, echoing back to us like a song. "China away from China, Taf." He said people shy away from what's different, that these Chinese could be shot dead—and not so long ago—if they walked down Main Street at night. So they had to build a separate town for themselves, a place where they could make their homes and work their trades, and here was where they did it. A whole town under a town. It made me feel sad, no sunshine, no fresh air, no berry bushes. No wonder I'd never run into a Chinese person before. They didn't have towns like this back on the Idle River, as least far as I knew.

"What kind of trades?" I asked.

"Well, Hop Sing, he ran a laundry through there. Just last year, he moved out to John Day to be with his own kind."

"You'd clean clothes down here?" I thought of how we'd scrub our cottons in the river and then lay them out on stones to dry. I couldn't imagine how you'd ever air anything in a cave.

"Sure. He'd roll up sweaters in a towel, dry in no time. No one washed wool better than him. I tried to get him work at the mills."

PB told me how Hop Sing, such a cheery name, ran a bathhouse too and cowboys'd stop in to clean up, having only the one outfit. You took turns, he said, one after another, and some men liked to wait it out, for it got cheaper the dirtier and colder the water got.

PB's voice got extra quiet then. "Remember I told you Mama got whupped at the cards?"

"I think so. Who beat her?"

"She was so good, no one'd play with her. She'd taunted Hop Sing and his customers, and the only one who rose to her challenge was my dad. Wasn't even much of a player, maybe he got bored with bamboo, I don't know. Anyway, this one night he got lucky. Down here in this very room is where he won my mother's hand."

"In marriage, is that what you mean?" It didn't seem such a romantic spot to me, but maybe it was different then.

"Exactly. She'd gambled away the last of her beads and leather, had nothing left to wager. Only herself."

I couldn't understand how you could do something like that. Solitaire was what my Ma played, and only when Hank was away.

"Not what she'd planned for herself, but I pretend they were happy, why not?" PB pulled me close to him; I was still shivering. "Especially when I came along."

"Everyone's happy when you come along," I said. And my love threaded his long fingers through mine. But I couldn't stop thinking of his father's foot mangled by barbed wire and the Chinese curse.

The first thing I set eyes on soon as I woke was my bird's nest. PB must have pried it back into shape, and the berries, what was left of them, looked good as new. I hugged the nest to me, as PB rested against my shoulder, and inhaled the sweetness of summer. It felt strange though down in this dark place. Almost like a death chamber. The walls looked like slabs where you write so-and-so died 1919, R.I.P. How odd to imagine people living without sunlight or rain, just thick, colorless air.

My stomach was starting to gurgle, for in all the fuss of getting ready that morning, I'd forgotten entirely to eat. I hoped Bob had fed my little girls supper, and Mrs. Hadley had gotten her calming pills in time. It could be evening easily, and surely Mais and Mr. D'd wonder where the heck I'd gotten to. There was no sky to tell what hour it was.

My head was busy imagining life above ground when PB woke. He must have seen the look on my face, for he immediately lit into a smile and plopped a kiss on my face. "Do you like your berry basket?" He seemed shy then, just for a moment.

"I *love* it," I nodded, and he began picking out the berries, one by one. "This one's blackberry, that one's raspberry; you probably know them."

"Yup, but I'm not sure of those."

And so he held each one up to my eyes, chokecherry, black thornberry, elderberry, which was called the music tree, 'cos he, or anyone else, could carve a flute out of its bark. Thimbleberry, gooseberry, juneberry. "Some, you can't eat." He pulled out a tiny circle the color of night sky—it looked like a grape—and said, "This is the birds' favorite. It's a huckleberry."

"Huckleberry." I tried to put my mouth around such a wide word, but before I got there, PB had set the berry between my teeth, and he was leaning forward, biting onto the other half. The skin snapped and a beautiful wet juice ran down onto my lap. And he just kept on sucking at it, coming closer and closer toward me, until finally his lips were right up against mine. I could taste the sharp flavor of the berry holding us tight together and my legs went gooey on me again.

"Best way to eat fruit," PB smiled, when he finally sat back, "is to share it!"

And I couldn't disagree, not for one single second.

"Mama used dry them, you know; she'd sit with a whip ready for any bird that might try to swoop in for a free feed."

I couldn't be thinking about his mother when my legs were half jelly and my breasts were starting to stand up all by themselves. It felt uncomfy in a way, maybe 'cos I wasn't used to feeling this. So I tried to concentrate on something terrible, like Lara Hadley, and I even said her name, or half of it, before PB shushed me with another kiss, and said, "She was my employer, that's all."

"But she said you were engaged."

"Engaged to sew her beads back on, you mean." PB said her nails would catch in the fabric, and unravel his handiwork. PB had lost his job at the mill when he refused Lara's affections. "Berserk" is how he said she went when he told her who his heart belonged to. "Went marching off to her father and said I'd been stealing supplies for my own business." I tried to laugh, but my body was still acting queer. "Not that she suffered long," PB went on. "She found herself a beau in Portland, and she's going to marry him instead."

And I sank back, exhausted, into gratefulness.

That night, at least I think it was night, for the light was leaving, I woke to PB playing his flute, soft, low sounds that haunted the air. Clem was curled up in a fist on his lap. I sat up and shivered at the sound he made, and its beauty, and the cold darkness of it too, how it nagged at the edge of my skin, how it could be the sound of death visiting.

"When I saw you, up on that stage, I thought I'd tear my heart out with my bare hands if I couldn't hold you ever again."

I was about to say he'd never have to do such a wild thing, when he set his flute down and felt his way down my arm to my fingers. "Come," he whispered, and I clasped the hand that seemed so familiar, it might just have been an extension of mine. "Clem, stay right here. Good boy!" He guided me back along the cobbled path we'd taken. It was really dark now and I stumbled over loose stones. "Hold this." PB blew life into a lamp and handed it to me. Its glow warmed the walls, and before I knew it, he had whisked me up into his arms and was carrying me back up the stone steps to the hotel.

"We're leaving?" I hoped we were; even though I was with my beloved, this place felt worse than jail had.

"Not quite . . . you'll see."

And in the next few minutes, I did. I saw something new, something beautiful, that lit up a whole new world inside of me.

PB set the lamp down on the top ridge of the rickety steps, and pushed his way back into the hotel, and up the staircase we crept, to where the swimming pool was. There wasn't a sound anywhere, everyone fast asleep in their beds.

"Let's swim!" PB whispered.

"Now?" I couldn't have been more surprised if he'd suggested we run away to China. "But what if . . . ?"

"No what ifs tonight. We're free! We can do what we want." I thought of Mrs. Hadley squirming in her bed and I wondered just how free we really were. And the Pearls, they sat like stones on my chest.

But the cheer in PB's voice nudged me on, and I followed him to the edge of the water, where I dangled my feet into the cool liquid. He peeled off his clothes in a flash and dived in. All I could do was gasp at his beauty, the sheen of his skin, the glitter of his cat eyes in the dim light as he surfaced and fished for my toes and began stroking them lightly. And then he was moving up my legs in slow patterns I knew nothing about. Only that the feel of his fingers set my whole body quivering like a silver fish about to be netted. I'd seen them drawn to the wild colored bait on the Idle River many a time, drawn and trying to get away, and drawn all at the same time, helpless in the hands of a force mightier than they could ever be. And I gave myself up, just like them, to the gorgeous newness, the slow tug of hands inventing new parts of me.

And as he eased me into the gentle waters, he slipped off my dress, so we stood there, two seal skins pressed close, and I could hardly stand for the shaking in my thighs. We never spoke, there were no words to say, we just held each other kissing every place we could think of. And PB wound my legs round his hard waist in a circle and I felt myself like a wild daisy opening, opening, opening until my own beloved filled all those wide spaces with the beautiful wedge of himself. It was as if our two lost bodies, fit snug like this, finally, after all our sorrowful wandering, had come home.

I kept my eyes closed, for I was seeing a whole other beautiful world there dancing before me. It was white and shimmery, and little floating things like seaweed twirling about and a light the color of honey rising up, up, up and opening out into a glorious pool, and this new place swished, weightless and airy, and maybe as close to heaven as I'd ever been. *I am a silkie upon the sea* swam into my head, then, and I knew exactly how a silkie might feel, to be trapped on land, too long bereft of froth and foam.

And then, just as quick, everything closed up and got dark, and I caught sight of a baby, or was it a boy, flat on his back, and his eyes were the shade of bruises. I suppose I let out a scream or something loud, for PB clapped his hand over my mouth in a hurry. "Shhh! Remember where we are."

I opened my eyes again, my body shaking even more now and PB was handing me my dress and nudging me out of the water. And then we were scurrying back down the stairs, sliding and dripping, two slinky fishes avoiding the hunt.

Chapter 26

"I saw you with that guy, the cop," PB said to me later that night as we were cuddled together inside a circle of stones to fend off the tunnel rat. "Clem spotted you first, didn't you, boy?" Clem's ears perked up. "Saw how he looked at you in the Rainbow Grill."

"He's real decent, PB," I said. "Been a good friend to me."

"I could see that, but he wasn't about to settle for plain friendship."

"Well," I hesitated, remembering how Bob had kissed me that time in the kitchen.

"But you don't love him in that way," PB stated rather than asked, as if he'd already decided on the matter.

"I do love him," I said, but not in the heart-pounding, leg-wobbling, head-spinning way I loved PB, and he knew it.

"All those weeks on the road I'd lie awake wondering if I'd be too late. I couldn't get back here fast enough."

"You're moving so fast, I can hardly keep up." I was half teasing, but part of me meant it.

And he tightened his arms round me so hard it made my breath flee.

Daylight streamed down through the glass squares above us, as we woke. I could feel my insides all squirmy and a rawness between my legs. And then my mind floated back to the soft beauty of the night before, and I smiled and stroked the secret places that PB had shown me.

"Good morning, my little berry fairy." His first words to me warmed me up so much the cold air on my skin couldn't hurt me.

I laid my hand across his chest and patted it. It felt hard, like a wall. "Morning to you!" But the words came out just like they did when I'd invite my little Pearls back to the land of the living, and my whole body ached for their bright faces.

"We're going to have to eat more than berries," PB said, "or we'll disappear altogether."

"That's what worries me. My girls will be needing me. We should head back up to the world soon."

But PB declared he had a better plan.

"You're not thinking of staying down here?"

"Course not—but I'm not planning on staying up there, either," and PB's fist rose skywards. "No one's going to hire me again in this town."

"Sure they will." I reminded PB of how I'd gotten the best job I'd ever had after spending two weeks in jail.

PB's voice was firm. "It's a matter of losing face."

"I can still see your face," I tried, but the truth was I couldn't. Only the blurred shape of it in the gray light.

"If Lara says I stole supplies . . ."

"But you didn't!"

"I know that, but who would believe me? Even if I found a job, no one would sell a house to me now. And I'm not sure I'd want them to."

I wished those laws for the Chinese applied instead to ruby-lipped women with mean spirits. Someone should have put a curfew on Lara Hadley long ago.

"The whole time I was on the road with Lara, I was looking for a place we could be together." He spoke of all the towns he'd visited, Echo, Boardman, Rufus, Hood River, the Rose City. Waterfalls galore, two rivers that made the Umatilla look like an insect. And houses so big, he said, you could almost fit the sky inside them. "One day, I'll take you there in my own car."

I drank in the music of his words, imagining all the land and sea and air left in the world for us to discover together.

"So, here's what I was thinking, what I've wanted to say for a long time. You and me, we should get married."

"Oh, PB!" I splashed his face with kisses. "Yes, yes!" I squashed down the picture of Bob's sad brown eyes. This was my own fairy tale come true. PB and me and our little papooses, and fields full of berries and tall trees to shade us, who needs cars, and gushing rivers to cool our feet. I was so caught up organizing the swirling pictures in my head that I missed what PB said next.

". . . with the new roads, it's not far to John Day. I've money saved. We could be there in a week."

"John Who?"

"It's a place, Taf, remember? Where my great-uncle Hay lives?" My beloved laughed and poked me gently. "Southwest of here. Blue Mountain country, more beautiful even than the Wallowas, I hear."

"What're you saying?"

"Come with me, Taf. Wing Wah's out there, my dad's friend. He owns houses all over the West, California, Washington. He'll know of something these hands can do, besides tickle you." He ran a bird's feather from my nest along my face, but I wasn't in a laughing humor.

"But I thought we were to marry."

"We will! In California probably, or wherever I can find decent work."

"Why not here?" I thought of Mrs. Hadley's wild cries before I left, and Pearl's worn crayons.

"Because." PB sounded impatient, as if I should know something I didn't. "You saw how people treat half-breeds the first night you came to town." PB stretched himself full length like a cat.

My hands grabbed onto the satin black of his hair. "Who cares about anyone else? We have us!"

"Listen, Taf, listen." PB drew back against the wall. "I just want to be able to buy us a little house, no more cow camps, with a fence round it so we can choose who we let in or don't, like everyone else. If I'm to have a wife, I need to provide for her."

"I already have a house. You can come live with me and the Pearls, and Mrs. Hadley." And Bob, I almost said, but slammed down on my tongue so hard it bled.

"Taf, I've made my mind up. No more Pendleton."

I thought of Mrs. Hadley screaming. I thought of the bony tilt of her husband, as he sat by her bed, like a lost crow. And the girls with scarves burying their mouths. My tongue felt like mud, clumpy and dry. I could barely catch a breath long enough to push the words out, "What if I say no?"

PB let out a breath that seemed to stretch all the way up to Main Street. "Then I'll go wherever Wing Wah needs help. We know we love each other now—that's the main thing. I'll save hard, build our house, and send for you."

"You wouldn't, you couldn't! We've only just found each other again. We've . . ."

PB laid his hand on my wrist, soft as a cloud. "I've never wanted anyone more than you, but I want to do you justice."

Justice, what was that, compared with love, I wanted to shout. Love was all I cared for, not a house, not the approval of others.

"Oh, Taf." PB had pulled himself up away from me; I could feel the cold air move in where his body had been. "I'd rather be with you—of course I would. But we're connected now, aren't we? There's a peace inside me where there wasn't before."

Peace felt as far away as winter geese to me then. I remembered the open road, how I loved the air on my bare skin. I let the vision come: me and PB, hand in hand, running through fields toward

John Day, Hood River, California, plucking fishes from rivers, dining on kisses and sunshine. An old familiar warmth erupted in my belly.

Then I thought of Ama and how she said sorrow would lurk at the end of any road I trod. And I realized then how wrong she had been. Sorrow bloomed without sunlight, without winding trails; sorrow fanned out before me right here, in this dark cave. Even as I knew PB could disappear again like a puff of wind and I might imagine I dreamed all this, even then, I was certain of one thing only. Even as my words snagged on the ridge in my throat, I coughed hard, and spoke. "I will not leave the girls."

"Couldn't the policeman . . . ?" Whatever PB was going to say, I cut him off. My fingers yanked on the tail of his hair, hard.

"Ow!" PB stood up and took a step back. "If there's one thing folks take kindly to, it's a prosperous family, Taf. Let me do one thing right in my life."

"Yes," I hissed. "And you let me." I slumped down onto the hard floor, a clump of dark hair in my palm. Every bone in my body shook, and it wasn't the cold. Clem leaned over and licked at my cheeks. I pushed him away.

"All right, Taf. I understand." He leaned over me. "I'll be back for you. Swear on my father's ashes."

"Here, till we're together again." I heard him say, but I didn't look up. I felt something slide under my knee, something small and cool. "I'll write from wherever Wing sends me."

By the time I sat up again, exhausted and empty, the room was dark as a death chamber and PB, my own love, and his dog, were gone. I tried sucking on his remnant hairs, but they tasted like salt, and I spit them out. I couldn't see what PB had left me, though I'd heard it roll like a marble over stone, and I didn't bother to search. It was the Incredible Disappearing Act of 1919.

Chapter 27

A gnawing hunger finally drove me up those steps again, not for food so much as to convince myself dusk could yield to dawn. Even at sundown, the light was dazzling. I had to shield my eyes with my arm as I slouched down Main Street.

For some reason, I had half a notion that if I walked back to the tavern, I'd find everything just as I'd left it. The Pearls on Bob's shoulders, Maisie still on stage singing, the mob never tiring of throwing roses at her.

And sure enough, there was a mob, or at least a large gathering of folks, many of them waving their arms like weapons and screaming black curses out on the air. I nudged and pushed my way through. The crowd ended right outside the tavern, with even more hulla-baloo there. Both doors were boarded shut, wooden planks nailed across them in an X. And there in a row like the pretty maids in the song stood a half dozen women, like soldiers almost, only instead of guns across their shoulders, they had signs fixed to what looked like broomsticks. "Hard liquor is illegal." One said, "Bring back our men. Farewell to the demon rum."

The women's faces seemed hard and pale, almost like statues you'd see in a park. I felt like Rip Van Winkle, waking up after a long sleep to find the world had rearranged itself in my absence. No one seemed to be acting their parts like they had in the long-ago past of last week, but then the thought flashed through me, maybe it was me who had changed roles.

"What's the problem?" I asked a man standing next to me, realizing I sounded just like Bob when he was on duty.

"Government's the problem," the man spat back. "Them women's the problem. Prohibition my ass!"

I was about to ask what that meant exactly when one of the ladies pointed her finger straight at me. "Look at that waif, for instance, in her ruined dress!"

Everyone turned to stare, and I looked down at Mrs. Hadley's berry-stained costume, and the rip where Clem's paws had caught. "I'll bet you're a victim of a drinker's home. Aren't you, dearie?" The scrawny woman in her stiff bonnet moved toward me, and clawed my shoulder between her thumb and fingers. "Does your daddy take liquor, dearie?"

Well, it was bad enough to be called a waif, and maybe she was right at that, but this stranger had no right whatsoever to accuse my daddy of something she couldn't possibly know.

"What if he does!" I spat back, and all my anger and sorrow at the unfairness of things came streeling out in that wave of saliva, all those past years of struggle, running after love, and love always outdistancing me, all those wasted, hopeless years. "Get your hands off." And I jerked the woman's hand free so fiercely I could hear something snap. Maybe it was her dress, maybe not, but out of the distance, I could see a familiar figure approaching: Bob, in his policeman's uniform, and what looked like a club in his hand. "Move aside, please. Move aside." He was heading straight for me.

I yearned to run, all the way to John Day if need be, but my feet stayed fixed to the ground. When Bob's warm eyes found mine, I could see the disappointment welling up round their edges. I felt like a dirty dishrag standing there, with a worn-out heart.

"Is everything all right?" The lady had fallen to the ground, clutching her arm. She was whispering words I couldn't catch. Bob and several other men bent down to assist her back to her feet.

"Lock me up again," I said. "Do the world a favor." But the words sounded sour on my tongue, or maybe it was how they landed on Bob, whose face darkened. When I asked about my Pearls, Bob had already turned away, and the question was swallowed up in the chaos. The man who'd cursed Prohibition stepped forward and said to Bob, "This young girl was being harassed. Your police force would be better off outlawing those temperance women than trying to temper booze."

Bob didn't say a word, only spoke gently to the woman, whose eyes pinched tight at the edges and fixed on me.

"I'm sorry about your arm, Missus," I tried, "and I don't know about alcohol but I can tell you one thing for sure. My body's off limits and you were trespassing."

A man with a face broad as a street appeared as if from nowhere, and took my arm. "Feisty girl you are," he said. "C'mon over here where it's quiet." Before I knew it, Bob had melted into the clouds of heads bobbing everywhere, and I was standing next to a wall. The wide-faced man was staring at me, chewing on a piece of straw, fingering it out of the side of his mouth. "I could use a few women like you."

"If you're talking about the Ho House, forget it, mister. I have a beau." Lord knows where that word "beau" came out of, nor who it was really referring to. At that minute, I had no one in the whole world, only my own sad and dirty self.

The man laughed and his face spread even wider so it had the look of a winter field, ready to be sown in. "Nah, a more glamorous job, I'm thinking. Women like glamour, isn't that right?"

"Can't say." I sat on the nearest stoop and rested my chin in my hands. Look where my first bid at glamour had landed me. Was I a woman, or just a lost girl hankering after a love that could never be?

I didn't know what the man meant, nor care to find out. He talked on anyway. "Saw your performance back there. Impressive for a girl in that fancy dress of yours." I wasn't sure if he was making fun, for my dress was scarred with berry juice. Oh, dear Mrs. Hadley, what had I done, taking her dress and ruining it, ruining everything. No matter what I did, sorrow met me at every turn.

The man talked on about Prohibition, which he said was the government denying regular citizens their rights to enjoy a cool drink on a summer's evening. I wanted to say leave me to my bitter thoughts, but instead, out of my mouth came the pronouncement that lemonade's probably still allowed.

"Sip?" The man brought out one of those hip flasks Timmy had and held it toward me as if it was water. There in the full light of day, and officers of the law swarming. When I didn't take the bottle from him, he set it down on the step between us. "Hot as roasted boar today." He swiped his arm across his grimy forehead.

I couldn't deny that, my skin moist as a sponge, nor could I argue with my dried-out tongue, which had been longing for a cold drink of anything.

"Near Beer, they call it." The man looked out into the crowd, and huge tears of sweat fell off his nose. "See, written right on it. Kansas brewers invented the name. Catchy, if you ask me."

"Near what?" I tried to sound like Jack, who found humor in things. "Near the law? Near the temperance ladies?"

"Near you!" He didn't move a muscle, but what he said made my heart jump a beat. My mouth was already dreaming of cool sweet liquid rivering through it and down my throat to the sea.

What interested me right then, though this man didn't care, was setting my life back in order the way it used to be just yesterday.

Everything had turned upside down and back to front, in the wink of an eye, and I wasn't liking the new vista. Once I wrapped my little girls in my arms again, I'd feel better. I would learn, in time, to settle. But still I kept sitting, silent and staring at a rock on the footpath, kicked aside by a passerby.

After a while, I felt like I knew that rock, its craggy contours, its beaten-down body, each scar it had never asked for. The man stood up finally, took the straw out of his mouth, and held out his hand. "Pleasure to know you," he said, his hand hanging in the cruel air. "My guess is my brews'll be in high demand. You want to earn a little cash, I'll give you a nickel for every empty you bring me. Ask for Alf at the back entrance to the Temple Hotel. Or Timmy." And he emptied out his pockets, tossing his coins into the air, and the sun made sprinkled silver of them as they landed at my feet. I stared at the dimes so long they became faces, Pearl A and Pearl B, and the nickel was Mrs. Hadley, and I gathered my three loved ones into my arms, and rocked them.

Sure as I sat there, pictures of my little ones scrimming across my forehead, who should walk by but the pair of them, one on each arm of a large woman whose face I had never before seen. She had on a gray coat, buttoned so tight at the collar, her chin collapsed into it. I leaped up, and moved toward them, but the look on that woman's face, was it hate or terror, caused me to set one foot back in the direction I came. A look that said, Don't you dare intrude. You've already ruined things. A disgrace, that's what you are. I could almost hear the words forming on her lips, and even then, I stepped forward. The woman grabbed the girls with one hand and swept them behind her skirt, using her free hand to shoo me away like I was a dog scavenging. I stopped, my mouth open, a moon full of grief, and no sound, not a single note, came out. Pearl B peeped out for the briefest second and her eyes caught fire. I could have sworn she was about to call my name, and I held out my arms like two wings, but the glow died, in less than an instant. And the twins, what was left of my life, turned into rag dolls trailing down the street in their new owner's wake.

I felt a slow, steady crack deep inside as I watched those girls dim into the crowd. And before I knew it, my hands took on a life of their own, grabbing for the flask as if it was an anchor. One swallow, and there followed an explosion in my chest, yellow liquid erupting up out of my throat, not settling down and soothing it like I'd imagined.

The old silkie song, more like a nightmare now, swam through my aching head. *Then he has taken a purse of gold, he has put it upon her knee, saying give to me my little wee son, and take thee off thy nurse's feet.* I ached for my girls, for Pearl A's joy and wonder at simple things, for Pearl B's leap when Bob came up the drive, for PB's leg cradling mine. I must have slid into a heap, for my next memory was darkness, and something nipping sharply at my heel. Before I'd pulled myself up to sitting, my arm smacked of its own accord at a wasp, or whatever it was, gnawing busily into my ankle. "Off!" I yelled, and sat up to find Clem before me, tongue hanging out of his mouth like a panting salmon.

"Clem, my pal! You didn't go with PB?" And the notion entered my head that my own love had left him with me for company. I tugged at his perked ears, and grazed my nose against his. He seemed to move back a little, maybe the smell of my Near Beer offended him. Near Death, they should label that stuff. And something fell out of his mouth, something round and gleaming. I picked up PB's nose ring. He'd left me two gifts, after all. I felt the tears come, but inside me.

"Looks like it's just me and you," I sighed, and Clem rested his chin on my soiled dress. An old man slept on the step right next to us. His snores seared through my head like arrows, each one pricking a hole in my brain. The street was empty now, still and calm. A broken board lay in three pieces on the road. Something was written on it, but it was too far to see.

The man's money jiggled in my palm; how far would it get us? The only thing I halfway owned was Ama's big coin, my lucky charm, still ribboned round my neck. As I ran my fingers along it, my little finger caught in the hole. It throbbed when I pulled it out. And it seemed clear as stars to me then what I should do.

"Let's go, boy." I hauled what remained of Taffy Hero, and pushed her legs, stiff as apple crates, over to Idle Hour Drugs and waited on the step till it opened. With my nickel, I purchased a notebook and pencil. Then I marched into Barber John's and asked how much he'd offer for my hair. He fingered its length for a long time, smiling; it felt nothing like in PB's hands, and I was glad.

I watched without flinching as each tress fell into a red heap on the floor. It looked like the makings of a good bonfire. "Don't you want to save some for a keepsake?" Barber John asked, as he counted out his bills. "Must've taken years to grow it all. Here, have one long strand, at least."

"I'd rather a cap, if you have one." My neck felt chilled.

"Take both, why don't you?"

And I did. And set out toward Reith, Clem close on my heels, toward the house where I'd left so many dreams sitting. When I'd last walked through that broken gate, I'd never imagined I'd be walking away forever. There was a light on upstairs in Mrs. Hadley's room; she was still there, still breathing. The window was open, and I heard a woman's voice, "Come along, girls. It's time for your bath." I had to turn away.

Old Ama had been generous to me, and like the girl who used her gift of cordial to arouse her sisters, I would spend my gift on something special. In that garden, where I'd once laughed and played with my little girls, I knelt in the warm, evening grass, and wrote to Mrs. Hadley and her precious daughters. I told them to take the coin to the bank; Bob would surely help them. They could do whatever they liked with the money, only I'd be happy if they'd buy themselves each a new dress. To be extra generous, I wrote, Buy one for the lady minder, too.

When I stood up, I saw Bob's bicycle propped against the side-wall, and for a flash, I imagined him marrying that tight-chinned woman, and felt inclined to scratch that last line out. Still, I wrapped the coin inside the note, and left them under a scraggle of wild violets on the front step, and walked back to town, satisfied.

Chapter 28

Grave's was all boarded up when I got there. The temperance messages were covered over by a huge picture of Maisie's glowing face. Grand Reopening, it read. Grave's Soft Drink Establishment. Friday, September 12. Hear Marvelous Maisie and her backup band. It was the first time I'd considered that Mais might find a replacement for me, or maybe she never needed me in the first place; she was just being kind. The Pearls had someone new to care for them, why shouldn't Mais?

I kept walking, glad of Clem by my side, as far as the Temple Hotel. Timmy was leaning into his carriage, rummaging around.

"Timmy," I crept up behind him. For once, someone was exactly in the place I'd imagined for them. Clem barked, two loud snips, and Timmy whipped round and his tin-colored eyes met mine.

"You! Looked like a boy."

"How far's California from here?"

Timmy shook dust out of his hair. "Too far for the likes of you and me."

Just like I'd thought, there was no point in following PB. "When're you going to the Wallowas? I want to go this time."

"Can take you as far as Minam; I've a delivery due there next Tuesday." He tossed his horse a carrot top.

"If you take me all the way to the Wallowas, I'll give you these." I held out all but one of my bills.

He lit a cigarette. "Well, well, you're a girl who knows how to drive a bargain. That necklace you had, now that might persuade me."

"It's gone, Tim. Gone." I pressed the bills into his free hand.

"Well," Timmy blew his smoke out straight into my face, but I kept my hand on his, money sandwiched between us. "Well, I suppose we can work something out. I've a lady friend out in Joseph."

"No!" Clem had leaped into Timmy's wagon. "No more animals." But he must have seen the two temperance ladies rounding Emigrant Street, for he shoved me in after Clem, and himself at the reins, and took off anyway at a terrific clip.

There was hardly room to sit down for all the boxes and copper tubes and old cookers stored under the letters. Tim's carriage had become a traveling store. "Bootlegger!" I yelled out to him, "What about John Craig?"

"What about yourself, missy? Times are hard; a man can't earn a decent wage hauling mail, you ask anyone. I'm doing this for John Craig, for myself, for all the downtrodden folk of America. Who says you can drink in Idaho but not in Oregon anyway? Bone dry state, my foot!"

The thick stench of whiskey or whatever it was took my breath away at first, but soon Tim's tobacco wafted in, and brought back a vision of Mr. D and my journey out here. All that excitement, and my chest full of possibility. Now here I was finally going to where I'd always been headed. That girl, in her green pinafore, seemed a long way from me now; I barely recognized her.

It was impossible to sit up straight with all the knocking around, and my behind hurt from tubes pushing up against me here and there. "We're on the winding road, Clem." I peeled off my hat and set it on his head, my hands fluttering. I'd forgotten just how burbling it made my body to be in motion, the scent of the unknown teasing the air ahead. For a brief spell, memories, good or bad, could fall away, leaving only fresh air and each new uncertain breath. I wondered if the returning soldiers felt like this when they journeyed homeward after the war, their lumbering histories for now left behind them. I let the gallop of hooves match the beat in my heart, faster, faster.

The land we whizzed past looked like nothing I'd ever seen, brown, then green, then almost blue. And the air grew sharper bit by bit. We bumped over the winding roads, hardly a house in sight, only enormous mountains, the kind you'd expect giants to inhabit, if you believed in giants, and their peaks were smothered in snow.

Summer snow, I'd never imagined such an occurrence. The road belonged to me, I felt it, like that whiskey cellar to the dauntless girl. I let the breeze make feathers of my hair. I couldn't sleep nor rest, just kept my face out the window and let the whoosh of air cool my face, until all light drained out of the sky.

"You get cold back there, use the plaid coat," Timmy yelled. "Dunno whose it is."

The coat might have belonged to Crazy Bill Locum, it was so large, but I put it on, glad of the heat, for no sun could reach us in the valley we were in. I launched into the silkie song; it seemed like a good one for the road. *And you will marry a gunner good, and a proud good gunner . . .*

I'm sure it was he . . .

I could have sworn I heard the words floating out on the air; they definitely didn't come out of my mouth. I sat up, and kept singing, *And the very first gun . . .*

That ere he did shoot . . . came the voice. I looked at Clem, then leaned out the window, but there was only Tim, whistling.

He shot his son . . . We were singing together, we were singing the lines of my pa's song together, *he shot his son, and the great silkie.*

"Timmy!" I scrambled out of the carriage and onto the ledge next to him. "How on earth d'you know my pa's song?"

"Your pa, eh?" Tim laughed, and spat out into the crisp air.

"The silkie song. You were singing it. You . . ."

Tim kept whistling the tune, as if it were Old MacDonald or any old nursery rhyme. "Tim! Tim!" I tore at his collar. "Tell me where you learned it."

"Thought it was from you."

I could tell Tim was enjoying my anxiousness.

"Or maybe that Welsh wool man?"

"Mr. Dacey? Couldn't've been."

I yanked at the horses' brace so hard, one of them stopped, and we bounced backward. "Whoa! Fire and tobacco, you, I always said so."

"Tim, you must've learned that tune from my pa. You must have met my pa on your travels, it's his song, it's his . . ."

Tim pulled the reins back and the horses took off again. "Be honest, think I picked it up off a cowpoke back in Sweet Home. Two-Time Sammy . . ."

"Sammy?" That wasn't my pa's name. "What's a cowpoke?"

"You know," and Tim made a motion with a stick to hit the horse. "They hang round railways, prod the cattle, make sure they're in line."

It didn't sound like what a cowboy'd do. I couldn't imagine my pa on his sorrel mare with a prod in one hand.

"Only Sammy, I'm sure it was him, now I consider it," Tim went on, and I didn't interrupt. "He was a chancer. Had a thing for the drink. He'd whack at those cows with his empty bottles. Liver trouble got him in the end. It'll get us all."

A cowpoke for a pa, or a friend of my pa. It was as close as I'd gotten to him, all this time, and when I faced the truth squarely, probably as close as I would ever get.

Still we rode on through the long night toward the Wallowas, Timmy whistling the silkie song, till I couldn't bear it any more, and begged him to stop. Finally, his throat gave up on him. And Clem and me rocked in the back, while Tim pointed out places to us— Lower Valley, Whiskey Creek, Lostine, and down that way, he shouted, was Hell's Canyon, the deepest gorge in the world, where folks ate rattlesnake soup, and the Seven Devils peaks ruled the land. And I was grateful for once that I couldn't see a thing.

Chapter 29

Welcome to Wallowa County, Land of Winding Waters. Come for a vacation, but please don't stay. The sign swung on its hinge like a wing.

"I thought we'd a stop-off, Tim."

"Minam can wait till the way back. Out you get. You're in Joseph, girl, the heart of Wallowa country."

"We're here, Clem. We're finally here!"

"Summer makes the journey easier," Timmy said. "None of those chinooks to blow us sideways. You take a good look at Joseph School up that hill there. Mown in half, it was, last year, by a chinook blew down off the mountains."

I set my first foot on Wallowa soil, Clem right behind, and it felt exactly like anywhere else.

"I could use a washup. But first I'm gonna . . ."

"Find me a woman."

Timmy waved me off, with his kerchief. "You want to ride back to Minam with me, be here at first light tomorrow."

We saw more horses lining the main road than people, and the few folks I queried about a cowboy named Stetson mostly laughed and said to try the rodeo circuits. Maybe they thought I was joking, me in my oversized coat and threadbare shoes. Only one woman had a suggestion to try Stetson's House of Prime, but she said that was over in Baker City and she thought the owners came from China during the gold rush. The First Bank of Joseph was closed, and the post office had a sign on it, Back Soon.

At the end of the road, a girl about my age rushed out of a building, and almost knocked me over. "Fresh air! Whew!" she said, and popped a hat on her head. The way the brim kinked up, it looked like wings about to take off.

She didn't apologize, and as I was setting myself straight again, she turned her back to me, and hoisted up her shirt. "Say," she said, as if she bared herself to strangers every day, "Say, could you just loosen this damn corset for me? It's murdering my ribs."

I remembered my own aggravation with Maisie's brassiere, and was glad to relieve this strange girl of her misery. "What a day. Fall's almost here." She let out a long sigh. "Sure wish I was out riding horses."

"Horses?" My ears twitched. "Don't suppose you know any sorrel mares round here?"

The girl moved closer. "You know something about horses, then? Ever heard of me?"

She turned to face me, pulling down her shirt again. She looked so hopeful, I wanted to say yes, but my head shook.

"Vera McGinniss." She held out her hand, and though her wrist was delicate as a china cup, her handshake was firm and strong. "Trick rider in Winnipeg Stampede, 1913," she announced. But her parents favored her sticking to office work, which was a more reliable occupation.

"Shame," I said, and left the girl to her regrets as I moved on down the street, Clem at my heels. I wondered what became of cowgirls, shed of their horses and dreams.

Clem and I had barely left the few stores and houses behind when we came upon the biggest lake I'd ever seen. Hundreds of Idle Rivers would fit into it. And mountains you'd expect would slit holes in the sky. My pa could be on any one of them, or dead of drink on some railway. Alvin had known instinctively what it had taken me three years to find out. I'd banked my hopes on the Wallowas, but the West was vast. A person could hide here his whole life long without witness, if he chose. Or trek through it, stubbornly searching for a thimble in a hay bale. Right then, I felt glad I hadn't taken to gambling like I'd allied to liquor. PB's mom would have whupped me in a second.

Even if I never found my pa, and I understood, finally, that I wouldn't, I swore off drink myself for the rest of my days.

Everything felt so huge here, you could get lost between one breath and another. The lake water held each peak in its bountiful mirror. And it held me, too, though when I leaned over it, I barely recognized myself. A defeated face with a clump of weeds for hair looked back at me.

Me and Clem sat on a rock and inhaled the air; it was sharp like needles and woke me up in a hurry. A very old man stood in the water struggling with a strange contraption; it looked like a three-legged animal, three saplings rising out of the water, and crisscrossing at the peak. But it mustn't have been anchored too well; it kept toppling. "What're you doing?" I asked after he told me he knew no Stetsons anywhere roundabout.

"Fishing for bluebacks, that's what. This thing's supposed to hold a fish trap. Works better in a stream."

I watched as he laid his trap over the sticks, but no matter how he positioned it, it wouldn't balance. "Damn wallowa." He spit.

"You said it," I nodded. PB had been right when he said it wasn't worth coming here. "Damn Wallowa, indeed."

The man turned to eye me, and his lure fell over entirely. "I wasn't meaning the place," he said, as I helped him retrieve his sticks from the icy water. "Wallowa's how the Nez Perce fished. They knew how to do it right."

"You mean this place is named after the Indians?"

"The mountains are, sure." I handed the ancient man back the last of his sticks. "Town is too, now I think about it. The old Nez Perce chief, he was Joseph. At one time, he and his people summered here. Course, they're few on the land round these parts any more."

"I know." I thought of PB's people banished from here, from this clear air and water, those arrowing mountains. The Wallowas I'd been hewing toward for years had been his place first. I thought of that pitiful fish trap, how it didn't understand its job, how it might as well have been trying to snare my own pa. Or PB. It didn't seem like it could even hold a foolish dream without having it slip through its cracks and drown in the deep, cold, beautiful lake.

Clem was nipping at the old man's trouser ends.

"Stop, boy! Sorry about that." I tried to nudge him away, but he wouldn't budge.

"Good-looking heeler, that! He must smell the cows off me. Used to be a cattle man." He looked out at the water, sadly. "Maybe I should go back to it."

How far Clem and I trod that day I don't recall, but the leather in my right shoe finally gave way on that long, hot search to nowhere. Finally I got so weary I clambered into a cart on a side road and lay on the cool slabs of wood, resting my head on my arms, Clem at my feet, and counted each mysterious star until I couldn't.

Chapter 30

Next morning I entered the post office and handed the last of my bills to the telephone exchange operator. "Pendleton Police Station, please," I requested. The man gave me a strange look, but got the connection and handed me the receiver. Nothing stirred, only the chump-dachump of my heart, and then, I heard, out of the air, he could have been standing right next to me, "Officer Dixie, how can I help?"

The clear, easy sound of his voice soothed me, and I longed to rush through the wires right into his arms, and yell, BobBobBob! just like Pearl B used to. "It's me, Taf," my voice fell to a whisper.

I thought I heard a kafuffle, like he dropped the receiver—something banged against a surface anyway, hard—then a crackle, and a cough. "Taf," he said. "Pearl." He said, "Where are you?"

"Wallowas." I swallowed. "Hush, Clem!" I shouted toward the doorway where Clem waited, restless. "Mrs. Hadley?"

"She's fine." He must have known my next question, for he went on, "and the Pearls are doing well." He paused. "They miss you."

And as if that was excuse enough, out of nowhere, poured the whole sorry story of trying to go back to them, and the childminder taking my place, and me and PB. I knew as I said it that I shouldn't, that Bob might still harbor a trace of feeling for me, but there was nothing in the world right then that could stop my mouth, and its tale of horror, how PB had found and then left me for his Uncle Wing Wah in California, and I'd looked up and down the length of Wallowa and never found my pa.

Bob swallowed, I could hear him, maybe he was chewing licorice. "A telegram arrived for you," he declared.

My heart pounded. "Who?"

"Mr. Dacey brought it over two days ago, said he didn't know how to reach you."

"Read it. Read it."

"Taf. Stop. Foreman's job in Canada. Stop. Free house. Stop. Meet me at 11 A.M. Stop. Echo Bridge. Stop. August 31. Stop. PB."

"31? 31? August's gone," I cried into the phone. "August's already . . ."

"Maybe he means next year . . ."

"How far's Echo?"

Bob said it was on the way to Portland or John Day, depending.

"Doesn't he say anything else? 'I'll wait, no matter how long it takes?' Didn't he ask after me? After Clem?"

"Telegrams're costly," Bob said, his voice watery. Then silence, like a phantom holding me upright until it took my last hope away. "Wait." I could hear paper shuffling; I couldn't tell if it was inside my head or in a police station miles away. "Looks like I missed this part . . . 'Tell Clem I love her. Stop. I love you, too. Stop.'"

I gasped.

"Forever. Stop."

"Tell me it'll be all right, Bob, tell me he'll come back . . ."

But even Bob, who was more cheerful than anyone I knew, said nothing.

"One day I hope you'll forgive me," I said, as the operator signaled my money was used up.

Bob's voice echoed back to me, calm as moss, "I already have."

As I laid down the receiver back where it belonged, I may as well have been handing over my entire life up till then. And what walked out of that Wallowa post office was a hollow shell, the tatters of an old fairy tale. Like Alvin's tree trunk, emptied of all its stories. Forget Taffy Hero. The true hero, after all, wasn't me. Bob couldn't have guessed that Clem was a he.

Chapter 31

That shell kept walking, out of town. . . . Clem, boy or girl, belonged here in Wallowa, I realized. It was a way, I supposed, to bring part of PB back home, a way of loaning peace to his troubled heart. I felt sorry he'd never come here, to this beautiful place where his mother's tribe had once fished. But if a house in Canada was what he wanted, I had to accept that too. I strung what was left of my hair through his nose ring, and made a scarf for Clem's neck.

When I reached the lake, I found the same ancient man bent over his wallowa. He wasn't having any more luck than yesterday. "I don't get it." He scratched under his cap roughly. "Time was, there were so many sockeye here, you could cross the damn lake on their backs."

"Well, if you want to go the way of cattle again, here's your chance." And before I could utter a word, Clem'd leaped into the water, like an overgrown baby, and retrieved one of the man's sticks.

It was as if he knew what was required of him, 'cos as I turned back toward town, he stayed, paws dug into the sand, his coat sparkling with water, and watched me, and didn't move, didn't wave his tail, even as I rounded the final bend, out of sight.

Nothing was mine, I realized. My pa, PB, the Pearls. They were all borrowed, like spring flowers, or winter snow. Maybe I'd always understood that, but fought it: the hard part was letting them go. It was as if I'd felt they wouldn't survive if I didn't keep filling them with love, as if they were pitchers, useless without me.

But life ticked on. A war come and gone, alcohol sold, then banned, four years since I'd fled the Idle River. It was time to be grown up now, I thought, and allow that folks love what they loved and not try to force matters. It took dauntlessness not to love. Or to love so much that you let folks go after their own dreams, while you went after yours. Maybe that was the admission fee to adulthood, even if I wasn't too graceful about paying.

As I walked out of town, I felt a shadow beside me, where Clem used to cling at my heels. It felt dark and cold. But I let it move alongside; there was no other choice. I'd let it stay until it didn't need me any more.

Hardly a hundred yards beyond Joseph a brown Maxwell slowed to a stop beside me, and I saw with surprise it was the cowgirl from yesterday. How long ago already that strange encounter seemed. There was a huge trunk in her backseat.

"Vera?" I asked. "Where you going?"

She threw her arms in the air. "You decide!" she said. "I've had enough of ledgers." She stepped out of the driver's seat, plopped her Stetson on my head. "Anyone who can clock up the longest telephone conversation on record in the history of Joseph earns a free hat." And she nudged me in front of the steering wheel, a place, I was surprised to learn, where I felt at home.

And as we sped along the road, the towering Wallowas behind us, I realized I'd no idea of where we were headed, nor did I care. It was the journey itself that counted. As I drilled my bare foot into the pedal, like Vera showed me, I had a vision of the silkie. Surely the best part of becoming human was the exact instant he shed his own skin, that pure excitement, before he took on another world entirely. Take old Ama as a young girl filled with dreams, leaving Spain. Or my dad galloping west on his horse, bareback. Or the geese, I realized, the spring geese, who always sang as they flew. No wonder I loved their arrival, that exquisite moment before they landed, before the silence and disappointment, when they could hardly contain their delight to be nearing the Idle River. *Taf! Taf! Taf! Taf!*, they'd cry, when they couldn't help themselves choiring, *Almost there, almost there*.

Biography

Annie Callan is a native of Dublin, Ireland. She is the author of *The Back Door*, a collection of poems; and her essays and short fiction have been widely published and anthologized. Her numerous writing honors include the Academy of American Poets Award, the William Stafford Poetry Fellowship, and the Heekin Foundation's Siobhan Fellowship for Literary Nonfiction. She now lives in Portland, Oregon.

Author's Note

Much of the Pendleton section of the book is based on true events. The town has held an annual rodeo since 1910. In the early 1900s, Chinese immigrants dug a series of connecting tunnels underground to assist in goods transportation for local businesses. Some of them ran their own businesses down there, for example, Hop Sing, who ran a popular laundry. In the early 1900s, the locally named Discrimination Law enforced a curfew: Any Chinese person found above ground between sunset and sunrise could be shot. Pendleton Underground Tours offers a guided walk through the area.

Vera McGinniss was a famous cowgirl of the time, and Doc Hay, a renowned Chinese healer.

Acknowledgments

This book grew out my residency in Wallowa County as the 1998 Fishtrap Writer in Residence. For that great honor, I owe Barbara Dills, who planted that seed of opportunity. And Rich Wand-schneider of Fishtrap, who made me so welcome; his enthusiasm, support, and knowledge have been immense. And the wondrous residents of Wallowa County, who made my stay both memorable and fond. I thank the land itself, whose magic conjured *Taf* into being.

Rob Clapp deserves huge praise for his many guided talks through Pendleton. His vast knowledge of the locale inspired much of the latter part of this book. I also am grateful to Jane Frink of Pendleton, who shared her memories of the war and Prohibition in Pendleton. And to Pam Severe of Pendleton Underground Tours, and the Umatilla County Historical Society, who provided background history.

I thank Laura Marcus for offering the folk lyrics of the silkie song at just the right time. There are many versions of this folk song; the most common is the Child ballad 113, a version of which is quoted here (Francis James Child, ed., *English and Scottish Ballads* [Boston: Little, Brown, 1864]). And Kevin Crossley-Holland deserves high praise for his intoxicating renderings in *British Folk Tales: New Versions* (New York: Orchard Books, 1987) several of which are woven herein.

I am also indebted to the patient and helpful librarians at Lake Oswego and Multnomah County Libraries. A generous residency at the Willard Espy Foundation in gorgeous Oysterville, Washington, lent me quiet and space in order to complete important research; I thank everyone at the foundation wholeheartedly. I am also hugely grateful for my luscious residency at Ucross Foundation in Wyoming, and how it nourished my western sensibilities.

The love and support of my friends is incalculable: Joanne Mulcahy, Bob Hazen, Melissa Madenski, Andrea Carlisle, and Barbara Burnett read various drafts, offered candid and helpful critique, and cheered me and Taf on. And for my adopted "family," Snow Thorner and Tai Khao, my gratitude is huge and constant.

Hallie and Dylan Madenski proved magnificent advisors through their candid readings of earlier versions of this manuscript.

I'm deeply grateful to Betty Beard, my incomparable landlady and friend, who provided support and sustenance during the final stages of revising. And to my generous neighbors and friends, the Stellways.

To Jim Heynen: bless you for guiding me to Marc Aronson, my insightful editor, without whom there would be no book. I cannot thank him enough for his patience, perseverance, and unflagging belief in Taf. The same holds true for Elizabeth Devereaux's thorough and inspired reading of the final versions of this manuscript. Also at Carus Publishing, Joëlle Dujardin deserves praise for her gentle, steady encouragement, and Karen Kohn for her visionary cover art. I thank Mary Ann Hocking also for facilitating practical matters. And Carol Saller for her precision and persistence in copyediting.

Stephen Johnsrud and Henry Carlisle have my heartfelt gratitude for their support during the final phases of writing.

And my agent, Elaine Markson, earns plaudits too, for her generous advice on business issues, and her faith in my creative work.

There are no words wide enough to contain my gratitude to those who saved my life, and as a result, my writing; Dr. Ed Goering, in particular, and dear Rosemary, who eased my journey back to health; my friend and chiropractor, Hari Das Khalsa, whose healing hands kept me in the chair long enough to usher Taf out of my computer and into the world; and dearest David Waldman, who continues to bring me back, again and again, to the essential.

And finally, an enormous hymn of praise to my dear sister Claire, who believed in me and *Taf*, from the very start, thank you, thank you.